MW00893500

NEFARIOUS:

Sailboat Racing In The Salish Sea

Antonio J. Hopson

Available as an audiobook on Audible

Front Cover Design: Anew Kyle. Nefarious: Sailboat Racing in the Salish Sea Antonio J. Hopson—2st edition.

ISBN: 978-1983177903

1. Sports & Recreation—Sailing—General. 2. Fiction—Action & Adventure. 3. Fiction—Romance—Contemporary.PN3311-3503: Literature: Prose fiction813: American fiction in English

Wildboy Concepts | Seattle Washington

AntonioHopson.com
antoniofiction@gmail.com

Acknowledgements

Thank you Dan, for showing me the race boats.

Thank you Craig, for showing me the words.

If you don't know where you are going, any road will get you there. I can't go back to yesterday—because I was a different person then.

—Lewis Carroll

You're so vain—you probably think this song is about you.

—Carly Simon

I've often thought the Bible should have a disclaimer in the front saying, 'This is fiction.'

—Ian Mckellen

CHAPTER 1

For no good reason, people tended to become a friend or a foe of Dan Swardstrom. He was not particularly benevolent, nor was he physically or intellectually intimidating, but there was something chancy about him. Perhaps it was the crookedness of his smile, the boyish, cocksure gleam in his mercury eyes, the way he positioned his body while sailing as if he were about to take a punch on the chin, or the way he somehow, through no fault of his own, ended up with your girlfriend sitting on his lap at the end of a party.

Despite his modest demeanor, Dan Swardstrom stood out among his peers; a consummate gentleman among pirates, assholes, vandals, and picaroons—words that accurately describe every one of his friends. His wintery hair and smart, mercurial eyes were deceiving. Your only warning of what he was truly capable of lay just below his right eye where a broken halyard once lashed out and left him with a compelling story to tell over a drink. When he smiled from the other side of a bottle of rum, the little scar frowned at you.

Today, he proudly steered his race boat through picturesque Lake Union, a Farr 30—a class of sailboat well regarded in the Seattle fleet. It was sleek and fast, designed to carve through water as smoothly as a Ferrari devours blacktop on a racecourse. The wind was at his back, blowing his thinning hair out in front of him, obscuring a fresh, excited face. Only a few scattered cumulous clouds speckled the sky. The sun was out, and the day was young.

"Sir, I need you to kill your engine!"

Harbor 1, the Marine Patrol unit that operates a 37-foot, cabin cruiser with twin diesel engines patrols the busy waters of Lake Union. It was called to the area to intercept a party boat, but what the captain found instead was S/V Nefarious; its sails stowed, motoring speciously along the cut at an easy pace. No wake. Five knots, not fast enough to disturb the charming houseboats or the posh, float restaurants with diners enjoying an early lunch. Why would a broken dock be tied to the hull of a sailboat? The captain put away his binoculars and picked up his bullhorn.

"Sir, did you know—"

"Yes," Dan said, nodding at the flotsam. "It's mine. My bowman neglected to untie us, and my crew didn't notice it until you started tailing us."

"Well, that solves one of our problems."

"Problem two?"

The captain motioned his pilot to close the distance.

"Have you been drinking, skipper?"

"Most definitely," Dan said. "Problem three?"

Harbor 1 drifted closer and the captain was not amused by the smirk on the skipper's face: a handsome face with a neatly trimmed, silver beard stuck to it. He set down his bullhorn and turned off his flashing lights.

"A woman reported that someone on your vessel yelled 'hot soup' and then emptied a bucket of urine overboard onto her kayak."

Dan scratched his beard.

"Yes, that's true," he said, "but, to be fair, she did not give me right of way while approaching my vessel."

The crew was quiet, like refugees caught in the night, and it was a miracle that they resisted the urge to sip their beers or drink from the lucky bottle of rum.

"Isn't your vessel equipped with a head?"

"Let me ask you this," Dan said. "Would you ask the owner of a Ferrari if there was a commode under the seat?"

The captain boarded Nefarious. When he stepped on a beer can, he sneered. This was unsafe. This was sloppy yachting. He removed a fresh citation from his pocket and looked hard at the refugees as they pretended to be sober.

"Skipper," he said while scratching his pen on the citation. "What is the destination of this vessel?"

"Race Week," Dan said.

CHAPTER 2

The pit-girl stepped up to the bar. Pink, fuck-tower, six-inch-heels with little tassels tied into bowline knots. Pink lipstick. Pink pantyhose, lacy and torn for fun. Pink eyelashes, and for good measure, a pink satin ascot.

"What're you having?" the bartender asked.

The pit-girl's blouse was a vintage navy uniform with silver first class stars buttoned to the sleeves, borrowed from Esther, her adorable godmother whose closet was full of swooshy, jazzy, swing-town fun. In her day, Esther took zero-shit from the world, lived free and loved free; she dated Negros, Degos, Wops, and, as it turned out, she had a real special thing for sailors in uniform.

"Let me ask you something," the pit-girl said to the bartender. "What do you think a woman dressed like me would order?"

The bartender looked her over slowly, pausing thoughtfully. Her sheer skirt was pink. Her vinyl nail polish was pink. Her blush was pink, and it sparkled on her pink, freckled cheeks like the Fourth of July.

"A Pink Pussy," he said.

"Good!" the pit-girl said and smacked the bar. "I'll have twelve."

The bartender began pulling out martini glasses and lined them up one by one.

"You're not from around here are you?" he said. "Mind if I ask you why you're in town?"

"Race Week," the pit-girl said.

CHAPTER 3

Ortun Hurley kissed his sleeping girlfriend on her fair-skinned cheek. He was restless and drowsy because the night before he'd dreamt of a watery chasm swirling downward into a warm, pinpoint of eternal light. The vision wasn't terrifying, but it awakened him suddenly, and for the rest of the night he grappled with an itch in his arm that radiated outward from his bones. Ortun knew it was that time of the year again, and there was only one of two ways to scratch the itch.

She awakened; reluctantly opening one eye and then the other.

"Good morning," she said skeptically.

Ortun was busted. He was already carrying his guitar, slung over his shoulder like a rock star, his canvas bag, and a six pack of Coors Light—on account that he was a diabetic.

"Where are you going?" she said sleepy and sweet, as if she didn't already know.

"Race Week," he said.

CHAPTER 4

The writer sipped coffee at Starbucks. He was irritated with the company for removing the nipples from their little mermaid insignia, and was busy drawing them back onto his paper cup when he received a text.

HI, DARLING, his girlfriend texted.

HIYA, he replied.

WHAT RU DOING? she asked.

WRITING, he replied.

The phone rang and he answered.

"No, you're not," she said. He could barely hear her through a crowd of singing sailors on the other end. "Are you drawing tits on coffee cups again?"

"Well, yes."

"Awww," she said sympathetically. "Pack your shit and meet me in Oak Harbor."

"What's going on?" he asked.

"Race Week," she said.

CHAPTER 5

Kai opened the curtains and went over the numbers again, this time without a calculator. A calculator could not gauge emotion. It could not approximate passion. Once you considered these intangibles, there was no other way around it. He gazed at the rising sun as it crested the rough-hewed Cascade Mountains. The scene was just like the sunrises he'd seen back home: golden-amber, glorious. He poured a fresh cup of Ceylon tea, creamed it, and watched the sun's colors brighten. In the courtyard, a tent was being perched and the morning's amber light made it look magical. Another year had passed and Oak Harbor was coming alive.

No, there was no other way around it. Not when you factored in heartbreak, envy, false hope and pain. The time had come to make a run at it. A real run. This year, there were no columns for hope or wishes on his spreadsheet. That kind of calculation, he had learned, was for sentimental fools.

Yes, Jupiter was a passion.

Ney, he thought, a fetish.

A pet tiger shark restrained by a studded, leather leash—which required blood sacrifice.

By his new estimations, being the owner of a Farr 30 triggered the same neural pathways as taking a cold shower while burning thousand-dollar bills; only each time you lit one on fire, the dominatrix you'd hired pointed at your junk and laughed. That's what it was like to sail a Farr. And the other skippers knew it, too. They used their boat as an extension of their cocks and every year a new gaggle of novices lined up in the crew-circle; all of them doe-eyed and ready to sail. So what if he only selected the pretty ones? Sure, the smart ones moved on, like Nefarious' pit-girl, but some of them stayed. Robin Mac Brádaigh was too good for the fleet anyways, so when she jumped ship after racing for Jupiter, he didn't take it personally. But crewing a woman had a tactical advantage. If you found a sturdy woman to man the pit, it equated to less weight on deck, allowing for larger men, who easily outweighed their counterparts in the amount of beer and steaks they consumed alone. Mac was a prize, and would soon turn pro. Earning her salt on a Farr 30 would get her a spot on a Santa Cruz 70 next season, then maybe a sponsored boat, then maybe America's Cup. Everyone around Mac knew what she was after, and it didn't take her long to master Jupiter, or its skipper.

Kai speed dialed his broker.

"Fly the kite," he said into the phone, the slang for raising a spinnaker with the wind at your back. "Fly it, now!"

"I haven't changed my mind," the broker said. "Numbers don't lie."

"You work for me, big guy!" he barked.

Kai called everyone 'big guy,' on account that he was short.

"You're not my boss," he said. "I'm the Skipper."

"Very, well," the broker said. "I'll deposit twenty-seven thousand into your Seattle account."

"Forty," Kai said.

"Fine," the broker said, and Kai could hear him typing on his computer. "That leaves you with little room, sir."

Kai looked down on the courtyard where Scamp Rum, the event's premier sponsor was untangling the main event tent. He sipped his tea and watched as the workers erected it, a hideous, maroon and gold monstrosity that looked like afterbirth. In Thailand, only the poor peasant farmers and fisherman, whose sad eyes misted in the sweltering heat, worked as hard as these flunkies.

"I don't need a lecture from you, big-guy," Kai said. "I worked my way up from the bottom rung! Lest you forget, you work for me. Now, give me my money or I'll pull everything! No more ballet classes for your pretty blonde daughters." The idea that his broker wouldn't have enough money to afford dance classes was ridiculous, but he cursed at him anyway." They'll have to learn square-dancing with hillbilly Bob, or 'drop it like it's hot' with boys from the south end."

The broker hung up the phone.

By now, the fleet was headed to Oak Harbor and the skippers would moor their boats in little rows resembling rice paddies along the harbor, but he had the best spot in the marina: Dock 1A. It was the spot where billionaires like Gates and Bezos parked their yachts, right in front of the bay side window of the clubhouse. Five hundred dollars per day for five days; chump change for the elite. Kai was not elite, not financially, and tuning the boat cost him a shit-load. In a month's time, he had replaced Jupiter's sails with faster Mylar sails, re-rigged her with halyards, glassy Kevlar, speed waxed the hull and hired a diver to clean her before every race. A halyard was a rope, and he learned the hard way that a real sailor never called them that. A halyard had a job, it was used for raising and lowering a sail, spar, flag, or yard on a sailing ship. His uncle taught him this on a junky Macgregor, a sailboat with a large enough engine to cruise long distances without raising a sail. No one ever took the boat, or his uncle serious. Uncle Aat was only a cruiser, but he loved the water. Upon immigrating to America, he opened a Thai restaurant in Tacoma and was content to make enough money to live aboard his boat the same way he did back home on the muddy Pak Nam Pho.

Bullshit.

It was time to kick it up a notch. Money was a means to an end. Use it, or die not spending it.

But half of his Race Week funds had already been spent on the non-material, professional sailors he'd hired to sail Jupiter to victory, and housing them was a small fortune. To keep them from consorting with the other sailors, he put them in Oak Harbor's finest establishment, far away from the marina. At this moment, they were probably eating Dungeness crab cakes and caviar like it was cornflakes.

Jupiter would win the day.

At last.

The flunkies in the courtyard pulled hard on the corners of the rum tent, filling it with air and space.

Kai smiled as he imagined the air being sucked right back out as he took the trophy into his hands at the annual, post regatta bash. As the winning skipper, he reserved the right to throw a themed party, and this year it sure as hell wasn't going to be a Dan Swardstrom toga party.

CHAPTER 6

The devil was bored, so he took up sailing and made friends with Dan Swardstrom. He mastered the craft instantly, of course. Really, there was no place better for him to be other than Race Week. July in Oak Harbor—when after the steeping tide had washed up a carcass—wrapped it in its clutches—left it to rot in the water that these men would sail upon— well, let's just say, he wasn't homesick.

The devil walked the shore looking for things that made him smile; a seagull tearing out the abdomen of a live crab, an eel that had culled flesh from a dead baby seal after a transient killer whale took a bite out of its flipper, played with it like a beach ball in the surf and then left it bleeding on a muddy flat. In a tide pool, he chased a sculpin into the waiting arms of an octopus. Bedazzled, he surveyed the cephalopod as it murdered the fish with its secret beak. When the butchery was complete, the water stilled and the octopus' skin changed from cinnamon to bright red.

"What ch'a doin' here, mister?" A group of teenagers with skateboards approached him and with eyes the color of the octopus, he turned to face them. "You a tourist? This is my ol' man's beach. No trespassers!"

"If we forgive those who trespass against us," the devil said, "our Heavenly Father will in turn forgive our trespasses."

The teenagers stopped.

"Never mind," one of them said, and they all backed away.

The devil smiled, looked them up and down and focused on one of the boys in the group who showed promise. The boy was wearing a leather flight jacket, stolen from a retired airman stationed on the island. The airman was a Vietnam vet who flew more than five hundred strafing missions and dropped thousand-pound bombs on villages, leaving only tears to fill the craters he left in his wake. In that jacket, the airman had fathered a dozen bastards, left their mothers with diseases, and once, on a dare, he drank enough whiskey to beat a nun. But this morning when the jacket embroidered with a laughing devil suddenly went missing, the sins of his past crept through his veins like poison, and crystals of fear took root in his heart.

"I haven't seen this in years," the devil said, and he slowly approached, touched the jacket and transported the teenager to a garage where the airman was coughing and gagging in a cloud of smoke. In that instant, the teenager understood who was touching him, and he saw how the jacket had insulated the airman from the hell he personally raised on earth. The airman had sealed his garage with wet towels so that the fumes from his running car would stop the pain that was caught in his heart, forever. The teenager coughed, tried to tear away from the devil's touch, but he was frozen, and the air was thick with poison and the motor droned like a death rattle. The airman fell to his knees and then to the floor. He called out, but there was no sound, no sweet air to inhale or scream into, and no one left in this world to care about him, or forgive him—only the teenager standing above him, cloaked in the flight jacket, gazing at him in horror.

"Don't worry," the devil whispered in the teenager's ear. "I'm only here for Race Week."

CHAPTER 7

The devil walked down Main Street admiring the quiet little stores that busied themselves for a week of sopping up the last dime of every sailor. Soon, the taverns would be filled and he imagined the whispered secrets and deeds to be done. Beer, amber to golden, would flow into pint or pitcher. Good whiskey would be ruined in syrupy cocktails and decorated with those awful little umbrellas. The odor of sex, salt, and fried things would linger and impregnate their clothing. They would carry the scent home with them and not recognize it until they were clean again, and caught a whiff of it on their pile of reeking laundry.

At the end of Main Street, he stopped at a vista and congratulated himself.

Even by his standards, Deception Pass was a marvel. These sailors would have to navigate it, a narrow pass that injected two hundred and

forty-five cubic feet of icy-water through a rock
forbidden for boats to race here, but sometir
right and a skipper might be tempted to catch a
its tidal surge. If they weren't mindful, The Eye would a₁
caused by an ebbing tide as the water drained back into the Salt.
Anything it saw was taken forever into its bottomless dream.
The Eye was not evil. There was no such thing as "evil," only carelessness. It
was the actions of people who decided to be near the channel that were evil.

On the beach, the devil smoked a Marlboro and watched a sand
castle disappear into the sea. The tide was coming in and the waves would
not be large in the protected bay, so he stayed long enough to watch the
entire thing fall flat. First the waves lapped at the walls, slowly eroding the
base as bits of it slipped under the murky water; drowning and dissolving
into silt.

The devil sighed.

This was only the edge of space and time; just one tiny portion of it,
merely a fractal, imbedded in a fractal that stretched out into an ocean that
opened into a sky filled with chaos. Outside of the bubble, there were stars
hotter than hell, and nebulas tearing at them, pulling them apart, and
recycling them into new stars. There were planets and mountains and
oceans for sailors to die upon, and for their loved ones to write stupid sea
shanties.

Power they could never understand. Not in verse, or song, or craft.

The sea was a force, but the violence it was truly capable of took its
own sweet time, and this is exactly why no one believed in him anymore.

tion takes its sweet time. There were no rivers of blood, or
r hellfire or brimstones. All those things were figments of human
ation. Real destruction was beyond their comprehension.

The devil spotted Dan in the marina and smiled.

"Captain," he said and saluted. "Reporting for duty."

"You again," Dan said. "I already have a tactician."

"Ah," the devil smiled, trying to make Dan smile so that he could
see the little scar under his eye. "Ortun! The musician. But will he actually
show up?"

"He texted me an hour ago," Dan said, not returning the smile.
"Says he's on his way."

"Is he up to the challenge this year?"

Dan knew what the devil was talking about, but he didn't let on.
Sometimes before your very eyes, Ortun was known to go AWOL, even
while you were talking to him. He was moody and emotional, which on a
good day made him a good sailor. But on a bad day, he was aloof and
required coddling. Dan was no good at coddling. He'd sooner massage a
fish.

"He did a fine job for at Swiftshore," Dan said.

"Swiftshore is for pussies!" the devil cursed.

"Listen," Dan set down his box of supplies. He'd heard enough. The
devil of all people, knew better than most that offshore racing along British
Columbia wasn't for pussies. It was premier racing; dangerous and fast. The
only reason he liked racing here was because most of the sailors were not
professionals and therefore, easily tempted by distractions. In the winter

they did not train, they did not travel to latitudes that suited their talents; instead, they drank, they slept, they remained walled by their professions. Some of the better ones moved up to more serious programs, but most were content to remain semi-pro. "You give me the willies, you really you do. Why don't you head over to the crew circle, see if some of the other skippers need an extra hand?"

"Oh, I only sail with Nefarious, you know that, captain."

Dan picked up his box of supplies again.

"Boat's full," he said.

"I can do mainsail," the devil said.

"That's like asking the Pope to officiate a farmer's wedding," Dan said. The devil could surely handle the position, no problem. Mainsail was more brawn than brain, a position that required a strong crewmember to keep the sail in its full, powerful shape. This was the gas pedal and what gave a sailboat it's power to accelerate or to slow down when needed.

The devil flinched and put his hand on Dan's shoulder.

"How are you this year?" he said, frowning.

"What do you mean?"

The devil knew the news before Dan, and he decided to let the surprise catch up to him at a better time.

"You know, Kai is really gunning for you this year," he said changing the subject. "He's got new sails, new rigging, new crew."

"Unless he's received a brain transplant," Dan said. "I'm not worried."

"Our deal is that you sail and you throw a party in my honor when you win," the devil said. "That's all I ask."

Dan straightened.

"I know the deal," he said. "I always sail to win."

The devil looked off into the perfect, blue sky.

Then he gazed out at the lovely green water.

"Have you ever built a sand castle?" he asked.

Dan stopped and opened one of the beers he was loading onto the boat, looked at the water with the devil.

"Sure, when I was a kid."

"When did you realize it was a futile endeavor?"

"What do you mean?"

The devil took a beer from the case.

"You know, when did you realize that no matter your efforts, the tide would soon come and wash your work away?"

Dan thought this through for a moment. "Honestly, I never stopped making them," he said. "I made that one over there just a little while ago."

"Ah, yes. A fine effort," the devil said spotting the lumpy mess. "But why?"

Dan thought again.

"I don't know," he was getting annoyed, and the scar on his face started twitching. "I suppose because every time I build one, I want it to be better than the one that was washed away."

The devil smiled.

"And how long could you go on doing this? Rebuilding and rebuilding, chasing after some ideal castle that can never exist?"

"Forever," Dan said and pulled a swig from his beer.

"Exactly," the devil said. "That is why I can only sail on Nefarious."

CHAPTER 8

In a waking, twilight dream, the writer drove at a deliberate pace to Oak Harbor and watched a hundred and twenty miles blur through his windshield. He drank coffee to stay alert, smoked cigarettes and tossed them out the window, worked and reworked the threads of words that rooted and sustained him.

No, he thought.

A peach is to be relished, not eaten.

And every verb owns a past, which you create. Then, he reasoned, a verb became an entity in time, hedged by the moment, with its future lurking near. Verbs were life, and all of them would be devoured by the past.

Relished, he decided.

He'd seen her first, inspecting a pyramid of sweet Georgia peaches in the fruit aisle at a grocery. In slow motion, he pushed his cart past her, fully engaged in the intimate embrace; a sassy, brazen assault on his senses. He, captured by this embrace, fell into a fissure, and now began to fill it with the greatest myth of all; the past-participial form of love.

There was something exotic about her, and there was something wrong with him, or worse, there was something wrong with the world he lived in. The writer adored her, and he knew well that she was not to be adored, only worshipped. In another life, she was born a princess in line to for the crown, and another, a pagan priestess, and another, the headmistress of a cowboy brothel, and in this life, she was a fiery woman-sailor who required sure hands, loyalty, collusion, but most of all, surrender. He knew this the instant he'd met her, and like any good writer, he opened Pandora's box and carefully observed.

Through the windshield he saw her pluck one of the fruits from the display—watched the pyramid collapse as a single peach, the one she was set to harvest, fell to the floor. He knew very well that archangels required sacrifice, and that his would be his heart.

Ripe.

Heavy.

The color of a California sunset.

The fiery orange of autumn.

The crimson red of blood.

The writer watched it come slowly to a halt at his feet, looked up at her, asking with his eyes if it would be permissible for him to retrieve the wayward fruit and offer it as sacrifice, as proof that she'd seen the moment unfold.

If she accepted, he could love her forever.

She agreed.

He retrieved the fruit.

Handed it over to her.

She smiled and took a juicy bite.

On the ferry to Oak harbor, he finished writing his poem.

Peach on a Tree

(A Note to Eve)

Not an apple...

a peach.

By design, better than an apple.

It is to be seized, savored

and rollicked on the tongue,

its nectar rived and quaffed.

Not the apple,

bitten and chewed

the way a cow masticates cud.

No. A peach is relished.

Silk on the skin, a sweet, slow game of

ambuscade!

Eve was wrong to choose the apple.

Perhaps the peach tree was hidden in another part

Of God's garden,

A place where she could not find it,

behind a wall of figs or mangos.

She'd never look there.

Had she done so, the bite would have been worth it.

She'd have kept her tears at bay.

Adam would have understood,

And so would his father.

We'd be thanking her instead.

Their first date was that evening.

"What exactly does a pit-girl do?" the writer asked.

The pit-girl put her hands in his.

"What do these hands feel like to you?"

He was honest.

"Rough," he said.

"Exactly," she said. "I tie shit down and it stays there until I want it to move."

"You tie knots?"

"I lock down the mast," she said. "And when the boat needs speed," she said releasing her grip on him. "I let it loose, a little at a time."

"Sounds like an important position," he said.

"You have no idea," she said, sipping a pink pussy.

Their next date was at the marina; he was lost amongst the hundreds of boats, all different, but the same.

HOW DO I FIND U? he texted.

FIND THE FARRS, she replied.

WHAT DOES A FARR LOOK LIKE?

She sent a shark emoji and he looked to the end of the pier where a crew was busy loading a slick looking boat with cases of beer. A Farr, indeed, looked as fusiform and sibylline as a dangerous shark. Sleek lines, white, flawless skin, a razor-sharp nose. Its mainsail was up, knife-edged, taut, and in the gentlest breeze, it pulled on her stays like an animal. "Are you ready for the ride of your life?" the pit-girl said, batting her eyes. It was a grey Seattle day, misty and windy, but she commandeered gear from the crew to keep him warm. This was his first ride on a race boat, a shake down before their summer racing season.

"Yes," he said.

The writer drove aboard the ferry, parked and looked upon the evening. He intended to get a cup of coffee in the galley, but instead he napped, dreaming in shades of change, tinged with melancholy. He loved his dreams. Even the darkest. The story his mind expressed without an editor: moods and shades and dancing light. Memories, long forgotten, retold as a gift, or a harbinger.

When he awakened, he walked the stern and looked back at the distant city, a lighted jewel captured in a ring of indigo. On the black water, far from the lights, the stars blazed like faraway demon pyres. New constellations appeared. Ones he'd forgotten.

He thought back to a time before pit-girl had taken a bite from that fruit. He was lost in his own sad sea, fraught with disappointment and a slow steady ache. Back then, the Seattle sky was forever grey, ever foreshadowing, ever and always hiding the light.

It was in his constitution to smile at the clouds; smile at the world, hoping it would burn a hole through his troubles. But at the end of it all, after his wife's addiction, infidelity and heart surgery for one of the boys, he sat on his patio listening to her words as she explained the divorce, where the kids would be, where the things would go, how the debt would be split. She'd already found a place to live and a friend to loan her money.

This was the past.

Before the pit-girl, that is.

She had found him holding his chin up, staring into a fire that closed in on him from all directions. The flames were close enough to hear: the snapping and hissing, the fall of burning cedar. And she was a forest nymph, bare feet, and nude slipping through the haze, nubile, her eyes smoky and wild.

It would be easy to find the pit-girl on the island. Find the seediest bar; enter. Follow the noise.

When he found her, she was hoisting a pink pussy, leading the crew in a sea shanty.

We're the crew of Neffy

wherever we may roam

we own the seas we sail on

so we're never far from home

Hey!

We're the crew of Neffy

we sail both far and near

and if we're late to the starting line

we'll be on time for beer!

Hey!

We're the crew of Neffy

You're in for a hell of a ride

and if you think you're gonna get sick

then go to the leeward side

Hey!

We're the crew of Neffy

we're here to have some fun

we've got the beer, a boat to steer

and a big ass bottle of rum!

The writer lifted his cocktail and joined in on the song. He only knew the "Hey" part, but it didn't matter. The crew sang merrily without him in their pink uniforms. Their sponsor was the William T. Hass Foundation for breast cancer research, and the debauchery that would ensue was for a good cause.

CHAPTER 9

Kevin Jonson followed an eagle in the sky—a dark shadow in the blackness of night. He watched it soar in moonlight, above the silhouette of a tall cedar, circle and then land in the dark branches. The whaler's moon was stuck in the sky, crescent with two jeweled stars hanging at its side.

A feather dropped from the tree, lit by the moonlight. Before it touched the ground, he stabbed his harpoon in the sand and caught the feather gently in his grasp, rolled the quill in his fingers, looked out at the straits.

The tide was flooding.

Makah relied on the eagle to spot the whale, signaling them that the time was right to enter the long narrow straits of Juan De Fuca, paddle into the flooding tide and ripping current, wait for the animal to breathe. The thunderbird hunted whale. It used two lighting serpents, tossed down from its wings to chase the animal into the waters of Neah Bay.

Sometimes his ancestors shadowed the creature for days, counting its breaths: waiting, paddling and waiting.

That was then.

Time immemorial.

As a child, his father taught him the art. It was fun to pretend. After harpooning the whale, divers tied stones to their feet and wrapped the whale in cedar rope attached to inflated seal stomachs and pelts used as buoys. They sewed the mouth shut so that it wouldn't sink, and towed it back to Neah Bay. If the journey was successful, they'd feast.

Kevin Jonson liked to imagine it all: the taste of the meat, the laughter and joy in the village, the song and dance and the smell of the animal's delicate flesh cooked over cedar planks. Sometimes he'd tie the stones his great grandfather had used to his feet, float below the surface of Neah Bay, neutral, adrift like a jellyfish. The stones strengthened his legs. He'd wear them around the village, tied to his ankles. During canoe races, he'd stand at the bow, practice his pose with the weights; perched, ready to use his entire body as an instrument of god.

The time was coming.

"Be sure to hold your arm like this," his father said, grasping the harpoon in his hands. "Hold it with the shaft straight. You are strong, boy. But you will need all of your weight to land on the whale to puncture its skin."

Father spoke in the native tongue, Qwiqwidicciat, which was taught in Neah Bay's only school.

"Yes father," he said in Qwiqwidicciat. And his father smiled.

Kevin Jonson raised the tri tipped harpoon, leaned into the shaft and leapt.

The sandy mud flat felt most like the skin of the whale. Lancing the animal would take great strength, an exercise of will and might, pushing the harpoon through the tough epidermis then blubber, muscle and bone. He would open the animal, exposing its inner dimension: blood and flesh, introduced to the cold sting of seawater. A red stream would spurt through the seafoam at the surface and the whale would release its energy.

He pulled the harpoon from the sand and mud, examined it. The mussel shells he had sharpen into razors, and the elk bone, crafted into barbs, stayed fast to the tip of the harpoon.

"You are ready," his father said.

Kevin Jonson disassembled the harpoon, breaking it down into three separate pieces. He marveled at the craftsmanship, a millennium of expertise handed down from one generation to the next.

CHAPTER 10

The pre-party was always something to behold.

There were never enough rooms in town to house all the sailors, so everyone had to find a place to be before midnight. Of course, the place to be was Dan's place, a seaside palace, rented from and old couple who got the hell out of town before the first Farr 30 arrived. They rented it, figuring why not make money in the process? Every year Dan rented it and ran a little den; part brothel, part hostel.

Ortun stepped off his girlfriend's boat. It was a cute little Macgregor, 12' but it took him places. Where it could not take him, he didn't want to go nor did he belong. Ah! What a night. The evening before the race. Cool air, inky black water rippled by a gentle breeze. But the drunk he spotted at the marina would never make it to proper lodging, not at this hour. He stepped up to the man, maybe a sailor, maybe a bum.

"Hey, sailor," Ortun chanced.

"You talkin' to me?"

"Yeah, I am."

"What do you got to say to me, kid?" the man said.

"You look drunk," Ortun told him.

"So, what?" the drunk said. "I'm on vacation."

"Well, this is Oak Harbor," Ortun said. "The cops here only get to beat the shit out of drunk citizens once a year."

"I don't care about no cops, or anything," the man said. "You wanna fight or something?"

Ortun took out his flask and shared it with the drunk.

"What is that?"

"It's gin," Ortun said. "I'm a diabetic."

"Who the hell puts gin in a flask?" the drunk said. "I thought you didn't want to fight."

"Listen, what's your name?"

"My name is Christopher."

Christopher straightened his jacket. There was a chill in the air, a sweet Canadian kiss running down the Fraser River valley. It was summer, but the cold air rolled under the blankets of July and cooled the evenings. The man shivered when the wind hit him and then watched Ortun a while; after he figured out he had nothing interesting to say, he took out a little little silk handkerchief and performed a magic trick. Ortun knew it was hidden in a fake thumb, he'd figured the trick out when he was a kid, but he applauded and smiled.

"Christopher," he said. "When the cops come to throw you in the drunk tank, I want you to say exactly what I'm going to tell you to say, you hear me? Nothing else."

"Ok."

"I want you to say, my name is Christopher. I'm here to race the boats. I can't find Dan Swardstrom. You hear me?"

"Yeah, kid."

Ortun was forty with a cleft chin and eyes the color of a glacier. He let the man take in his face, remember it. The poor bastard was probably a bum, but one never really knew during Race Week. He popped the drunk's collar and patted him on both shoulders.

"Say it back to me," he said.

"My name is Christopher. I'm here to race the boats. I can't find Dan Swardstrom."

"Very good."

In the distance, a foghorn sounded. It was a lonely bull stag, calling out to the night in secluded sorrow. A single, sweet, lamenting note that flooded the empty streets and found every nook and every weed and then disappeared back into the starry night.

CHAPTER 11

Ewan and Duff Hooker relaxed in the hot tub. They were brothers, orphaned and reunited by an uncle who found them when he needed cheap labor. He waited until they were both of working age, found Ewan living on a farm baling hay in Oregon, and Duff shoveling fish in Alaska. He moved them to Everett where he ran a hot tub wholesale, servicing and supply company. The uncle was rumored to have died, leaving the brothers his business, but in fact, he was retired in Mexico, drawing from the company's funds, which only partially explained why Hooker Hot Tubs and Company never prospered. The two fought any chance they could—they fought over money, or beer, chess, cans of tuna, who looked more like their father, whom they'd never met.

A drunk sailor from 65 Red Roses was sitting on Ewan's lap.

"You can't fuck the competition," Duff said.

"Who says I wanna fuck her?" Ewan said.

The girl was nibbling on his ear.

"Yeah," she said. "But if you do, you better screw me good."

"Well," Duff said. "If you're aint gonna screw her, pass her over."

"What was that?" Ewan said, attempting to unlatch her top. "I'm sorry, I have a filter installed that makes it hard to hear people with an IQ lower than seven."

"Huh?"

"I said I have a filter installed to ignore people with an IQ lower than seven."

"Huh?"

"I said—"

The pit-girl appeared from the den. She took off her clothes without spilling her drink.

"Hi boys," she said. "Ready for tomorrow?"

"Hell yes," Ewan and Duff said.

She entered the hot tub the way a princess might.

"Hey," she said to Ewan. "You can't fuck the competition."

"I'm not going to fuck her."

The pit-girl smiled.

"Well pass her over here."

Ewan obeyed.

The two women embraced and kissed hello.

Duff rolled his eyes.

"How many tits have you motor-boated?" he asked the pit-girl. "I mean really? How many?"

"More than you, asshole," she said. "Now why don't you fuck off?"

Ewan and Duff watched the girls make out while listening to jazz playing in the den. The blue lights in the hot tub accentuated their bodies, Star Burst 28-LED color changing spa lights to be exact, turning the water into a beautiful, swirling mess. They maintained and regularly cleaned the tub, free of charge, and did so for health reasons more than anything else.

"What are the conditions tomorrow?" Duff said, attempting to make conversation.

"Light wind," the pit-girl said between kisses, "becoming south-west to ten knots in the afternoon."

"My favorite," Ewan said. "A slow motion chase!"

"All of Dan's money," Duff said. "Just to race at the speed an old man can walk."

It would be a slow course, but sailors raced the course they were given, and like a rack of billiards are busted up at the start of a game, a player—a real player, never re-racked the balls.

"You'll have to un-fuck the mast," the pit-girl said. "Dan didn't tune Neffy for a slug race."

She slipped a hand under Cybil's top.

"Hi Darling," she said. "I'm Mac."

"I'm Cybil," she said.

"Duffy, grab your phone and text Max to get up here before he misses all the fun," the pit-girl said, and then to Cybil. "He knows a trick that I want you to see."

CHAPTER 12

The den was busy. A rolling, rollicking cloud of consciousness intersected by laughter, funneled through stories, food and drink. On the way to Oak Harbor, the skipper of Blue Lullaby fished for Dungeness crab, steamed them on the dock, iced them and brought them to the party ice cold. There was Andy's smoked cod, the flesh so delicate, each bite melted in your mouth without the need for butter. The gin was cold and the beer was crisp.

The writer was serving fried calamari.

"Ah," the devil said. "Devine."

"Thank you."

"What's your secret?"

"Secret," he said. "No secret."

"But the batter, it's like silk."

"Yes," he said aloof. "I use donut batter."

"I see," the devil said. "Unconventional."

"I like to surprise people," the writer said, and then went back to writing on his little pad of paper. "I have an eye for the dramatic."

"I see," the devil said, and he dipped a morsel into the writer's aioli and let it slowly dissolve in his mouth. "I am a man who likes surprises, too. Without surprises, life just unfolds, seemingly without meaning, does it not? A math problem with a solution, you see? And being consciously aware or unaware of our ability to detect surprises is what separates us from the animal world."

"I suppose you're right," the writer said, not impressed. Tying sentences into knots was not interesting, nor were wordsmiths or other writers. When people discovered his profession, they often tripped over themselves attempting to be eloquent, which was annoying and inauthentic. In his mind, the only reason he wrote was to console the innocent, or to corrupt them. "But I don't think every surprise is a blessing," he said putting away his pad of paper. "Some of the worst things in life, happen by surprise."

"Oh really?" the devil said, surprised. "But you see, through the misfortune or fortune of our actions, there is an unending string of events that we pretend are not of our own doing. It's rather simple, in losing what we have lost, and in gaining what we've gained, we are guilty of a great lie."

The writer smiled politely. He hated puzzles. He knew, or thought he knew, that the solution to all puzzles were inevitable, whether they eluded him or not.

"There is no such thing as a lie," he said. "Everything is true."

The devil laughed.

"I like you," he said. "Tell me about this amazing aioli."

"Mayonnaise, lemon, Old Bay seasoning, sweet pickles and a touch of whiskey."

The devil licked his fingers.

"How did you come up with such a concoction?"

"Easy," the writer said. "You take the basic ingredients and change it until it tastes good to you."

"A desecration," the devil said. "You take the classics, and make them taste better?"

"No," the writer corrected. "You take the classic ingredients and you make them taste different."

He watched the devil finish the appetizer, delighting in every bite, and he was just about to fry another batch when the pit-girl interrupted.

"Darling," she said wrapped up in a robe. "Did you get Duffy's text? I want you to meet someone."

The writer grinned. It was obviously the woman who was wrapped around her, kissing her neck.

"Cybil," she said. "This is Max Rigby. He's a writer."

The woman stopped kissing her neck and moved on to his.

"I told her all about you," the pit-girl said. "I told her all about us, how we like to have fun."

"You did, huh?"

"We're taking her to my room, sailor," the pit-girl said, winking at the man who was eating calamari.

"I'm not a sailor," the writer said.

"But I only fuck sailors!" Cybil said.

"Ahoy!" the writer said.

The writer feigned nonchalance. He was self-conscious about these things. He was dating the pit-girl of Nefarious and now he was being ushered off to a threesome. Somehow, the sailors did not hate him. Maybe it was because he cooked for them, or drove them to their boats, or pleasantly talked waitresses and bartenders into not calling the cops when the crew was out of control.

"I'm sorry," the writer said to the devil. "I didn't get your name."

"I'm the devil," he toasted. "You have better things to do than to discuss aioli, do you not?"

In her room, the pit-girl peeled off her robe. It was dark and the sweet scent of their excitement filled his senses. They were busy kissing and pawing at one another like teasing cats, giggling and fashioning each other's hair and letting it fall back on their shoulders into a beautiful, black and red-haired mess. The writer poured a glass of whiskey and watched for a while; he watched the women admire each other from limb to limb as they slowly engulfed each other in a passionate flame. Before his eyes, their bodies became one flame. Sultry, curved locks of hair on white breast, rouge rounded cheeks and a mist of sweat covered them, dappled in moonlight. The beauty; it troubled his heart.

"Remove this woman's bra," the pit-girl said. "The way the cheerleader taught you in high school."

The writer closed in on the playful shadows.
"That was a long time ago," he said, ten years her senior. He still had his drink in one hand, but with the other, he unfastened the woman's bra.

"Yes," the woman moaned.

"See, I told you," the pit-girl told her.

She flipped the woman on her back and tore away the bra.

"Oh yes," the woman said.

They were both young, and he a voyeur. This kind of love . . . this kind of passion, he thought, was it the beginning of the end of him? A last look into the temple of pleasure before he turned and faced the life that waited for his return?

He sat on the side of the bed and watched his lover seduce the woman; her silver words and low-loving laughter caused his heart to roll out of rhythm. He watched as she ran fingers over her taut skin, down her neck and down the valley of her breast.

"Look at her tits, darling!"

The writer warmed his hand on his thigh and stroked her breast with the back of his hand, and then the front. He'd become a connoisseur of breast recently, these being some of the finest; pert and firm, with rosy nipples. He squeezed and stroked until he found a rhythm that corresponded to her breaths. He watched her hips roll and thrust.

"I'm going to tie you up with a round, turn and two-half hitch," the pit-girl told the writer in a husky voice. "It is a highly useful and reliable knot, but it is a constrictor knot, meaning the tighter you pull on it, the tighter it gets," she easily rolled off the bed, dragging a rope behind her. "It doesn't jam. It doesn't give in and guess what, lucky boy? If you can get out of it, you may join us."

CHAPTER 13

At eleven 'o'clock, the doorbell rang and Dan opened the door. It was Christopher.

"My name is Christopher," he said. "I can't find Dan Swardstrom. I'm here to race the boats."

"You found him," Dan said. "Welcome!"

Dan ushered Christopher through the door, took his coat.

"This is Christopher," he announced to his guests. "He's here to see the race boats!"

The sailors cheered.

"Conditions look fair," Dan said, hanging up his coat. "Looks like it's going to be a slow-motion burn."

"I'm here to race the boats."

Dan poured him a drink from his finest bottle of whiskey. He put two ice cubes in the glass and handed it over.

"I always pour from this bottle the night before our first race," he said. "I figure, my crew will take it easy on the good stuff. They have a lot of class. Are you a rigger, a mainsail? You don't look like a tactician."

"I'm here to race the boats," Christopher said, then drank the whisky and chewed on the ice.

Dan poured him another.

"Are you Gardyloo? Bat out of Hell? Moonshine?"

"I'm here to race the boats."

"Ah," Dan said. "You're scouting us and you don't want your skipper to know you're here? Very good." He topped off Christopher's drink and smiled. The man was unshaven, wrinkled clothes and he smelled like a distillery. He could have been a sailor, or just a bum. Dan waited patiently for him to say something but he didn't. Instead, Christopher finished his drink and performed a magic trick.

"I've seen that one before," Dan said. "The handkerchief is in your fake thumb, there."

Christopher frowned.

"My cook has prepared some calamari," Dan told him. "And there's a shower upstairs. Good hunting, tomorrow!"

Dan watched Christopher put a hand full of fried squid in his pocket and disappear upstairs.

"Who's that?" Duff said.

"Christopher," Dan said. "He's here to see the race boats."

"A rigger?"

"He didn't say."

Ewan interrupted.

"Never mind that guy," he said. "Did you hear that Kai is bringing in a pro? Some guy named Kevin Jonson."

"A pro, huh?" Dan said, pouring himself a drink. "No need to worry, boys. No one knows the course like Ortun."

"He's Indian."

Dan paused.

"No shit?" he said.

"Yes—shit, Skipper." Ewan said. "And another thing, that kid you brought in from Vancouver? He hasn't showed up. Rumor has it he ditched us for Jupiter."

"Kai is trying to take us out early, eh?" Dan said, drinking up. "We're gonna need another grinder."

CHAPTER 14

Ortun arrived at midnight, late. His Irish blood forbid him from showing up early, and it also kept him from ever saying goodbye. Now that the pre-party had died down, he could slip away and prepare for his set under the rum tent. On the beach, he lit a small fire and played his guitar to the dancing flames.

The pit-girl's new boyfriend joined him.

"You're a tactician?"

"Among other things."

"Tacticians are the north stars of the fleet, yes?"

"Or something like that," Ortun said, his voice trailing off.

He played a romantic Spanish guitar solo, something that eased the evening through the cold fog creeping in from the east. Ortun was a handsome man, lean and upright with and icy-blue eyes. He didn't seem to care though, the writer thought. In fact, he seemed to be amused by anyone who fell for the trick, always with a rabbit grin and sharp questions.

"You direct the helmsmen through the course?" the writer asked. They'd met on the dock the day of the shake down, when he nearly shit his pants. "You find the wind, tell the skipper when to tack and when to fly the kite."

"Sure," Ortun said, watching the flickering flames. "I guess there's a bit of luck too, if that's what you're getting at."

A moan came from an open window, and they paused to listen to the woman's slow, orgasm—a song of pleasure, a chant, and a lullaby, echoing softly. When she picked up the beat, Ortun played faster.

"The bravest men are the ones who take roles that required luck," the writer said. "Generals, lawyers, fisherman, lovers."

"You flatter me," Ortun said. "But I'm a better musician than I ever was a sailor."

"And I am a better cook, than I ever was a writer."

The writer tipped his cowboy hat and bid Ortun goodnight. Ortun kept playing as he moved into the cold fog and crept up the stairs towards the chants of pleasure. He watched stop and listen outside the door for a while, waited for the sweet lullaby to end and softly entered.

"You are but a dream, inside of a dream" he told the writer, "and dreams of the future are better than the history of the past."
Ortun played his set alone in the darkness awhile—sad, moody melodies lost in fog and consumed by goosebumps on the water. The notes moved through him peacefully and left him pacified without the need to think, only to feel. When the world was black inside, he put away his guitar and gently stamped out the little fire.

CHAPTER 15

Kevin Jonson prayed over a small cedar fire in front of the bus stop. It would be a two-hour trip to Oak Harbor, through the winding roads of the cape. It was a sunny morning; no gales to chill the noonday sun, or late morning fog to keep in the cold. The sun felt good on his shoulders and the cedar vest he wore felt smooth and warm on his skin.

He heard the bus shift gears on Old Cannery Hill, change gears on Main Street near the museum and a moment later, it stopped in front of him. He opened his eyes when the door hissed.

"Hello," the devil said, looking him over. "I'll pay you one-thousand dollars for your vest."

Kevin Jonson entered the bus and paid the devil his fee.

"I have no need for that," he said refusing the money.

Today he wore a Makah hunting vest, made by his grandmother, each stitch woven from pitch, harvested from the phloem of the tree. The cedars on the reservation were kept a secret and only the elders decided if harvesting bark from them was appropriate.

"My father warned me about you, so don't bother," Kevin Jonson said, and he sat, closed his eyes and continued to pray.

"Prayer is a cry of weakness," the devil said over the engine. "It is trickery, a way to avoid the challenges and responsibilities of life."

Kevin Jonson kept his eyes closed.

"I choose not to avoid any of life's responsibilities," he said.

"Then life as it is doesn't frighten you?" the devil asked. "You find peace within the hell fire that is the universe? The ever-and-ever sea of stars, churning out flesh as matter, falling as ash into a dark void?"

Kevin Jonson opened one eye.

"There is no void," he said.

"Your creeds tell you this to comfort you, but I've seen it. Great civilizations, fruiting like apples then falling into a lather of energy that cools into darkness," the devil tapped the compression breaks as he headed down Wakashan Hill. "There are no archangels to cry for, no rapturous deities to worship. What is left of them at least, will fall with the ash into the same void."

Kevin Jonson opened both eyes.

"If I can see it—it is not a void."

"Really?" the devil said amused.

"My father warned me that you would tell me this," Kevin Jonson said. "But, so long as I can see, and feel, and hear the void, then there is no void. The stars do not live in a void that creates stars. People do not live in a void that creates people."

"I see your point," the devil said. "You can't get nothing, from something."

"Yes," Kevin Jonson said.

The devil accelerated and drove onto Highway 2. After he eased the bus into traffic, he offered the warrior some food.

"Do you have a need for breakfast? I have some of Polly's smoked salmon."

He threw it to the warrior.

"I always have a need for that," Kevin Jonson said.

CHAPTER 16

Dan Swardstrom traced the keel of Nefarious the way he traced the back of a woman, a sensuous affair where, if it was done correctly, neither participant knew who was the receiver. To find beauty in its most raw form, one "thing" must admire and the other "thing" must submit. So far as he knew, a Farr 30 was the ultimate submissive. In the great dance, she was willing to turn on a dime, always on his cue: the simplest, tiny fraction of input, sent her waiting, wanting form into the wildest maneuvers. Anything he asked.

Whenever he wanted.

The trick was to ask her very, very, very sweetly.

The other skippers didn't understand this about their fleet. They were coarse and direct. Blunt instincts better suited for a hooker wanting money. No. A Farr 30 was a lady. The princess and the pea.

The devil joined him. He was dressed in a bus driver's uniform, but Dan paid no attention.

"Yes," the devil said. "The Farr is a divine creation."

"You're still here?" Dan said.

"She was designed to resist the coefficient of drag—a dimensionless quantity, affecting anything with mass," the devil said running his hand along the hull. "A puzzle I cooked up."

"Yes," Dan said. "One of your better inventions."

"You'll never figure it out, you know," the devil taunted. "It's what keeps you coming back for more."

"I know," Dan said. "But it keeps me busy."

The devil smiled.

Their relationship was not unlike that of a Labrador and its owner—one who throws a stick into a river and is amused by the endeavor. Dan was a pet, something to toy with, entertainment even, but the moment the stick left the master's hand, the master relinquished all control, and it was entirely up to the dog to return.

"I met your cook," the devil said chewing on a piece of salmon jerky.

"Rigby," Dan said. "What about him?"

"Mac's new boyfriend?"

"Yes."

"I don't like him," the devil said.

Dan was mildly interested.

"How's that?"

"He's neither good nor bad," the devil said. "And I don't like people who think of me as merely a genie."

"He's just a good cook and shore support."

"He's a writer, masquerading as a cook."

"I don't read," Dan said.

"He wrote, Aquarius."

"Oh yeah?" Dan said, "Never heard of it."

"You'd like it," the devil. "He's a romantic fool, like you."

"I've never been one for romance," Dan said still touching his boat. "He's a good enough cook, however. That's useful to me."

"I don't mean romance, Danny," the devil said. "I mean sentimental, in a manly fashion, ergo, the great liar Steinbeck, or the greatest liar of them all, Hemmingway. You see a boat race the same way they see a brothel or a bullfight."

"Never had time to read for pleasure," Dan said without a care, he only read navigation maps, marveled at their attempt to reconcile the infinite. A good map provided all the drama he required. No need for poetry, not when you considered the topography of a seafloor, then set a current free to run wild in its canyons. "And I didn't need to read Rigby's books to have him haul shit around shore-to-shore or to cook food."

"Yes," the devil said, "but did you know that he's every bit of a liar as any writer ever was? Even as a cook he lies. For instance, the recipe for his calamari was stolen from a ninety-two-year-old woman from Ottawa who he feigned losing a scrabble game to, just to keep her talking while he charmed the ingredients out of her."

"Evil bastard."

"Or his aioli?" the devil explained. "It is so delicious because of a woman he allowed to fall in love with him, long enough to know her secret ingredients: cream cheese and sriracha sauce and fresh mint."

"All's fair in love and war," Dan said.

"And he used to steal school busses."

"What?"

"When he was in high school, a hood rat, he figured out where the drivers hid the extra key. He'd take his dates out for a spin and have sexual intercourse with them in the back seat."

Dan smiled.

Maybe he and Rigby were the same kind of romantic.

"Rigby's a puzzle," Dan said, getting back to work, "one that I don't have time to solve."

"Martina seems to get along with him just fine."

Dan stopped touching his boat and turned to face the devil.

"That's none of your business," he said. "Rigby and her are friends. They help with shore support and take care of the crew. That's all."

"Yes, of course," the devil said with an easy smile. "But that business at Round the County?"

"It was just drunken fun, you hear?" Dan said in a stern voice. "We were all a little crazy that night, including me."

"My apologies," the devil said throwing a stick into the water for his Labrador to fetch, "but just remember I told you this—your cook has green eyes like myself, and as Caligula once told me, Corves osculum corvid non-erupt—a crow does not pluck out the eyes of another crow."

Dan leered at the devil's green eyes. They were indeed like the writer's, the kind of green that hid under winter snow—a seething, passionate, hungry-for-light shade of green that waited patiently for the ice to thaw. And now, after considering the devil's eyes, he could see it.

"We all need puzzles to solve," the devil said lighting a Marlboro, "and Rigby has one hell of one to solve in the pit-girl, doesn't he?"

"Yes," Dan admitted.

"You tell him now that he's let her out of the bottle," the devil said taking a drag from the cigarette. "There will be no putting her back inside of it."

CHAPTER 17

Dan Swardstrom sat down at the table. He was happy to be together with the crew again, they'd all trickled in little by little, all, minus their stolen grinder. Jupiter's new sails would have no slack in them, and considering the slow conditions, he needed a strong man on the wrench, very strong, to keep his aging mainsail tight and fast.

"Skipper," Ewan said. "Can you believe this shit?" He was irate, and busy shaming a waiter. "This place doesn't serve mimosas."

"No, sir," the waiter corrected. "We don't serve mimosas by the pitcher!"

"What the hell kind of establishment is this?"

Dan handed over a bottle of O.J. and champagne he'd brought for his main trimmer.

"Ewan," he said. "I got you."

"Thanks skipper," Ewan said popping the cork. "I have to stay hydrated."

Dan waved the waiter away.

"Listen," he told the crew. "Problem-one, what are we going to do about Kai's new tactician."

The crew looked up from their breakfast and some even set down their glasses of mimosas.

"Who is it?" Ewan said, emptying a vase of flowers and mixing up a strong mimosa.

"Some guy named Kevin Jonson."

Ortun bowed his head and whistled.

"I heard of that guy," he said. "He's a native. Sailed in the world's back in '11. He knows every current, every back eddy of the Salish. The dude sails shirtless so that he can feel the direction of the wind on his skin."

"Fucking hell," Ewan said, he whipped out his phone and group texted the crew of Tupac, WHO THE HELL IS JUPS NEW TACH?

"And get this," Ortun said, "he fucking sails with a sacred harpoon."

No one at the table knew what to say about this.

"What?" Duff said after a beat. "I thought the Indians around here were fisherman and farmers. Am I to take it that blubber is no longer a profitable and delicious business?" he said, taking a drink from his mimosa, "and now the they're taking our jobs?"

"No," Ortun said. "The dude doesn't race for money, he chooses a boat and he sails for free."

"A pro who sails for free?" Ewan cursed. "What the fuck?"

Dan was not surprised. This kind of shit came with the territory. He once sailed with a Venetian who used a gondola oar to signal a tack or to jibe. He'd stand at the stern of the boat and sing his commands in the style of Italian opera. He didn't accept money—his payment came in the form of his captured audience.

Dan poked the writer.

"Didn't you write a book about the Makah?"

"Yes," the writer said. "I lived out in Neah Bay for a spell. Tried to write about whaling, but they went underground when the government revoked their hunting rights using the Marine Mammal Protection Act of—"

"Fascinating," Ewan said. "Please tell us more about obscure federal laws protecting cows that turned into fish, Mr. Rigby."

The writer began to finish, but the pit-girl squeezed his hand.

"Fuck right off," she told Ewan. "He was asked for help—and he's trying, aren't you darling?"

"Don't worry," Ortun interrupted. "He hasn't won a championship race yet. As a matter of fact, at world's, he hit and nearly killed a grey whale, go figure. Got a DNF for his troubles."

The crew was reassured by this.

"Hey, skipper," Ewan shot off, reading a text from his phone. "The guys on Tupac say that he can grind, too. HES A KILLA. U BETTA LOOK OUT, MOFO."

"A grinder too?" Dan said, cursing Kai. "That's why he stole our guy. He'll be double handed every set."

"Shit," Ewan said. "Let's head over to the crew circle and scrounge one up."

Dan's phone beeped and he looked at the screen.

It was the devil.

U STILL NEED A GRINDER? he texted.

YEP, Dan replied.

HOW ABOUT MY FRIEND? The devil asked.

WHATS HIS NAME?

BONESTEEL.

SEND HIM TO THE DOCKS, Dan said.

CHAPTER 18

Kai met his tactician at Dock 1A.

"You like this boat, big guy?"

"Yes," Kevin Johnson said. He set his harpoon against the hull of Jupiter and ran his hand along the inline of the keel. The beautiful boat was out of the water on her trailer, and looked as graceful as Eschrichtius robustus, the grey whale, taken by his tribe years ago and memorialized at the museum. "But it's not properly tuned for today's conditions."

Kevin Jonson stopped at the centerboard.

The Farr 30 has a large lead bulb attached to a steel cast fin, which made it look like an upside-down shark carrying a missile launcher. The cast fin was bulbous and weighed down significantly, allowing the boat to stay upright in windy conditions, but it also created drag.

"Oh, yeah?"

"Yes," Kevin Jonson announced. "The bulb needs to be more hydrodynamic."

"Ok, I have something special," Kai assured him.

Kevin Jonson followed the owner to a locker in the back of the trailer, who turned a combination lock this way and that and then opened the doors.

Kevin Johnson tried not to smile.

The new keel bulb was shaped like a teardrop, tapering off to a sharp point. A titanium coating covered the lead, and there wasn't a scratch on it.

"Have you used this before?" Kevin Jonson said.

"No," Kai said. "I don't think it's legal."

"I've used them at World's," he said. "Same spec requirements here at Race Week, but not many owners can afford it."

If the Farr 30 was tuned correctly, it rode high out of the water so that the only drag it created was produced by the bulbous centerboard. When the conditions were right, and the equipment was top notch, it could hydroplane, leaving only the bulb in the water. This gave the passengers the sensation of flying.

"You're the boss, big guy," Kai said, closed the locker and scrambled the lock. "Say," he said, looking the Indian up and down. "What's with the suit? And the rocks tied to your ankles?"

"It is the native dress of my people," Kevin Jonson said. "Surely you understand?"

Kai figured out what he was saying.

"Sure, I do, but I'm from Thailand," he said. "I left home to get away from all that nonsense."

"That's how we are different," Kevin Jonson said. "I am home."

Kevin Jonson retrieved his harpoon and looked around the marina.

"We need more men here, to help us attach the new keel bulb," he said. "But we're going to put it on backwards."

"Why on earth would you do that?" Kai asked.

"Because, I'm the pro, remember?"

CHAPTER 19

Low tide in Oak Harbor is called "breakfast for crows" by the sailors. Every stinking, rotting thing that ever lived and died in the ocean washes ashore, finds some snag, or nook as its final resting place before its final communion.

The devil smiled.

He sat and watched the crows. In their black eyes, he could see morning's sunrise into sweet rapture. A hopeful chirping began, and the creatures in the thicket picked and preened through phantom pictures of meals and activities that they might find on this new day. Somewhere in their cognizance, they visualized the dropped sticky sweets left on the beach; or the butt-ends of crumbly hot dog buns; purple gum; or chicken bones with gristle. They dreamed, or perceived to dream, of fattened squirrels and cats that might be left dead in the city's streets, spines, a limb or two— something that would sustain them, body and soul. In their mind's eyes, they stood over the carcasses and culled flesh from the bones and then flew into the clouds with dangling entrails.

Beaks clattered.

Some of the creatures were not interested in food at all. Some dreamed of sex—sex in the trees, sex on a telephone wire, in an old dusty attic, on a chimney. While the sun continued to rise, these birds preened themselves in foppish detail and picked obsessively at feathers in the pits of their wings.

And there were those who dreamed of war—war with big birds, war with little birds, war with medium birds, and war with a fence post. They schemed: a fierce talon in the breastbone followed by deathly pecking? Or a beak in the skull followed by a deathly clawing? It mattered very little who their foe would be, so long as blood be spilt this day!

The sky ignited; rays of light began to crest the city's skyscrapers, sending golden warmth to the moss-covered thicket. Shadows from the new light drifted through knotted limbs and made branches crawl like snakes. In a moment, it would be time to fly.

The birds readied themselves.
Some bounced on their perch, exercising cramped muscles, some called out crass serenades, exciting themselves, and others dropped onto rooftops and began pulling at shingles small and loose enough to molest.

The sailors heard the cawing; the clatter, clawing and the torn, fallen shingles sliding into tin gutters with a clang! Dreary-eyed, they pulled on halyard, adjusted mainstays; started their motors and joined the murder.

The devil lit a cigar and took a sip of whiskey from his flask. "Race Day," he said aloud.

CHAPTER 20

The writer kissed the pit-girl.

She was the worst kind of addiction. The kind you didn't want to quit. The kind that flooded you with waves of pleasure so intense that you got the shakes while you waited for the next flood of endorphins to hijack your brain. Until then, you waited. You waited until you were alone with her, and she only had you as a novelty. No race. No sailors. No navigation charts. Just you and her, drinking coffee, flirting, holding hands...

"What's wrong, darling?" she said.

"Nothing."

When she called him darling, she seemed more mature.

"You are the worst liar I ever met."

"I'm the best."

She was not amused, but she held onto her contempt. There was a dark demon lost in her golden eyes—a powerful succubus he knew was hiding.

"Why didn't you help me with that pretty girl last night?"

The writer scratched his chin.

"I couldn't get out of your knot."

She frowned harder.

"But that's an easy knot, and you know it."

"I don't like easy puzzles," he lied. "Just the hard ones."

A horn went off in the distance. The starting clock. Race boats were given thirty minutes to dash onto the course and begin jockeying for position. Unless you were a sailor or a passenger on the committee boat, it was the only part of the day that looked like a race. Even worse, the race course changed every day—from some obscure peninsula, to some harbor, to some desolate inlet—and from what he'd gathered, each race increased with difficulty and started further away from shore. This, he deduced, was why there were few spectators at Race Week, only sailors and their lovers, the one's too insecure to stay at home.

"Not now," she said, her frown turning angry. "Not before a race."

"Every day there is a race," he said. "We won't talk for a week. Race Week, remember?"

"If you have something to say, Max, say it," she said. "It will get that nasty taste out of your mouth."

They were a cactus and a tree—two entities, too incongruent, too different to know the other any better: a fish and a rattlesnake, a mosquito and a steel bull. Perhaps, he thought on the ferry ride to Oak Harbor, there was no hope of benefiting one another. Everyone around them seemed to know it, and maybe they did too.

"Are we fighting?" he said.

"Out with it," she said.

He lit a cigarette and looked into the smoke. If he left her now, left Oak Harbor for good, he'd save himself the agony, and maybe even some of his dignity.

"You were the hero last night," he said into the cloud of smoke. "It was your show, you know? You were Homer and I was Odysseus."

It had only been a few months since they'd met, and the truth was, she was too young to indulge, too old to flatter. Her youth was a nice change however, but in the back of his mind, he knew better than to steal a ripe strawberry from his neighbor's vine—yet he'd think about the taste forever. Wake to the smell of strawberries warmed in the noonday sun. Wish, hope and imagine the taste.

"Don't do it now Max," she said. "Not before a race."

The writer knew better.

He smiled.

A break up before a race was too harsh. Messy. A dangerous distraction on the Salish Sea. Mean. And maybe he was wrong about Robin? Maybe he was wrong about last night? The way he defied her. Maybe he could tolerate being her lucky plaything a little longer? By the end of Race Week, there was sure to be enough drama to write stanza after stanza before his heart could break. And what was the worst that could happen? He'd done it before. He could do it again. The heart was an organ that did not break, it bruised and got better.

The pit-girl smiled.

"Ok darling," she said. "The gear will be dockside at two-hundred hours. Dan will need you to break down it and set it up before the race tomorrow. Dinner will be ready at five, yes? The crew will be hungry, especially Duffy."

"Aye-Aye," he saluted. "Bullets."

A silver bullet was awarded to race boats for winning a heat. A prize that some sailor wore around their necks or as earrings.

"Bullets," she said turning her back.

No one was better at saying goodbye with her ass than the pit-girl. Even in sailor boots, it looked like she was walking away with the highest-heeled pair of fuck-you shoes in the universe.

The writer sighed and returned to Dan's den where he'd watch the start of the race from the balcony, sit in the hot tub and drink Dan's Irish whiskey, perhaps with a little coffee stirred in; take some notes and then a nap. For fuck's sake. He'd need his beauty rest. Race Week had only begun.

CHAPTER 21

There is an energy that rises on the first day of racing, a potent vim that floods in with the tide, settles and fills every crack and crag. The sailors zip and tie shit down, and fasten, tuck and pull on anything that will give them an edge, or comfort. They are serious, but jovial. The day will be long and the water waits. It sparkles with promise and holds the stories they will share when after the tide has ebbed, night has fallen and the course resets.

Dan was worried.

The new grinder hadn't showed up, and his pit-girl was extra grumpy and officious. Rigby was useful, but their augments were a distraction to Mac: always existential, mostly filled with subtext. It was easy for him to understand from the outside. Mac was a lightning rod, and every sailor in the fleet wanted at her: she was hot, yes, but he saw in her the potential to actually lead the fleet of sailors she fucked around with.

"Have you inspected Jupiter's keel yet, skipper?"

The pit-girl almost never called him by his title.

"No," he said.

"Well maybe you ought to!" she said, and peeled away.

Mac never dated sailors, she only fucked them. This was a fatal flaw, and she knew very well what a man would tolerate, so long as he had access to her bed. They'd let a pretty girl get away with the most outrageous behaviors: locking them in a "friend zone", calling them the wrong name during sex, having a psychotic break in public. But the cook, he'd call her out on her infractions. He'd been around a few pretty women and knew better, or did he? Somehow, he walked the line between anchoring Mac and giving her enough rope to drift amongst the sea of testosterone oozing out of every sailor.

Dan stopped to have a word with Kai.

"You stole my grinder," he said. "Bad form, sailor."

"All's fair in love and sailing," Kai laughed. "Conditions look light, so don't be a baby."

"We found another this morning," Dan said. "Your petty move won't amount to much."

"It will," Kai challenged, "without a good grinder, Dan's monster will appear."

Dan paused.

"What are you talking about?"

"You blow your starts," Kai said. "Everyone knows you suck at it. They call it your monster, so I decided to hit you where it hurts, big guy."

Dan didn't flinch, but he imagined a scaly thing standing on his deck.

"Word is, we found a good one," he said as calm as he could muster, but the scar under his eye started to twitch. "Bonesteel, ever heard of him?"

"Oh sure," Kai said. "He's good, but I have plenty of other surprises for you, Danny. Don't you worry.

"Like your Indian tactician?" Dan said.

Kai stopped untying a bumper.

"What about him?"

"Ortun sailed against him once," Dan said. "Hell of a fine sailor."

"The best."

"That money can buy, right?"

"You got it big guy," Kai said holding up the bumper. "You'll need plenty of these, today."

"You like it rough, do ya?"

"All I can get, Danny."

Dan stepped closer to Kai.

"Can I ask you something?

"Go ahead, big guy."

Dan didn't want to offend Kai, but maybe he did.

"You placed second in worlds last year," he said. "A great showing. You won Swiftsure, Round the County. You even placed at Van Ise."

"Unlike you," Kai said, "I have a serious program."

"But, you never hired a pro, did you? You never stole my crew. What is it about Race Week this year that's got your panties so tight?"

Dan was serious, and he almost never was.

Kai took his time answering.

"This is the race that's the most fun," he said finally.

"To sail?" Dan asked.

"No," Kai said, "to win."

Dan tried not to change his temperament, but his words were terse.

"I don't get it, Kai. You win a lot of races. And you win without taking cheap shots—like, your bulb there," he pointed out. "Why is it on backwards? You could hydro, run into another boat and puncture the hull."

Kai stammered.

"My pro tells me they do it at worlds," he said. "How many times has that boat of misfits gone to worlds? Once! And you only placed ninth. Take it to the committee if you're afraid, Danny."

"I'm not afraid," Dan said. "But everyone will keep thinking you're an asshole."

"I am an asshole," Kai said, and smiled. "I'm an asshole who spends his money on a pro. But you! Instead of new sails and a decent crew, you spend your money on party-houses and chefs."

"Rigby? Chef?" Dan corrected. "He's a cook and he works for free."

Kai shook his head disappointedly.

"You don't care about winning," he lectured. "You're like a thirteen-year-old man-boy. You only care about having fun. Your program isn't serious, Danny. This year, I'm going to show everyone that you're a fraud and that you're out here just fooling around."

"Sailing is supposed to be fun."

"No, it's not, big guy. It's a sport."

"It's a way of life."

"It's a competition," Kai said. "A competition you're going to lose."

Dan turned to head back to Nefarious.

"The cup's been mine the last four years," he said, "and I've had a lot of fun doing it."

"Not this year," Kai said following him. "You're Roman Toga party this year is going to be a big downer without a trophy, isn't it? In fact, I'll let you in on a little secret, big guy. Some of the other skippers back off at the end of the race so that you can win. And do you know why? Because they can't afford to throw a fun party like you! How's that racing? Not this year! This year, I've already rented the Admiral Room for my party—a black tie party, with a champagne fountain and fondue, seafood, and a giant fucking chandelier!"

Dan was stunned. He knew exactly what Kai was doing. This was not a "black tie" crowd and dressing them in suits would be stabbing the fleet in the heart.   "You'll be hearing from the committee about that bulb," Dan cursed.

"Good hunting, big guy," Kai said laughing, then strutted off. "I predict that you'll want to be all alone on the night of the big party. In your boat, alone, watching my party from a distance! Then you'll want to go home and think about what's important in your life. How you failed.

Maybe instead of boats, you'll leave this all behind you, leave your boat right here in the marina for scavengers to pick through because you just don't care anymore."

Dan hurried to the crew circle to find the pit-girl. Problem 1, he thought, find the grinder. Problem 2, beat the hell out of Kai for causing Problem 1. Problem 3, rent tuxedo, just in case Problem 1 and 2 are not solved immediately.

When he found the pit-girl, her eyes were glowering.

"Where's the grinder?" she said.

"My friend said he'd be here."

"You're friend and your grinder aren't reliable."

"It's their nature," Dan speculated.

"Honestly," she said, locking eyes with him. They were a strange color, gold when she was angry. "I can't crew for you if your guys are gonna flake on us. The season is almost over, and I need a winning boat to catch that gig at worlds—I hear Rolex is looking for a pit—"

"I'm not their mother, Mac," Dan interrupted. "I don't wake them up and fold their pajamas."

"Maybe you should."

"Maybe you should remember who's skipper."

The pit-girl stopped and smiled. Not a real smile. The corners of her lips fought hard to hold up her cheeks and, instead of letting them fall, she took a sip from her flask.

"Aye-Aye, skipper," she saluted.

CHAPTER 22

Bonesteel.

A menace.

A magician.

Bonesteel.

Devilishly handsome, fatally serendipitous. Six pack abs, wired directly into his amygdala. Biceps made of gold. No one has ever seen the man without a tank top. Not in a restaurant. Not at a funeral. That's how he rolls.

Bonesteel.

Nobody does it like Bonesteel.

Best grinder in the fleet, they say. Stamina. Vicious. Virile. Viral. There is a story going around that he's already had two vasectomies.

Bonesteel.

Is twenty-five.

Father of two and one-quarter bastard children.

Bonesteel.

Officer Bonesteel. Discharged from active duty. Begged by his commanding officer to leave before he brought down the entire Royal Navy. Bonesteel. Released on his on his own recognizance, as if he ever had such a thing.

Bonesteel.

Scared by a flaming drink.

Beardless from a fire.

Oh!

It was an enchanting night!

And it happened that Auckland 's mayor had decided to see his town from a perspective seldom seen by him—not from downtown where he spent most of his time in the shadows of pre-colonial buildings. Tonight! Tonight, he would watch his metropolis from across the bay where it seemed to pulse, breathe and live.

The mayor would sit at the bar next to Officer Bonesteel.

Bonesteel had just returned from a year tour of duty, where he worked twelve-hour days on a remote island as punishment for violating several of the navy's code of ethics, including the invasion of his superior officer's daughter's vagina. He had grown a beard and none of the women with whom he had been acquainted might recognize him. And, better still, none of their boyfriends or husbands of fathers who had seen him slipping away through the backyard while buttoning his trousers could sucker punch him in the kidneys, or cold-cock him on the crown. It was a relaxing evening, and he thought fondly of friends he could call that were not married or too ashamed to see him.

"'Evening sir," the bartender said. "What'll it be?"
Bonesteel thought for a moment, his eyes walking around the swanky lounge.

"I'll be havin' a go at that, mate."

The bartender followed Bonesteel's glance, at the far side of the room, a waiter was making a show of a flaming drink. The brandy's blue flame leapt and flickered seductively. The smell of cinnamon filled the air.

"You bet-cha'!" the bartender said enthusiastically. "Comin' right up!"

The mayor looked up from his fine scotch to watch, and with a mild sort of interest, he mused over the presentation: the quick, stylistic rub of a lemon wedge around the rim of a wine glass, a dip into a saucer of sugar and cinnamon, a splash of sherry. It was all done with proud bravado. The mayor watched the bartender swirl the velvet mixture romantically, sniffed the air lightly and allowed the sweet smell to perfume his senses. The bartender added the 151.

"Smells good!" the mayor said.

"Just wait until I light the thing!" the bartender said. "You'll think you were a' smellin' Heaven!" Then, while smiling a little smile, the bartender whipped out a match. As the drink was designed to do, everyone at the bar waited in anticipation, and then, with a bit of pompousness, the bartender struck the match. He grinned a little grin and dunked the ignited end into the concoction.

And this is when Bonesteel's face caught fire.

After the glass exploded from the too-sudden movement of molecules, little shards of hot razors covered the Mayor's fine Italian double-breasted suit. It all happened and ended in an instant, and the expression on his face was that of horrified surprise.

"Oh! Ohoo! Oh!" the mayor said excited. This would no doubt ruin his fine, scotch-induced mood. "Oh!"

While the bartender apologized and cleaned the politician, he failed to realize that one of his customer's face was engulfed in a cool blue flame. By the time he noticed, it would be too late! Ezekiel Bonesteel's beard had been burned clean off his face.

At the end of the bar, a man yelled while shaking a fist, "That's Ezekiel Bonesteel! The son-of-a-bitch nailed my wife!"

CHAPTER 23

Dan watched the young man approach from a distance, the only sailor without a home. Late. Sunglasses. Neon-white lotion on his nose. Tank top on a day when the sun hadn't broken through the marine layer.

Bonesteel walked right up to him and dropped his bag.

"You my new, skipper, bud?"

"You must be, Bonesteel."

Bonesteel saluted perfectly.

"You have as many wheels as a fucking canoe there bud!" he said.

"What was that, sailor?" Dan couldn't place the accent. New Zealand? Australia? South Africa? It was someplace where white people originally didn't belong.

"You got a dial-tone there, bud?" Bonesteel said. "Hard to believe you're a skipper."

"You're late," Dan said. "The crew is waiting. You'll have to figure them out on your own."

Bonesteel saluted again, then he flashed his massive biceps.

"I heard Nefarious has as many ponies under the hood as my sister's hair dryer. Good thing I was only fishing for snakes today," he said, and kissed both biceps. "Not anymore."

"I don't understand you at all, sailor."

Bonesteel slapped Dan hard on the back.

"The skipper of Jupiter called your skiff a fuck-bud, and he made me run upstairs and put your socks on you at Round the County. Remember, bud? In that kind of wind! I'm puttin Nefarious to sleep, he yelled at me! And he did it too, bud. Second tack to port. He came at cha' with a full kite and you fell down and skinned your knee like a brat. That was these beautiful girls," he kissed his biceps again. "I put that sail up on you, yes I did skipper." Bonesteel smiled proudly then picked up his bag and headed down the dock. "And if you think I won't do the same to Jupiter, then you're as wrong as my jerky hand."

Dan scratched his head.

What an asshole, he thought, he'll fit right in.

CHAPTER 24

On the deck of the committee boat, the devil watched the fleet jockey for position. There was only a light wind, but if he tired of these conditions, he could always change them. The marine layer had not yet burned off and there was still a thick cloak of fog resting on the water.

Jupiter was off to a good start, but the beginning of a race is diabolical, deemed one of the tensest moments in all of creation, a tightrope walk between passive and aggressive.

PUSH DAN. MAKE HIM BLOW HIS START, he texted. The tacticians sailed with their phones in waterproof cases. They were always on the lookout for tips from fans or skippers who were willing to keep the race competitive, and you could count on more chatter from the less serious boats, wildcards and spoilers.

WILL DO, War Canoe texted.

ROGER THAT, 65 Red Roses texted.

It wasn't necessary. Jupiter took the lead, positioning themselves to cross the starting line first, a devious move to push ahead early, stealing wind from the others. Race Week was no fun at all unless he toyed with his pet, and Nefarious took the bait. But was Kai faking? A one-buoy penalty was exacted for crossing it too soon, enough time to lose the entire day. Yet it was worth the risk! If done correctly, a good start could win you the day. Often, it was the only excitement of the entire race, sweetening the victory that much more.

The area judge prepared to raise his "go" flag, and any tactician worth his weight would be watching him through binoculars.

The devil grinned and put his pinky in his gin and tonic, stirred the lemon, and a dark tendril sank from the marine layer, ruffling the water.

Nefarious saw it, and instead of avoiding it, they moved to gather the energy.

GOOSEBUMPS ON THE WATER, Deadliest Catch texted.

WE C IT, Bravo Zulu respond. LET DAN AND KAI HAVE A PISS FIGHT! I'M NOT GOING TO SCRATCH UP MY GEL COAT AT THE FIRST SIGN OF SCRAPS.

Four boats moved windward, Blue Lullaby, Bat Out of Hell, Bad Blood and Deep Pickle. Two of the skippers feigned a tack, driving right at Nefarious and then backed off. But not Kai. Jupiter pushed hard ahead, right at Dan, a few boat lengths. He caught the fresh air an instant before Nefarious and cleared the anchor line.

LOOK AT THOSE BASTARDS GO AT IT, Critical Theory texted.

The devil smiled when Dan threw a protest flag.

"Oh, Baby!" he said. And sipped from his gin and tonic.

The area judge raised the "go" flag, irrelevant to the rest of the fleet. In today's conditions, the race was already decided.

A surprise!

The area judge set his go flag aside and raised the caution flag as a committee member talked in his ear.

I C IT, texted War Canoe.

WTF texted Cherish.

The devil made his way from the mini bar to the back of the boat.

"What's going on, Edmund?" the devil asked the area judge.

"Hold on," the area judge said. He picked up the microphone and spoke to the fleet. "Be advised, grey whale on the course, moving east of your position at Strawberry Hill. Your boats are to stay fifty-feet to avoid any contact as you maneuver for a restart."

"What the hell is this?" the devil said. "You can't do that."

"The marine mammal protection act says I have to."

"Those pinheads! Bullshit."

"Not bullshit. It's the law."

"Law?" the devil said. "There is no such thing as law, just silly rules attempting to keep the universe from its natural state of order, bedlam! Are you kidding me? What about the ozone? Huh? You guys don't care about that shit. Or global warming? Your boat's fuel is doing more damage to those sea cows than a sailboat."

The area judge raised his postponement flag and reset the course, sending the devil back to the mini bar cursing.

"What the hell has happened to you people," he said to a stranger sitting at the bar. "You yellow bellied, snail-skulled little rabbits. I gave you the apple! You took a bite, and now look at you! Afraid to play tag with a whale."

"Who the hell are you?"

The devil looked up from his drink.

"Behold," he said. "I have created the smith that bloweth the coals in the fire, and that bringeth forth an instrument for its work, and from the fire, I have created the will to destroy."

"Right," the stranger said. "Can I buy you a drink?"

"Make it a double," the devil said.

A call went over the short-band—an urgent demand for Jupiter to steer clear of the whale.

"I say again, Jupiter. You are to stay fifty-feet from any whale," the area judge said. "What are you doing out there Kai, sightseeing?"

The devil stood up and moved quickly to the rail. Jupiter was tacking windward, directly at a breaching whale. The area judge blasted his horn and the creature's slick skin disappeared below the surface just before Jupiter intersected its path.

"Restart the goddamn race," the area judge said. "And make Kai round a buoy to let them know not to fuck with me again."

"For Christ's sake!" the devil said. "There's a Farr 30 rep here! He's scouting the course for worlds! Don't be such a pussy."

CHAPTER 25

Dan looked for his monster. Found it. Standing on the deck in all its scaly glory. He cursed Kai for creating it and looked the other way. The crew knew it was there. It sailed with him at the start of every race. Starts were not Dan's forte, nor was ignoring the obvious. He'd blown just about every important start, but even with the ugly thing ting on deck, the miracle was that he still managed to win. Once the monster left, he'd positioned himself for a strong finish.

"Fly the kite," Dan said.

The crew looked confused.

The restart was on and the clock. A power move on a spinnaker set was a gamble this early. If executed, it could make the start a mini race for position on a short course, giving them an advantage in the straits. If not executed, they'd be stuck out front with their underpants on the mast.

"You heard him!" Ortun said. "Smack it up there, for your skipper."

The crew scrambled to raise the spinnaker.

"What's up?" Ortun said to Dan.

"They look rusty," Dan said of the crew. "Hair of the dog. Too much fun last night, I guess."

Ortun looked confused.

"No more than usual," he said. "It's Race Week."

Dan watched Bonesteel set the winch, the forward position that would raise the spinnaker. He was ready before the pit-girl had fastened it to the halyard that would draw it up to the top of the mast—but Ewan was busy tying his shoes, two bunny-ears and Duff was making fun of him.

"Get your asses in gear," Dan told them.

The whales had cleared the course, but Kai was downwind. He had not yet tacked for his run back to the starting line because of the penalty.

"What's that bastard doing?" Dan demanded.

"He has a penalty-buoy to round," Ortun said. "He must have something up his sleeve."

This was an insult. Somehow, Kai had gotten under his skin on the dock. "Fly that damn kite!" Dan said, turning Nefarious to catch the wind.

Bonesteel leaped into action.

"Grab your monkey by the tits!" he said, and the crew instantly responded to his barking. "Do it, buds! Do it!" Ewan left one of his shoes untied and Duff leapt to the bow to grab the top of the spinnaker from the pit-girl. She pushed it through the hatch, scrambling as if she held two arms full of lava. Duff attached it to the main halyard. "You fuck-buds! I can pay a stripper two loonies and get kicked in the nads."

Dan eyed Kai from across the breach. Jupiter was tacking away from the whale, and lining up to steal the wind that would fill Nefarious' spinnaker.

"No way," Ortun warned. "Forget about it Dan. "We missed it!"

There was one chess move left, to put Nefarious on the line where it wouldn't be rolled by Jupiter. Dan aimed Nefarious against the wind. Crazy Horse and Tupac stayed out of the pissing contest, backed off when they saw him coming.

LOOK AT THEM GO, texted Bravo Zulu.

Bat Out of Hell and You're a Wolf pushed forward, sucking up wind, shadowing Blue Lullaby, leaving a lane for someone to slingshot into.

"He's trying to pin the line," Dan said.

The spinnaker filled.

A thump and a splash.

"No! No! No!" Dan said.

OH SHIT, texted Tupac. DAN's GONNA PITCH FORK.

Nefarious' ass came high out of the water. The bow caught a sloppy wave and spilled over the deck. More wind took hold of the spinnaker.

"Kill it!" Ortun said. "Kill it now!"

The bow dug in, tripped like it was wearing new shoes and Nefarious stopped moving forward. The spinnaker pulled the stern higher, more water spilled over the deck and the next thing Dan saw was green water smack him with an ocean-sized kiss.

CHAPTER 26

"Wipeout!" the devil said. "Did you see that?"

The devil called for the bartender.

"Dan just lost the race! No, he just lost the week! That's a DNF for sure," he cheered. "A round on me," he announced. "Top of the line. Whatever the fans want."

The devil fixed his tie in the mirror, reached for a bottle of champagne and went to find the area judge.

"Edmund," he said. "Did you see that? Oh my! What a delightful surprise! No way they make up an entire race. They splashed out like a fat girl in a kiddie pool."

The devil whipped out his phone and texted Dan, WIPEOUT!? UR AN ASS DAN!

"Looked pretty bad," the area judge said. "Lucky no one was hurt."

"Oh, they're hurt," the devil said. "The fleet will be an entire race up on them. A wipeout at the start of day one! They won't make it up, Edmund. They'll be the laughing stock of Race Week. What was Dan thinking? He won't be able to host a victory party this year!"

"Who says Kai will win?" the area judge said. "There's thirty boats here today."

"Of course, Kai's going to win," he said. "Dan and him are the only two who care about winning Race Week!" the devil said, and he poured two glasses of champagne. Oh sure, he knew that compared to a supernova it was a puny affair—an event happening on a speck drifting in dark energy that met another dimension in a web of dimensions—each hidden inside of a hole that folded into another dark speck inside of a cell that lived on a fungus that decomposed the bodies of its lost cosmic children. But Race Week was the only event in the universe that he allowed to surprise him. "A wipeout! Kai must have gotten in Dan's head this morning. What a chump!"

"Dan's no chump."

"Oh really?" the devil said. "Are you one of those Dan supporters who throw the race just to have a party at his house? Really Edmund. The area judge?"

"I'd never throw a race for Dan."

"Do you know how he received his scar?" the devil asked, and then told him the story. "It was given to him by a hooker in Tijuana whom he drunkenly forgot to pay. When he left the brothel, she called him a *barato gringo* and threw a bottle of Corona at him."

The area judge frowned.

"Beer, Edmund?" the devil offered.

"No thanks," the area judge said "—you sick bastard."

CHAPTER 27

The area cordoned off for the post-race ceremony was empty. In a few hours, the marine layer would burn off and a vacant, weedy lot would be filled with sunshine and sailors, rum and beer, silver bullets and a dazzling gold trophy. The bullets would be awarded to the victors of day, but the trophy would go to the team that won the cumulative shortest time it took to sail five races during the event. Making time, anyway a skipper could do it, made the difference between sixth place and first. When after it was all in the books, at the end of the race, the Farrs were so well tuned that, assuming all five of the races were completed, a first and second place competitor might only have a few seconds between them.

The "Rum Tent" was set, and the stage electrified, ready for the band to plug in—Ortun's band, who came every year and led the sailors in revelry—sea shanties, country, rock-n-roll, anything that got them to move and drink and sing and dance. "Medicinal Sailor and The Propagation Blenders" arrived with a professional "We're gonna rock your scallywag asses" attitude, and Ortun always wore his top hat. He was the lead singer, and when he wasn't racing boats, you could sure as hell bet he was playing music or nailing some pretty-young sailor new to the scene.

A row of sponsor booths was set up, selling everything from equipment for boats to insurance for sailors. A few charities attended, sailing lessons lesson for inner city kids, clean water for Africa, and the William T. Hass regatta for breast cancer. "Save the Boobies", was their motto, and "Willy For Tits," and their official color was pink. The pit-girl was an advocate, aggressive enough to register the entire fleet for the fundraiser; she strangled money out of every sailor—from the lowest crewmember to the doughy, middle-aged owners and skippers.

Esther, her neighbor was a stage-four survivor who loaned her vintage clothes from the forties, ensuring that every event the pit-girl worked on behalf of Willy T, she jump-started the heart of every sailor. Esther had stolen or caressed the uniforms from dozens of sailors, officers and enlisted alike. She dyed some of them pink and adjusted them so that they would fit the pit-girl's sensuous frame. While sewing, she told stories, of course. "This here is Captain Zajaczkowski's uniform, a handsome Pollack with a swimmer's body. He had a thing for expensive, thigh-high stockings. He'd bring me a pair from every port he visited, and by the end of the night—darling, I'm telling you, we'd have taken them all for a spin in my boudoir. Now I don't know, if you know how many ports a sailor stops when he's out on West Pac deployment, but rest-assured, it's almost more than even I could handle in one night."

The pit-girl would listen to every word, relish the stories, but it made her sad that Esther was alone in the world, even then, as her lifestyle didn't afford her a kindred soul. In the forties, she was a radical, a woman who dared to live her life the way she loved, hard and long.

The yacht club stood guard over the whole affair, a laurelled and conservative organization, that didn't quite understand why their annual race had become the frat-party event of the summer. Race Week had morphed from supine to delirious, from Jimmy Stewart to Jimmy Buffet. There was a time when Sean Connor and his team trained here, using the

Salish Sea as a proving ground for the America's Cup, or the time that Gary Jobson broke the course record during a storm in a pickle-fork. The Club Members celebrated Race Week inside, in a lounge, away from the Rum tent, with brandy warmed by Sterno and served with Russian caviar. It was flanked by the committee room, leading to a hallway of trophies and models of old wood-hulled boats; a dark and quiet place where only the members can haunt. The spider webs are covered in dust and the tables have little doilies on them. It smells of absinth and pipe tobacco, and is decorated with pictures of lost, forgotten crews, dusty trophies with names engraved in brass plates oozing with green copper. The writer stared at the trophies, tried to bring them to life again, but the names were oxidized from the air and salt, and the turquoise crystals erased the grooved-out names.

Heat 1A started. Race Week had at long last begun. The boats would not return until the sun had charred the other side of the bay and fallen into majestic violet. In twilight, they would all get drunk, then the next morning: Race, Party, Play. Repeat. Heat 2A would start tomorrow, and so on, every day a new course, reconfigured to make the day seem fresh, a new challenge, a new drama.

"Is time's only purpose to keep everything from happening at once?" the writer said to his drink.

There is a stranger next to him, dressed in an oxford shirt. He is not perplexed by the question—he even seems to understand.
The stranger turns and examines the writer.

"You're not a sailor, are you?"

"And you are?"

"That's how I can tell you're not!" the oxford man said after sipping his brandy. He relaxes after a moment, decides that there's nothing better to do. "Time is the one thing that a sailor has the luxury of forgetting, which is why of course, they like to race their little boats," he said, and waved one of his bony hands in benediction. "We are all too aware of the eternal nature of time."

The writer let his mind wander to a place where time no longer waxed and waned like the phases of the moon. His headache retreated, and his stomach eased and then he landed on Nefarious, a second cruise after the pit-girl had taken him on their hellish training run. During this outing, there were no stopwatches, no shouting, and he was properly introduced to the lot of men while sailing the smooth waters of Lake Washington. It was calm on this day, like a glass of Chardonnay at dinner. The pit-girl was proud to have netted a non-sailor then, a juxtaposition to the revelry of her life. A serious person who needed a lightning rod in his ass.

"Gary Jobson," the stranger said.

"Max Rigby," the writer said, and glanced at an aged picture of a handsome sailor on the deck of a tri-hull behind the bar. "That's you, isn't it?"

The oxford man smiled, looked at the picture of himself.

"That was a long time ago," he said. "When a sailor is on the water like that, we don't age."

"And what happens when you're off the water?"

"We are one with time," the stranger said slowly, "the water is our elixir. And like dancing with a bear, it is what makes us special and curses us all at once."

"Interesting," the writer said.

The stranger smiled wanly and ordered another brandy.

"And how do you stop dancing with that bear?" the writer asked.

The man sipped at his drink and licked his lips.

"You stop dancing with the bear," the stranger said a little rough. "When it's goddamned good and ready."

"Do you mind if I write that down?"

"Ah! Very good! A writer," the stranger said. "You ever been published?"

"Yes," the writer said.

"Then I don't mind."

CHAPTER 28

Kai steered Jupiter downwind. The wind had settled a bit, but his new spinnaker was full—a tall, metal-gray sail with a colossal image of the planet Jupiter emblazoned in the center. This amazing sail made him the king of kings.

Nefarious was nowhere to be seen. He had missed the exact moment of the wipeout, but heard the chaos over the radio. Edmund spit several expletives in the microphone, heard throughout the fleet; he was a man who'd seen everything bad that could happen to a race boat, and this was the worst. A DNF meant that Dan's sissies would not be able to make up for an entire day's sailing, they'd have to limp to port, dragging their ass lower than a snail. Too bad it ended so soon. He'd have enjoyed torturing Dan all week.

"Why did you tack at the whale?" Kai said to his tactician. "I'll be protested for sure."

The Indian thought for a moment.

"I was not tacking at the whale," he said. "I was tacking at your competitor. When we blew by them, I wanted the crew to see their suffering. It's good for moral."

"You're a good," Kai laughed. "I thought you were actually going to ram the stupid animal!"

The tactician looked away from the spinnaker, eyed his skipper.

"Whales are sacred to us," he said.

CHAPTER 29

Dan watched Jupiter sail to the front of the pack, a full spinnaker pushing into the distance and rounding Strawberry Hill. When it disappeared, his eyes withered and sank to his feet.

Nefarious had right sided, settled back the way the good girl was supposed to, but her deck was a mess, and the crew, while safe, was in shock.

The pit-girl crawled from the pit, her golden-eyes on fire.

"What the fuck happened?" she demanded.

When the boat tipped, she was rolled forward to the front of the cabin, pinned to the bow and enough water entered for her life vest to activate.

"We blew out," Ortun said.

"No shit."

"Easy," Dan said.

"I could have been killed!"

"We all could have been killed," Ortun said, opening a lite beer, on account that he was a diabetic.

The pit-girl climbed to the top of the cabin and looked out at Strawberry Hill.

"Where's the fleet?" she said, and with the binoculars, she found the little specks in the distance. "Goddamn it!"

"That's a DNF for sure," Ewan said, completing the task of tying his shoes.

The pit-girl jumped onto the deck.

"What the hell's gotten into you, Dan?" she said.

"Watch it, sailor," he said.

"You watch it!" she barked. "You risk flying a kite at the starting line? What the hell are you doing? We got a whole week of racing in front of us, goddamn it!"

"Hey bud," Bonesteel said. "That's the skipper's skirt you're tugging at!"

The pit-girl turned to Bonesteel.

"Shut the fuck up."

"Hey!" Duff said. "It was Ewan's fault!"

Ewan didn't look up from his bunny ears.

"Fuck you," he said.

Dan's phone beeped. He looked at the screen and stepped down to the deck, soaked, hair matted to his brow, skin pale and the little scar under his eye was shaking. He held up his phone, smiled like a madman and made an announcement.

"I'm having a baby," he said.

Ortun spit out his lite beer.

The pit-girl gasped.

Ewan and Duff turned their head like confused puppies and they all watched Dan, waiting for the punchline.

"What the hell are you talking about?" the pit-girl said. "Like, a baby? Like a little human thing?"

"Yes," Dan said. "Martina is preggers."

Bonesteel grabbed hold of his belt.

"Yee—haw," he said, and humped the air in front of him. "She won't be the only knocked-up lassie at Race Week."

Dan's lowered his head again and went below into the cabin, closing the hatch behind him.

CHAPTER 30

Kevin Jonson returned to the helm and watched the wayward whale cut into the Elwha Delta. Though they appeared docile, they were once called devilfish because of their fighting behavior when hunted. Its dark slate-gray color appeared above the waterline, and then disappeared like a mystic siren, lost in the silken sea. He had never seen one as close as he had today, close enough to see the characteristic gray-white patterns, scars left by parasites which drop off in its cold-water feeding grounds. His father told him all about the whales, and how to respect them. Their entire culture revolved around the creature, and the Makah flag embodied the tribe's quintessential essence: a black whale, with a single sentient eye, its sublime body arched, its tale set to thrash. Above the creature was the thunderbird, holding two serpents. The thunderbird helped the Makah find the whale, and set two bolts of serpentine lightning loose into the sea.

Twice a month, before the government revoked their treaty rights to hunt, the village would send a team of whalers out for days to chase down a creature. During the journey, songs and dances were written and performed about the hunt—each performance a cultural data file with information that helped the next team track and kill and divide their sacred spoils. Back then, song and dance was their museum.

But the hunt would end.

Abruptly, a senator decided to acquiesce to pro-whale lobbyist, even though the grey whale was far from extinction. The senator's constituents had never tasted the succulent meat of this mammal, but they'd eaten plenty of cows, pigs and lambs.

People were hypocrites.

They selected animals to eat that they saw merely as animals, and nothing else. But the world was filled with many sprits—everything alive had a consciousness. Pigs were not any more, or any less conscious as a whale.

He was a hypocrite, too.

Kevin Jonson had never eaten whale. He once asked his grandfather to describe the taste of the meat, and the old man answered with a single word: dark.

On an east tack, he lost track of the creature in a silty delta. Apropos of a Makah song, the whale disappeared in Elwha land. Many generations ago, a whale that the Makah had wounded and fought for days washed up on Elwha land. The chief—though there were no chiefs in Makah culture—offered to give the Elwha, a fishing tribe, the spoils so long as their sacred whaling equipment was returned. The Elwha chief declined, and the Makah slaughtered him and his emissaries, removed their heads and stuck them on sticks facing out to sea so that their relatives would recognize them as they paddled ashore.

Yes, the Makah were headhunters.

And proud of it.

Kevin Jonson looked out at the delta and couldn't help feeling that the Elwha were involved in Makah business once again. The whale avoided Jupiter, and perhaps it even knew to stay out of the straits where it would be safe in the murky Elwha delta.

He grinned.

Every year his family sang the song at Makah days in front of the Elwha's sheriff and deputies. They were many generations at peace. But still he grinned.

If the whale was unwise enough to enter the shallows of the delta, it might do it again tomorrow. If his timing was better, he could strike the whale in the cold, clear water of the straits before it disappeared.

The treaty rights had a clause for sick whales that washed ashore. Once government scientist determined the cause of death to be natural, Makah could harvest the meat.

Who else could remove an eyesore from public lands better than his people? And what's more natural than death by sailboat?

Generations of not being hunted made the whale stupid.

It was time for them to wise up—to live up to their sacred nature.

CHAPTER 31

The pit-girl entered the cabin and smiled.

A real smile.

Maybe.

Dan smiled back at her and she handed him her flask. He shook it, but it was nearly empty.

"I'm sorry, skipper," she said. Her red hair caught some of the breaking sun. "You can't win them all."

"I don't know why I flew the kite," he said, and pulled the emergency bottle of rum out of the Boatswain's locker. "Do you know about the monster?"

The pit-girl frowned. Chewed on the inside of her cheek, then smiled.

"What are you talking about?"

"The one that the other skipper's say is on deck with me at the start of a race—you ever heard them talking about it?"

"No," she lied.

"Well," he said. "I thought I could make it go away this time. Not fuck the start this once."

"You should have stuck to your old habits," she said. "Luck is not chance—it's' toil." She wanted to blame Martina for the bad luck, for distracting her skipper during a race with baby-shit. "When did you find out?"

"Last week she missed her period, took a test," he said. "I told her to text me the instant the doctor called."

The pit-girl stood and slapped him on the back.

"You're a good man," she admitted. "If you have a daughter—you have to name her Bullet."

"No, that's the worst."

"Bullet Swardstrom!" she suggested.

"No."

They met at Nationals. Nefarious was down a position and the crew was overweight. Ewan and Duff did not respond well to the extreme weight loss regiment Dan had put them on and he was desperate to find a pit. Dan was hardly ever serious enough to make them diet, but they'd become a sloppy mess during their road trip to the Bay Area, hitting every bar along Interstate-5. "You mean beer doesn't count as water?" Ewan complained. "You should have said that, explicitly."

They found her in the crew circle, big eyed and new. She had sailed on Jupiter as mainsail, but the crew figured out she was banging the skipper. This, made the deck hierarchy awkward, if not damned annoying. No sailor liked to see their skipper's brain hijacked, especially by a nice set of tits.

"How much do you weigh?"

"That's none of your damn business."

"I'm the skipper of Nefarious."

"Never heard of it."

"We're a serious program," Dan said. "And you look serious."

"Do I?"

"Well," Dan told her after giving her a demerit for wearing make-up on race day. "Serious enough," he said.

The pit-girl sat down and put her arm around Dan. There were worse starts to Race Week, she imagined. And so-what if at the end of the day, they lost time. Nefarious could make it up—would make it up! It might take a sobering loss of dignity, but that's exactly when they responded best: mostly sober, and under pressure. Emotion was the best teacher and by her estimations, there was no other way to learn. She took the bottle of rum and opened it with her teeth. She drank. Handed the bottle back to her skipper and stood.

"You know," she said, "there are worse things than having a baby."

"Like what?" Dan said.

"Like not finishing this goddamned race."

CHAPTER 32

Ortun sat on the deck preparing his set list for the Rum-tent. He thought, perhaps country western with an electric guitar would suit the mood. Something laidback, yet energetic. Old country—Patsy Cline, Buck Owens, Hank Williams—something that touched the melancholy of the day.

He watched the fleet disappear behind Elwha Point and wondered if they felt it too. Leaving Nefarious behind meant that the trophy would go to Kai, and with it, the epic end of the revered Swardstrom party.

Nefarious had taken it the last four years in a row, and that was a long time for a sailor. The craft and art of sailing was in many forms a type of procrastination—time wasted, time spent caught in the temporariness that existed between utility and futility. On deck, when shit wasn't busy happening, there was plenty of time to think: forced meditation, every bit as sublime as a monk trapped in an abbey. The fleet would be thinking . . . devising ways to beat Kai. Now that Nefarious was out, they had time to reflect on the wasted energy of a not so serious race: half hedonistic, half prom.

Dan's baby would cost the crew a new mainsail, a new boom, a jib . . . expenses that kept them just competitive enough to be taken seriously. These costs were his and his alone. Sure, he'd tell them that nothing would change, but it would soon change. If racing a Farr was like burning thousand-dollar bills in a cold shower, then a sailor raising a baby was like throwing money into a volcano.

Dan would choose the latter, of course.

At the end of the week, the trophy would be Kai's.

Race week would revert to its more serious station on the circuit.

The reign had ended.

This was better, he thought, better than Dan just leaving to raise a family.

This was dramatic.

Ortun finished devising his set: George Jones, Ray Charles, Guy Clark then some Johnny Cash. He would close on a high. The fleet would need that after watching Nefarious limp back to port.

Dan stepped from the cabin.

He smiled like a boy.

"Hike that kite up there," he said.

The wind on the Salish had picked up, with little whitecaps running toward the Elwha head—plenty of wind to chase the fleet.

"You heard the skipper," Bonesteel said. "Let's give these teets a good scrubbing!"

Ortun crumbled his playlist and pulled on the mainsail halyard: Led Zeppelin's "The Immigrant Song" was playing in his head.

CHAPTER 33

The marine layer burned off and the sky opened like a lucid, polished agate. The seagulls took a break from their stubborn and stupid cawing and the starfish sojourned to cold, deep water. The fleet was tangled in an air-water mix that moved over their hulls like molasses and the boats dodged and parried like slow-motion boxers jabbing and missing one another through crystal until, finally the onshore flow stagnated and sank upon them. Their sails lofted and relaxed. The lapping of water could be heard.

Bat Out of Hell threw up a flag with a shrimp on it and lit the barbeque. It was the unofficial half-time break, and they had a flag for chicken, pork and fish. Rhett, the skipper called for the first beer, and ice chests all over the fleet opened. The crew took off their gear and lazed on deck, lotus-eaters that they were. The ladies were in neon bikinis, tanning. When they peeled off their layer of Gore-Tex, their male counterparts were always surprised that, in fact, the cursing, sassing, spitting tars that sailed beside them were divine creatures of feminine form.

Rhett's wife was a Brazilian whom he met at nationals in Rio. He talked to her in broken Portuguese, convinced her to position the mast on account that she would look good on his pole. Ivonne was bronzed like the bark of a Jabuticaba tree and her presence on a boat brought with it a light, festive atmosphere: she played sultry music with provocative drums that made your hips want to hump and grind. Ivonne could cook up a Gaucho barbecue like nobody's business, and she fed the crew polenta that stuck to their bones like a black-haired lover on the breast of day. Her beijinho was silky-sexy-smooth and dissolved into a rich, milky crème under your tongue long before your teeth realized there was anything left to do.

She stood on the bow, nibbling a skewer of delicate, pink lime-and-chili-marinated shrimp.

"Dan Swardstrom!" she said.

"No, no—hun" Rhett said. "Nefarious pitch-poled today."

"Look," she said. "The mast! It's a Farr."

Rhett found his binoculars.

"Son of a bitch," he said. "It is Swardstrom."

Rhett handed the binoculars over to his tactician, who handed them to The New Bambi, who handed them to over to Scary Bacon who gave them to Space Camp in the pit.

"He's moving," she said.

"Bull."

"He's running three degrees, about to tack."

"He'll lose his speed," Rhett said. He commandeered the binoculars, and in the little circles he watched Dan's crew lean over the windward side. "Hike it, bitches," he said. "Hike it for your skipper!"

The Farr was moving, even as they tacked through the molasses. Some crazy bastard was cranking the sail like he was possessed by the devil himself. He pulled the slack taught, and deftly ducked under the mast as the crew switched sides. The boat changed directions, catching the baby's breath of wind that pushed them another fifty yards.

"Give me those, minha docinho," Ivonne said. "Oh, look at him grind, he's so strong."

The grinder was already working the next tack, his muscles as taut as the sail. The sail tightened.

Nefarious accelerated.

They changed directions again and the crew switched sides.

"Hike it bitches," she said. "Hike it for Danny-boy."

Rhett looked for Jupiter, who was raising their mainsail.

"Looks like the party isn't over," Rhett said, pouring out his beer. "Why are things so serious this year?"

"Minha querida," she said and kissed him on the cheek. "You don't want Kai to throw the party, do you? You don't even own a tux."

CHAPTER 34

A man turned to the devil at the bar.

"My name is Christopher," the man he said. "I'm here to race the boats."

"Are you kidding me?" the devil said. "What the hell are you doing here?"

"I'm here to race the boats," the man said.

"You're bored, like me. So, you came here, didn't you?"

"I'm—"

"I know exactly who you are," the devil said gathering up his drink. "Go find your own little corner of the universe to haunt! This one is mine!"

The devil went to the bow of the ship where he could see Nefarious slowly edging back into the race, one tack at a time. Bonesteel was working his ass off, the little brat. He never listened to his uncle did he? He didn't vote for George W. Bush, didn't attend Harvard, didn't play hockey, didn't watch reality television shows on Tuesdays, didn't eat Brussels sprouts. The little shit. He knew how important this race was to him, which was exactly why he was here. The devious son of a bastard.

The devil smiled just a tiny bit.

Children were forces of nature; their inevitable rebellion is exactly why they were created.

Nefarious edged closer to Saratoga Passage, where an ebbing tide would jetstream them back into the race. Oh, there was no chance they'd take Kai, but maybe Blue Lullaby or Gossamer. That would keep them in contention for Tuesday's race into Penn Cove, a bar fight, something that Nefarious excelled at.

The area judge sat down next to him and smiled.

"Looks like Dan's going to race today."

"He'll never make up the time."

"Like hell," the area judge said. "He's passed Rhett."

"Rhett is already tuned for nationals," the devil said. "He doesn't care about Race Week."

"What makes you think Rhett isn't getting his ass kicked?"

"What makes you think he's not letting Dan back in?"

"Because that would be bad form."

"Bad form?" the devil laughed. "You sentimental fool. These sailors don't have morals. They have wind, and just like everything else in the universe, it is blind and unforgiving."

"Better to have the wind, than nothing else."

The area judge poured from the devil's bottle and left him alone.

CHAPTER 35

The skipper of Tupac watched Nefarious round Ponell Point with a westerly pushing the Farrs into the straits. Low tide was 5:17 a.m., and now the evening's tide flooded like ink from an octopus into Saratoga Passage. Half of the fleet flattened out their spinnakers and the other half dropped their kites, tightened their mainsail and cut into the ebbing tide. During the day, algae foamed on the shore and baked onto the rocks. When the tide flooded in, the crusty layer was dragged back out to sea, bent and fragmented, twisted into willowy lines that broke the green water into a matted mosaic. Nefarious was far behind, flanking the fleet, a lone white dot on an emerald sea. It was admirable that they were still in the hunt. Racing with no wind, spoon-feeding their sails to move through molasses on a sultry, sky blazing-day at the end of July.

"Damn," the skipper said. "They's still at it."

He handed his binoculars over to his boy Demetrius.

"You right about that, shit," he said. "They's gaming."

"Maybe we ain't gonna party at the yacht club this year."

"Ah hell, no," Demetrius said. "I got a tux."

The skipper looked towards the finish line, where Jupiter was just about to cross.

"Danny-boy's got a whole day to make up," he said. "That niggah can't catch Kai. Keep your tux. I know your ass rented it anyways."

CHAPTER 36

Jupiter crossed the finish line and turned windward to see the scattered dots left in its wake. No one applauded on the committee boat, save a dapper looking fellow holding a bottle of champagne under his arm. He popped the cork and it landed on the deck.

The area judge raised his flag and sounded the horn.

"It's a preliminary result," he said. "You have two protest flags."

Kai looked at the fleet. The closest boat was Absolutely, ten minutes out.

"I've got plenty of distance," he said picking up the cork and tossing it into the water. "Today is mine. The week is mine."

Kai turned his Jupiter back at the committee boat for the passengers to have one more look. He was not a good helmsman, and the reversed keel bulb caused it to slip sideways.

"Get the hell outt'a here," the area judge said. "Turn to port!"

Jupiter continued to slip, and the crew moved away from the portside. The captain started the engine and a puff of smoke left the stack of the old, wooden showboat.

"Turn to port!"

Kai watched his precious boat close the distance the way that a diver watches a shark approach.

The passengers took a step back and set down their drinks and the captain blew his horn trivially.

"Holy-Fucking-Shit!"

This is when the harpoon appeared.

It sank into the side of the wood hull—a dull, dead ring and stayed there. It was designed to stick to bone and there was never any doubt. The passengers watched it sink into the ribs, hold fast and solid. It was still vibrating when the tactician grabbed hold of it, used his muscled arms and shoulders to push the two boats off course.

Jupiter's inertia eased, and the bow passed safely through the cloud of blue diesel smoke.

When they came out on the other side, the passengers applauded.

"Finally," Kai said. "Some appreciation."

CHAPTER 37

The writer lowered his hat and watched the fleet returning to Crescent Bay. The cowboy hat he fancied kept him from aging in the sun and hid the puffy crinkles gathering in the corner of his eyes. He was exactly ten years physically delayed, which made it possible for him to hook up with the pit-girl, but the crinkles were a reminder that time is a commodity, traded like sugar, a guilty pleasure, consumed and soon converted to vice. How sweet it was to taste her.

A dark and lovely bar.

Under bricks, where the angels who art in heaven, cannot see.

She turned to assess him: fit to sail, she decided and approached him, still assessing.

The pit-girl had not known this at the time; he had instantly fallen for her. But he feigned delight, not in a fake way, not intentionally. His face was the face of a Buddha, she had told him, and open to surprises. He agreed with her—ten years of marriage had left him lusting for them, but he never let them happen, never took the chance of surprising himself.

He did that night.

He touched her face the way that he wanted to be touched.

He pulled her closer and closer and he kissed her the way that he needed to be kissed.

He pulled at her blouse and slipped his hand under her bra and absorbed her warmth the way that he needed to be absorbed.

She relinquished; let him have control.

Let him unspool her with wet kisses.

Let him brave himself a lover, who explored his deepest fantasies.

Let him find his passion, and follow it down the nape of her neck with bites, a trail that ended at her ankles.

He found a way to make her wait . . . and wait . . . until it was time to beg . . .

Yes, my beloved. She'd say to him. Yes. Anything. Anything you wish.

And then . . .

Sailing season began.

The writer sighed.

He found two drinks, drank them and sat down near a tree to write a poem.

Fall with me...

Into a mystery

Where so quiet

We lay

And think

In that metal leeway

Without a ridge

or cover

Here . . .

Our hearts are synchronized . . .

Cockled to time

And the sound of a single

falling

penny. . .

Into this vessel

Of walls riveted with

metal and hope

And things to cherish

It falls.

And we are falling too.

Waiting for it to land

And sing

Then dance

And settle

And lie down carelessly

Anywhere to rest

.... awaiting

the sound of another.

I will listen with you.

And whisper out beyond these walls

To tell you…

…I heard it too.

He closed his notepad, stretched his legs and wondered the grounds with the other non-sailors—service workers and shore support, the wives of sailors—waiting for the fleet to return. Ortun's band was setting up, waiting for their lead singer.

When the boats landed, the crowed ripened and became lively. The writer bought more rum, stood under the shade of the rum tent.

Ewan appeared with two cups.

"Here," he said.

"I already have a drink," the writer showed him. "And I'm already drunk."

"Take it."

The writer drank one of the cups, ditched it, reloaded. Maybe another would bumper Ewan's edge.

"Let's talk about that piece of crap you wrote two years ago."

"Aquarius?"

"First try!"

"What about it?"

Ewan looked over his nose at the writer.

"Did you know it was a bunch of sentimental crap while you were writing it," he drank down one of his cups and started on the other, "or did you figure that out after it was published?"

"I knew it was crap while I was writing it."

The writer drank.

"I don't believe that for an instant," Ewan said. "Here's how I figure it happened. You were born a romantic fool, then you figured out you could string together sentences, and then you said, I need to break everybody else's heart because I can't be content with just breaking my own."

"If that's true," the writer said. "Then what business is it of yours?"

Ewan raised his finger; he had an insight into the mind of the writer, or thought he did.

"It wouldn't be my business at all if you weren't using our pit to break it," he said. "I don't know if you noticed, but things are intense this year. We need her mind in the game—so you be a good spouse and keep our girl happy and mostly sober."

The writer drank.

"Just so you know," he said. "I was set to leave this morning."

"You're still here," he challenged.

"Yes," the writer said surprised. "I am."

Martina appeared—pretty as a summer day is long.

"Hello green eyes," she told the writer.

"You look thirsty," the writer said, and quickly offered her one of his drinks.

"No thank you, Max," she said. "Dan and I are preggers."

Ewan eyed the writer, to see if he already knew.

"He told the crew today," Ewan said. "Congratulations."

"Thank you, I'm pretty sure we were drunk when it happened," she winked at the writer. "If I did my math correctly, I seemed to recall a debauchery or two happening that night."

They all toasted, she with a water of bottle.

"As a father," she said in her cute German way, "Dan will need to learn much from you."

The writer knew he wouldn't be around long enough to see a cute little Dan and Martina mash up. A crew stayed fixed and the coming and going of their shore support remained transient.

"A baby sailor!" he said.

"Well," she said. "If it's a girl, then no sailing for her. I know what this fleet does to girls."

"He doesn't have a clue," Ewan chimed in.

"Oh, Max knows very well," Martina said.

"Yes, I do," The writer said.

The writer left and found a nice place to sit and think with his two cups of rum and coke. He leaned up against a tree and dozed off into an intoxicated, delirious sun-drenched dream. Rolling clouds boiling at the horizon, taking the shape of objects he could only recognize the instant they disappeared, currents speeding by, night and dark, night and dark, the stars rearranging themselves.

And then the world stopped spinning, and the clouds froze in the night, lit by a blazing moon. Everything stopped. Nothing moved. No sound. No wind. Nothing, only frozen shadows. He tried to stand, to walk away from the freezing shadows, but his hands were tied in bowline knots and he could not move. His chest tightened and his breaths became short. He looked down at his feet, more bowline knots.

The writer began to panic, called out for his ex-wife by name, but he could only hear the heart in his chest, a cannon set to explode. He called for the pit-girl, called for her again and again until a lithe form appeared in the darkness. It approached as one of the frozen shadows, silken and obscure.

Closer.

He could smell rum and the sea.

"Help me," he said.

"I will find the tallest ladder," the figure said. "But I will not allow you to step on my head."

"I can't move," he said. "Your knots are too tight."

"Knots are supposed to be tight," it said. "A knot is the promise of a sailor, his word to his shipmates—his covenant."

The writer did not understand, or care. He wished for the world to spin again, for the stars to move and the clouds to boil—anything but this—to be stuck in in time forever, tortured by a sky of darkness, a sky of sorrow, a sky of unending change where the stars did not set and the sun never rose.

He violently tugged against the knots.

The shadow drew closer, so close he could feel its breath but he could not see her through a dark, ornate mask.

"Mac," he said. "Untie me!"

As the shadow removed the mask, it laughed, and a cold chill crawled up his spine.

The stars stayed fixed.

The clouds still frozen.

In the moonlight, he saw that it was he who was laughing from behind the mask.

CHAPTER 38

The pit-girl leapt on to the dock and immediately looked for the writer. She looked for him after the last bad race; scanned the marina for his open, waiting smile. He had a face like Buddha, exultant with an edge of despondency. At Swiftsure he'd meet her at the dock with a cold beer and a flower he'd found on his way to the dock.

What was he up to?

Where was he?

A baby.

The pit-girl shivered. An image of a cherub faced-tot appeared inside her skull. The only worst luck on a boat was a banana. Sure, there were plenty of fathers in the fleet, but those boats weren't serious. A serious program meant you were not anchored to responsibility or the protocols of offspring. She had chosen Dan specifically because he was the least patriarchal man she had ever met, a veritable anti-father who once stepped outside of a bar to get some fresh air and ended up buying drinks for a sixteen-year-old girl who was crying. He asked what was wrong and she told him that her mother was inside getting drunk. Dan didn't know what to do, so he put his blazer over her shoulders, brought her in and told the bartender that she was his date. The bartender winked and brought them two martinis. He told his date about Jung's "The Girl" and that the only way the mother could teach her daughter not to drink was to get drunk and to show her how bad she was behaving. When the mother spotted them, they all drank and laughed together.

The pit-girl disapproved.

"Fuck Jung," she said. "Two wrongs don't make a right."

"No," he dead reckoned and then drank. "But two wrong tacks means you're headed in the right direction."

It was just one of many moments where Dan attacked life using the skill set of a middle-school boy carrying a case of beer and a pack of condoms. Even with a white beard, he retained the boyish charm of his youth, and managed to own a Farr 30. Not as easy as it sounds. By her count, there was only one skipper in the fleet who knew exactly what to do with a race boat, a pack of condoms and a case of beer.

And then came Martina.

Just as sure as she planned to have Dan as her skipper, she planned to not fuck him. It was a calculation. They were not connected, not that way. Not the way that he was connected to Martina.

When she was around, he aged. Not the way that boys aged into a man, but the way that a man turns into a gentleman around a princess. The pit-girl was no princess, but she liked to be treated like one, so long as it wasn't obvious. Wasn't it like this for every woman? But worse than that, Martina treated Dan like he was a prince.

The pit-girl eyed Martina on the dock, smiled.

"Hi sailor!" Martina called. She was headed to Nefarious holding a tray with two cold glasses of champagne. "Tough day out there!"

"Where's Rigby?"

"I saw him sleeping under a tree," she said. "I think he's drunk."

The pit-girl chewed on her lip.

"Congrats on the baby!" she said.

"Danny told you?"

Of course, he did, you twit.

Dan appeared. He met Martina with a kiss on the cheek and took the glass of champagne.

"When did you find out?"

"The doctor called today," she said. "I told him to not worry about it until after the race, but Dan wanted to know the instant I knew."

"How sweet," the pit-girl said.

"I'm so happy," Dan said.

"Oh Danny," she said. "I know you're scared."

The pit-girl listened, but didn't interrupt.

"I've done scarier things," he said. "Like pitch a boat."

"No, you haven't," she warned, "but I appreciate the optimism."

"We'll have to get married—and all that Jazz."

"I do," Martina said instantly.

Dan got down on one knee and took off his class ring, put it on Martina's skinny finger.

"Can Mac be my best man?"

"Of course!"

"Did you hear that?" Dan called out to the sailors. "I'm getting married!"

The sailors cheered, and Duff led them through a chorus of the Nefarious song.

"Here Mac," Martina handed over a glass of the champagne. "I can't drink this, so you have it."

"Thank you," the pit-girl said, and curtsied.

CHAPTER 39

Dan hugged Martina and smiled at the pit-girl. He couldn't tell if she was more pissed about him having a baby or blowing the start. If it was the latter, every skipper knew that if you didn't blow a start occasionally, you weren't racing and If was the former, the same rule applied.
They shared a serious glance, one that in a moment relayed everything right about the moment and everything wrong.

"Be sure to give them a piece of your mind at the protest," she said.

"Protest?" Martina said. "You came in second to last, today."

"That's not the point," the pit girl-said. "It's the principle of the matter."

"But what good will it do?" Martina smiled.

"Maybe knock Kai down a buoy," the pit girl said.

Dan's head spun back and forth; he was caught in a gravitational wake, like the moons of Jupiter, where geysers sprayed out into space.

"We still might be able to catch him by the end of the week," he said. "It's a long race."

"Atta-Boy," the pit-girl said.

Martina guffawed.

"Is this about that silly party?" she said. "Who cares if he wants to blow all his money on a champagne fountain?"

"A champagne fountain?" Dan said. "He has a champagne fountain?"

"Seriously," Martina said. "You will soon have more important things to spend your money on." She rubbed her belly—flat and tight as a main sail on a forty-five-degree tack.

Dan shot the pit-girl another look, and Martina caught it.

"It is about that party!" she said pouty, a strange thing coming from a German. It made her sound like a good witch. "You beat him at Van Ise. You beat him at Round the County."

"It's Race Week," he said.

The pit-girl jumped in.

"Ah, Martina," she said. "Let him have some fun. You'll have him changing diapers instead of a mainsail in no time." She swooped under Dan's arm and carried him away. "C'mon, we have to get to that protest."

Dan let himself be hauled away by his best man, but first he kissed Martina, downed the champagne and threw the glass onto the deck of Jupiter where it shattered.

"I'm going to kick your ass tomorrow," he told Kai.

Kai's head popped up from the cabin.

"The only thing you'll do tomorrow with that foot is put it in your mouth," Kai said.

"Yeah, yeah," Dan said.

CHAPTER 40

The writer awakened under a tall oak tree, its black branches splitting the sky; blurred hues sharpening into pure light.
The warmth on his face was good.
The world was moving again and the shadows were gone.

At his feet, he found a tuft of fresh grass, light green and new. He smiled at the blades dancing in the wind, reassured that the dream had thawed, and the eternal dusk was at bay.

A flower!

Swaying in the gentle breeze.

The yellow cup of a dandelion.

It was glorious—a visual poem that caused the compass inside his head to spin and his eyes to water, and as the blur opened, he was miraculously transported inside the flower, where, imbedded in its flesh—speckled with stars, he could see a resplendent, spinning galaxy. Inside of the minute peddles, he witnessed nebulas giving birth to billions of planets—each of them, a tiny dot teaming with oceans of lava, or sky, or salty water with specks of life projecting their will and wishes into a tiny, distant world.

He tried to wiggle his big toe and found a giant leather sandal, and in amazement he watched an exquisite dragonfly delicately land, flutter away and drift among the branches of the great oak. In the clouds, he gazed upon the fleet returning to port, their dart shaped hulls drifting above him in a sea of stars.

Someone tapped the writer on the shoulder and he turned to greet the person who needed his attention—a grizzly bear.

"What the fuck?"

The bear grabbed him by the shirt; pulled his body into its warm fur.

"Ok, ok," he said. "Easy does it."

Though he knew it to be another dream, he was caught firmly in its grasp. The bear's arms were locked around him—shaking him?

No.

He could feel his feet being dragged through the cool grass, and in the distance, a band was playing. The smell of rum was on the bear's breath and occasionally, a claw scraped his foot.

"Are we dancing?" he asked the bear, which answered with a growl and a fancy spin that nearly took off his arm.

The writer tried desperately to keep up with the beat, but the bear had no rhythm.

"Madam," he said. "Who's leading?"

Clearly, it was the bear.

CHAPTER 41

The pit-girl pattered down the dock ahead of the crew, full steam ahead. Her black, all weather, polyvinyl boots tight on her calves. She brushed through the crew of Tupac, who knew to let her pass and without a word.

"Great day out there, Jabari," she told the skipper.

He did not take the bait. Instead, he let her words waft in her wake, like chum.

She gained on Rhett and Drunk Bob, who heard her coming too.

"Off to the committee?" Rhett said.

"You bet your ass," she said. "Someone with balls ought to."

Rhett whistled quietly.

"Edmund's not going to be in a good mood," he said. "Not with these conditions."

The pit-girl stopped and turned slowly.

Rhett and Drunk Bob stopped walking.

"You think it's ok for Kai to use whatever water he goddamn pleases?"

Rhett took Drunk Bob's beer and dank.

"No," he said. "I mean, yeah. He came close to the line, but hell, you know it ain't racing unless you lose a little paint."

"That son of a bitch forced us to crash a squall," she stomped her boot on the dock and some lazy seagulls took flight. "We pitch-poled!"

"It looked like Dan was pussy-footing around," he said. "Should have boxed Kai out. What's gotten into him?"

The pit-girl blinked.

She saw a tree crash, but could not hear a sound.

"Beer?" Drunk Bob offered, cracking open a can from the cooler.

CHAPTER 42

Edmund sat in metal chair with an asshole-serious look on his face. His acid reflux was acting up again, and the bitter taste was sitting on his tonsils. If he could just keep shit straight this one last year while the Farr International World's Federation representatives were here, he could retire, set this course right again, make it serious.

Sure, he had a hand in its undoing: Race, Party, Play was his idea for the banner. And yes it brought in money, but he had plenty of that now, and so did the other city councilmembers. Maybe he could he could put the genie back in its box? Return to the glory days, when the plutocrats came to Oak Harbor to race their J Class Hanuman yachts.

Edmund leaned back in his chair and groaned, wondering who'd be the first numbskull to enter the empty auditorium.

The pit-girl arrived.

"Let's have it," he said.

She smiled.

It was animated and large, like the lips painted onto a deranged clown.

"Edmund," she said. "This is a big mess, isn't it?"

Edmund grimaced and looked at his assistant who pretended to have a stack of paper to sort.

"You are a hot mess, sailor."

She slapped him the way that Esther slapped bad sailors. Edmund spit out his orange juice and the smell of vodka filled the room.

"Come on now," she said, taking hold of his tie. "Let's be friends."

Dan opened the door.

"Mac!"

The pit-girl tightened Edmund's tie.

"You just make sure you call 'em nice and square," she said. "Just like this pretty little knot."

CHAPTER 43

Dan entered with a copy of the US Sailing Federation's rulebook already opened to page two hundred and ninety-one, where he'd found an obscure tenet. It described a situation where the area judge retained discretion over the right of way of boats being "forced" off the starting line. He read it aloud to the near empty room.

The pit-girl had a firm grasp of Edmund's tie.

Dan snapped the book closed.

Closed the door.

"Give me this room, sailor."

The pit-girl looked over her shoulder at him, apologized diminutively.

"Sure, Dan," she said, and released her hold on the area judge. "You're the skipper."

Edmund loosened his tie, eyed his assistant who was conveniently thumbing through his stack of papers again. He turned to watch the pit-girl curtsy, pass Dan and then brush by Kai as he entered the committee room.

"Wait a minute, big guy!" Kai demanded, and hurried to the committee table in front of Dan. "This isn't supposed to start until both skippers are present."

Dan watched the pit-girl leave, slam the door.

He was pissed.

"Never mind," Dan told Edmund, and threw his open rulebook on the table. "The ruling stands."

"What?" Edmund said, "Since when do you get to reverse what I've already gone ass-backwards on?"

"When?" Dan said. "Since I became skipper of my boat."

Edmund could see the contempt in Dan's eyes. His eyes were narrowed, rigid, and cold. He'd seen this before; skipper's attempting to tame Mac.

"Are you withdrawing your protest?"

"Yes."

"Oh no you don't'," Kai interrupted, his face turning red. "I won't let you take the high road."

Dan stepped in front of Kai, though a bubble of cologne.

"Are you wearing perfume?"

"Yes, you mongrel."

"On race day?"

"Don't you dare walk in here and try to manipulate the area judge into giving you an advantage?"

"Advantage?" Dan said. "I'm withdrawing my protest."

"You want the sympathy vote," Kai accused.

"I vote with my boat," Dan said indignantly.

"Do you see what he's doing?" Kai told Edmund. "He wants the fleet to hate me! Hate me enough to sabotage my party."

Dan rolled his eyes.

"You're really a desperate little man," he said, and tried to wave off some of the cologne. "I don't give a damn about that party," he lied, and everyone in the room knew it. "But I do give a damn about my pit coming in here and having a word with you on my behalf."

They all agreed.

"Not very manly," Kai said.

Dan told him to shut up, and leaned over the lectern. He was close enough to smell the vodka on Edmund's breath.

He whispered.

"I don't give a damn what she told you, or threatened you with. You make sure you do the right thing and let ruling stand," he said.

"What are you telling him?" Kai said to Dan, and then the assistant. "This is an open forum. Are you recording this?"

The assistant didn't look up. In fact, it looked like he was having a bowel movement in his khakis.

Edmund stood.

Rhett and Drunk Bob opened the door, sat quietly in folding chairs. Drunk Bob opened two beers and passed one to his skipper. Two more skippers entered, followed by their crew and the devil entered, crossed his legs and smiled.

Edmund took in a deep breath to speak. He felt sorry for Dan, could understand how bad it would look if he reversed his ruling. But the pit-girl never made a threat that wasn't followed by action. She was hell on wheels, with a bottle of gin. Her threat made sense now, and it drenched him in sweat. She cursed him. Cursed him with her soft lips and wet mouth. She was evil, but he could not blame the devil because he warned him, and now was sitting in the room smiling.

More people entered the room.

Edmund cleared his throat.

"The ruling is reversed," he said. "Jupiter is to be penalized two buoys for tomorrow's race."

He slammed his gavel, a crab cracker.

"Ain't that some shit?" the skipper of Tupac cursed.

The room erupted in chatter.

"Dan's a pussy!" Drunk Bob yelled, and threw his beer can. "The area judge is Mac's bitch!"

Someone threw a folding chair.

Edmund's troubles had only just begun.

CHAPTER 44

The devil drank from his flask and screwed the cap down tight. He ducked and let a flying chair pass as he read the little inscription carved onto the side of the flask: "You will outlive the bastards!" He smiled again and recalled a conversation he'd once had with a snowflake. What could he say? He was bored and there wasn't a damned thing otherwise interesting to do.

"Why do you persist?" he laughed at the snowflake. "At this moment, you are melting."

The snowflake knew who his was, but could not veer away, so he leaned into the decent.

"Weee! Weee!" it yelled.

The devil matched its speed and tried to see the point in enjoying the inevitable. Nothing. But as he fell, he began to admire the blades of ice protruding from the snowflake's body, splendid forms catching rays of light that, through its two hundred and sixty-eight molecules of water, became rare and radiant possibilities he could not predict.

Beauty!

Purity at its finest.

But he was no fool.

"You are transcendental," he taunted.

"I am an individual."

"You are dying, and every crystal will melt, sorted and dispersed, far and wide. Did you know that this molecule here," he touched the thing, melting a crystal, "it was once the drink of an ancient pharaoh, and then urinated on to the corpse of an enemy. Or this one here, it was lactate from an otter with an unfortunate mutation that kept her from feeding her pups? They all died, one by one to starvation before they even learned to play tag."

He laughed.

Beauty, he thought! Purity.

Ha!

The universe is a wicked place.

"And this! You have no idea that this will live in the mind of a great dictator, it's polarity will fire the neuron that helps him take his army into war. Millions will be lost. But worst of all!" the devil said in a sad, little voice. "The rest of you will amount to naught. A mere drop in a vast ocean that will soon—very soon to me—be evaporated into space, and time, and nothingness!"

"Weee!" the little snowflake said. "Weee!"

"Fool!"

"There are no others like me!" the foolish snowflake said.

"You crave death."

"I crave life."

"You will disappear!" the devil said. "Look! It's happening now! Your existence is destroying you!"

Fascinated, he watched two blades of ice fall away and dissolve into the either.

"Weee!" the snowflake continued. "The privilege of a lifetime is being me…"

The devil dodged a beer can. Some of its contents landed on his blazer. He thought about the water droplets for an instant and then smoothly wiped them away with his handkerchief.

He stood to look for Dan Swardstrom in the ruckus.

If Dan was too proud to do sail with him, then perhaps the skipper needed the privilege of knowing himself a little better.

CHAPTER 45

"Wake up!"

"Madam, please!" the writer said.

"Madam?"

The pit-girl frowned and waited for the writer's eyes to open.

He was napping against a tree.

"Max!"

"Mac," he said finally. "What are you doing here?"

There were two dreams, two places, and two different time streams to slip into. He was standing in the doorway watching his ex-wife read to his children. The other was in a forest, where he danced with a magnificent bear.

"Why weren't you at the docks when we pulled in?"

The writer stood, dusted his jeans and fixed his hat.

"I had no idea you were back," he said. "I must have dozed off."

"Martina was there," she said, her frown still set. "She was there with a tray of champagne."

"Sounds nice."

The pit-girl put her hand on her hip and let a tear roll out of her eye.

"Ah babe," he said. "What's the matter?"

"We came in second to last, today," she said. "A total fuck-wad of bullshit!"

He moved to soothe her, but she slapped his hand away as if the entire matter were his fault. "And there was no one on the dock to greet me."

Next to a compliment, the writer liked an honest rebuke. But this was not a rebuke, it was pouting. The nuances of Race Week were complex and required timing. Boats came and went, and they all looked the same. At Swiftshore, Martina attempted to teach him how to recognize the mast of a Farr, but he was not interested in mastering the technique. Instead, he diverted her attention to Germany, where she grew up the daughter of a business owner, drinking good beer with her father and discussing his car dealership. At the age of sixteen, she was able to close a deal on a '94 Mercedes 500E, balance a spreadsheet, and order new inventory. "I'm not impressed with luxury cars," she told him. "But I like what's under the hood."

The pit-girl set down her gear down.

"We needed you, Max," she said. "Shore support, remember? There's shit to be done."

"I'm new at this," he said.

"Easy, Max?" she said. "Nothing about Race Week is easy."

They were talking about the end again, and like the dream, he was stuck in two realities and couldn't move both ways at once—to end it or restart it. What was so difficult about learning the masts of sailing ships?

"Have you started dinner?" she said, seeing the opening in his resolve.

"Lamb chops," he said picking up her bags. "Herb-crusted, lentil and baby carrots."

When he looked up, a beefy sailor interrupted them.

"Davey!" The sailor slapped her ass and she turned to greet him, screamed with glee and jumped into his arms.

"Mac!" he said, and spun her. "I heard you pitched, today!"

She was ecstatic.

"Someone has to race here," she said. "Might as well be Nefarious!"

"You call that racing?" he said, eying the writer, not sure who he was. "I call that swimming."

"Oh fuck you!"

"No fuck you!"

They hugged again, and the writer set her bags on the dock.

There seemed to be a lot of sailors she allowed the pleasure of slapping her ass without one returned across the face—Dan, Ortun, Edmund, and now Davey—and he'd learned through trial and error that these relationships were never to be questioned. If he did, the demon-succubus would appear.

"This is Max Rigby," she said. "Max, this is Davey. He's a pro—races pit for Jupiter."

Davey shook the writer's hand hard. It felt like a vice wrapped in burlap.

"Hey there Max," Davey said. "You a sailor?"

"No," he said. "I just fuck the pit-girl."

Davey froze.

"Don't you love him?" the pit-girl said. "Look at him! He's adorable!"

Davey man-hugged the writer. The sailor's body felt like an ironed bed sheet, filled with chipped, lead weights.

"Right," Davey said. He looked to the pit-girl, who threw her arms around the writer to steady him. "Nefarious has got her work cut out for her, eh?" he said changing the subject. "I heard the ruling stood and there was a fisticuff in the committee room!"

The pit-girl's expression changed.

"That bastard!"

"No," Davey said. "It wasn't Edmund. It was Dan."

"Dan reversed the decision?"

"No," Davey said. "He withdrew his protest."

The writer watched her eyes muddy. The demon took form. It crawled out of roiling clouds of grey, spread its wings and tried to soar—but its weight kept it from flying and it tumbled through darkness sky and hit the ocean with a clap.

The water swallowed it whole, but the demon reappeared, stabbing the green water with arms that belonged to an octopus.

The writer looked at Davey.

He'd seen it, too.

CHAPTER 46

The devil sat down in a plush leather chair outside of the locker room, velvet. There were two.

Dan was wrapped in a towel.

"Let's talk," he said.

Dan dried his ear, sat down and smiled at a bottle of seventy-year old scotch sitting on the table.

"Mind?" Dan said.

The devil waved his hand.

"You withdrew your protest, didn't you?"

"You already know I did."

The pet was misbehaving. A stick wasn't working; it was time to try a carrot.

"I've come to make a proposal," he said.

"I won't' sail with the devil," Dan said, pulling the cork out of the scotch. "And I won't have a race called for me by member of my crew without my permission."

"I prefer antichrist," the devil said, and sipped at his drink. "I'm going to sweeten the deal."

"How's that?"

"I want to give you a bigger, faster boat." The devil looked his glass and the image of a sleek, Class 40 mono-hull appeared. "Her name is Wildhorse."

Dan gazed at the image—a fine boat, sleek and sexy. Its sails were new and erect, and the kite was emblazoned with a fierce horse running wild.

"I only sail Farrs," Dan said. "Don't need a bigger, faster thing."

"You're full of shit," the devil said.

"You of all people should know better," Dan said pouring the scotch into a crystal glass. "The aim of sailing is not seduction—its adventure."

The devil snapped his finger and the boat disappeared.

"Yes," he said. "I Figured as much. So I'm going to ask you, pretty please, with a cherry on top—to try a little harder out there."

Dan smiled like a good boy, but the scar under his eye frowned.

"I'm trying as hard as I can."

"You know," the devil said. "I saw this coming. I mean. Of course I did but I thought if I tested you a little, maybe threatened to take the party away from you and your friends . . . well, I thought maybe it'd light a fire under your ass."

"You win some you lose some," he said sipping the scotch.

"Oh bullshit!" the devil said. "You never would have said that before you started thinking about offspring—don't you see it? Your lackluster sailing is letting everyone down, Swardstrom. We'll all miss the best party of the year."

"I figured Kai's party is more your style," Dan said, petting the fine velvet chair.

The devil laughed.

"Kai wouldn't know hedonism if a goat was sucking his cock," he spat. "The deal was, I give you a boat and you sail it—you throw parties with no rules."

"Yes," Dan said. "But you didn't say I had to win."

The devil grimaced.

"No, I didn't think that would be necessary," the devil poured himself another drink.

Outside, Ortun's band was starting their post-race set and he could hear the crowd buzzing.

"Sailing without intent is unpardonable," the devil continued, "is it not? Who, or what are you sacrificing—Dan? Whom are you giving yourself to lose to?"

"Sacrifice?" Dan asked.

"Yes," the devil said. "Sacrifice. You are all being hunted," he said with insight into the matter that his pet did not understand, "and it's only a matter of time before your passions catch you. Do you ever look over your shoulder? Try to see who it is?"

"I never look behind me," Dan said.

"Yes, you remind me of a friend who once needed to negotiate with a Russian general," the devil said indulging himself in another scotch and an anecdote. "But first, the Russian wanted to have a drink with him."

"And?" Dan said, savoring the glass of fine scotch.

"My friend refused. He told the Russian that he had no desire to drink with

him or any other Russian son of a bitch."

"I have sailed against Russians," Dan agreed. "Your friend sounds like a smart fellow."

"No," the devil went on to say. "He wasn't—you see, a war between two superpowers was at stake, and my obtuse friend was as humble as he was intelligent." The devil rubbed his glass and an image of General Patton appeared. "The Russian was not insulted in the lease, and accused him of being just as much of a son of a bitch as himself."

Dan finished the scotch and poured another shot.

"And how did Patton handle that?" he asked.

A smile crept into the devil's lips.

"He told him, 'I'll drink to that—one son of a bitch to another.'"

Dan held up his glass and the devil met it with his own.

"Here's to son's a' bitches," Dan said, "sailors, and to you."

CHAPTER 47

The sun fell over the horizon and Scorpio crawled into the sky. The air was dry and the distinct smell of rum sat heavy upon the party like a plump, nesting bird. The smell poured out of the sailor's skin and their clothes and their spilled, half-finished plastic red cups. Fruit flies delighted in the tang, and drank the nectar from the cups until they'd had their fill, and fell into the concoction drowning in their happiness. The rum enticed butterflies to venture near, but there were no flowers, only the red cups, and the trampled dandelions hiding near the fragrant trashcans in the lot reserved for campers and tents.

Ortun strummed a few cords and howled into the microphone.

"You sailors are a fucking mess!"

The crowd cheered.

He eyed his band and tipped his hat back—a tall magicians hat, and counted them off.

A low note.

Something to catch crowd's ear.

A tease, just a taste.

Maybe it wasn't even a note.

"You're all a fucking mess tonight—and I love you."

The bass player watched the audience, eyed them intently until he found a funky beat. When they started to groove on his rhythm, Ortun bobbed his head.

"I like that—I like that."

He looked back out to the drowsy crowd, made love to them with his eyes.

"I know it was a tough day for a lot of sailors out there today. Myself included—but if you sailed today. You won. Do you hear me? We're all fucking heroes! Every last one of you smarmy bastards."

The crowd cheered.

Ortun played another note and looked up at the sky.

"And you're all galaxies. Every one, do you hear me? And friends— galaxies are all different, aren't they? Have you ever seen one, or thought about one? Gravity pulling a billion stars into a fiery center. You see—my friends, they can only exist because of two opposing forces—the need to come together, and the need to fly apart."

He hit a clear note on his electric guitar—a cosmic tone that rolled out of the amplifiers and caused the nesting seagulls to stir.

"Do you ever feel like you're doing the same goddamned things them stars are doing up there? Do ya? That you're all a part of a vast cosmic fugue spinning in on itself without purpose—and maybe—just maybe, every once in a while, you need a little light to shine in on your dark corner of the universe? Well, if you do, this song is for you."

Ortun started into his song, Nine Ways to Love a Puddle.

He sang…

Love it like it's new,

Love it for what it is.

Love it like a crow, drinking it down apropos.

Love it for its potential, to melt away the snow.

Love it when it's gone.

Love it when it's wrong.

Love it at night,

when it doesn't have to fight

the purity of a mountain lake;

it'll reflect them stars just as they are

—as they were meant to be seen.

Love it in the rain,

when it wants to grow, and splash your ass . . . wake you up!

Love it the way you need to love it,

because tomorrow it may go.

Ortun stopped on a final cosmic note, danced, and then let the band finish the song the way they wanted—which was different every time they played it.

CHAPTER 48

Dan watched the Moon appear in rum tent and smiled as it began to disappear over the horizon. It was confirmation that the long day had ended and a new one was near. Ortun's band was jamming, and soon, as if synchronized by the same chemical reaction of a closing lily at nightfall, the sailors would taper off into their births to sleep.

It was only the first race, and there was plenty left to be had.

Race. Party. Play.

Now and then, a sailor would find him in the dark, pour some of their rum into his cup and pat him on the back. It was a sanctimonious sharing of blood between his brothers and his sister, the last few boats always receiving the sacrifice.

He accepted the sacrament with goodwill with grace.

Sailing without intent is unpardonable, is it not?

True or false, the devil had put a scare into him. While sitting in the velvet chair, drinking fine scotch, he was captivated. Though he'd known it since the day they met, his sponsor was a bored and cynical man, cursed to live life through the trials and tribulations of those who dared to live their lives without fear of him. But the questions tasked him—one in particular.

Whom was he giving himself to?

For most of his life, the answer would have been Neptune, King of the Sea. But now, every fiber in his body resisted the urge to sacrifice himself to the sea. Yes, there was the child to consider. But how could something yet to exist, have such a power over him? Something that asked him to live pure, to provide a home, free of scandal and debauchery.

There were many such instances, too many to note: the time that Ewan brought a stripper and her friend to a party at his home and made a makeshift pole for them to dance on out of a brass stairway railing. It didn't hold their weight and the stripper broke her coccyx after falling and shattering Drunk Bob's eye socket. Strippers were now banned from his parties, but not "dancers". Dancers were allowed, so long as they kept their clothes on and both feet on the floor. There was the constant discovery of

Ortun's insulin needles that turned up from time to time, under the sofa, in the garden, floating in the hot tub, or wherever he'd pass out. There was the fact that every frat boy and sorority sister with a father in a yacht club knew where the free booze was—the twerps dressed in turtlenecks, skipper hats and pipes to fit in. But they never did, and when a few of them were caught making out with the crew, they too were banned.

It had all become so complicated, Dan thought as he watched the moon sinking. The same moon that once inspired him as a child to see beyond the horizon, to set sail and watch the constellations change into new mysterious forms. After the Argonauts finished sailing the seven seas and reclaimed the Golden Fleece, he wondered they felt the same.

And what was this week but an attempt to set sail for the first time he'd ever cut the engine and caught his first wind? To live the kind of life that wounds and stabs him, but resurrects him after each new day on the water. A blow on the head. A bruised intercostal. A life of disaster! And every time, he'd fall in love again.

But now.

These stars were a rerun.

He'd sailed in every competition there was: The World's, San Francisco, Denmark, Australia, New York, Normandy, Peru. No, he did not win any of them, but that was not the point. He'd only cared to win one: Race Week.

In the past, losing a race hurt more than watching his father wither away like a neap tide, erased into a stagnant sea. The old man forbad him to sail. It was a sport for the rich, nothing that the son of fisherman should aspire. But he did. Every time he watched a sail boat slip effortlessly through the abyss, he stopped to admire it, even as his father cursed them for closing off good fishing grounds.

But the sting of losing was soon replaced by the thrill of new experiences, a statement he could feel his father scoffing at from beyond the grave.

Jake Taylor Swardstrum was a salmon fisherman, a trawler who didn't hate his life, he just had no keel. He'd fished his entire life and never once did Dan see him enjoy the life of a man of the sea. He stayed on his boat, even slept there, and just maybe only shared his bed with his mother to consecrate a son. The very idea of chasing fish out of the south sound was preposterous. Why on earth would we head north? The fish come here, Danny Boy. Now gut that son of a bitch! Them fish are yer' college books!

The old man was right, of course.

The spiny inlets of the south sound were woven into a mat of eelgrass and estuaries, a fertile landscape dotted with rusting bridges and buildings falling apart one brick at a time. The smell of mud, baked in the sun, or drenched in clean rain diluted the sickening smell of diesel the engines. Sometimes the pit-girl complained of the salty mess, but Dan never hated it and never would. It always reminded him of leaving home. Leaving the inlet. Leaving the land-locked sound, and heading out to sea.

College was easy.

He never went.

When the old man passed away, he left his wife with enough money to live a comfortable life, in a quiet home in Olympia. Dan sold the fishing boat and moved into an apartment overlooking Shilshole Bay Marina and from his balcony, he watched the sailboats race the way a cat watches a mouse. He drank beer, and sipped at margaritas. On the corner was a Caribbean sandwich shop that stuffed roasted pork with crackling skin into bread rolls and wrapped them in brown paper. Dan saved his money and lived a rich life. All he needed then, was a solid first mate: himself.

During racing season, every weekend, the Farr skippers manned their boat with rail meat. This was a free ride. Free lessons. Free scouting. Only a few boats were considered to have a serious program.

Dan kept his eye on Ballistic.

The skipper of Ballistic was a refined man, a construction businessman who could afford to pursue his interests—winning. He'd won at Yale, he'd won at being handsome, he'd won at third grade, won the pretty wife contest, but he could not win at sailing. Dan admired him for his effort, and knew that, though he was a tactical pilot, he had no instinct for the curling mess of green water under his hull, every bit as important as the wind. But when the skipper did win a race, which was far and few in-between, the crew celebrated with gusto. Their victories were sweet wine, always procured from sour grapes. A fool's wine was better than no wine at all, the skipper would say, but this was not the reason Dan joined the crew. Before he was asked aboard, he'd spent a year studying the physics of sailing and was able to easily apply it to his knowledge of driving his father's boat. Yes, the diesel engine pushed the hull through the rip currents of Puget Sound, but to understand yin you needed to feel yang. Dan knew long before the skipper knew, that he could add value. He puzzled over turbulence when he poured beer, watched the currents of suds the way he watched over the sides of his father's boat. When the marina closed for the day, if he didn't have a date to invite back to his little apartment, he'd climb the fence and sneak through every compartment of Ballistic until he could freely move about in the dark without a shuddered step, or a fumbled halyard. He'd test the lines; lean over the rails until he felt the braided wires imbed in his gut enough to leave bruises that he was proud of.

The skipper took him aboard. Picked the scrawny kid out of a group of well outfitted, trust-fund boys. Told him later while celebrating that the reason he was asked to join was because he thought he could out drink the bastards.

Dan toasted the moon and watched the last of it fall behind the tree line.

Sailing is a song, sing it. He thought, remembering the words of his skipper. Sailing is a game, play it. Sailing is a challenge, meet it. Sailing is a dream, realize it. Sailing is a sacrifice, offer it. Sailing is love, enjoy it.

He poured another cup of rum and listened to his tactician finish his set. There was still the "raft up", party to attend and a morning race he hoped would remedy the day's debacle.

Race, Party, Play, he told himself. Repeat.

Martina found him and threw her arm around his waist.

"Do you think that we'll miss this?"

Dan, with the stars in his eyes, smiled at her, and the little scar frowned.

"I'll always be a sailor," he said. "Doesn't mean I have to be a rake."

"There is no such thing, honey," she said.

Dan rubbed her belly, took his eyes off the constellations.

"I can't wait to meet her."

"And how do you know it will be a girl?"

"Ah," he said. "It's the curse of a pirate."

CHAPTER 49

Starry nights on the water are magical.

No one notices the stars, but they are there—pins of light stabbing into darkness. The darkness is true, but there is a collected, wash of light. It is there, and just as true, though there is much more darkness.

The water reflects this beauty, but tonight, the stars win. They are there, reflected in the water and shining in the sky—strung out like pearls. Perfection. The fleet is bathing in their wake, tied together, starboard to port—a million-dollar raft of fiberglass and Mylar—drifting jewels, rolling on dark swells.

It was a rule that the last few competitors stayed anchored until everyone drank their fill and, at the end of the night, the drunken sailors climbed from boat to boat, without falling overboard. They held onto their red plastic cups and deftly maneuvered over wires and halyards, cleats and booms. Their laugher hit the water hard and softened instantly on the swells.

There was the smell of BBQ. Rhett flew two flags, a chicken and a cow. Ivonne tended grill. She pretended that the hot dogs were dicks and stuck them in every ear that came near her before cooking them. Every time she did it, she laughed like it was a new experience. The women dressed in pink tutus for cancer, and the new ones to sailing were advised to kiss the skipper or the mast of every boat once they were aboard. Some of the skippers were old enough to blush each time they received a peck on the lips.

The writer watched the party with a melancholic eye. He watched the stars. Watched the people ignoring them. He stood with his feet slightly apart, to steady himself on the swells. Though he not could see it, a whale song found its way through the hull, through his feet and into his bones. It seemed they were in the same mood.

The new grinder was speaking.

"Fuck if it's stunned," he shouted. "The gas was cheap today! But we'll piss more than a dog tomorrow!"

More laughter.

Hers.

His.

Hers again.

The pit-girl was having a good time on a boat someplace in the mess, and findings his way to her through the unsteady maze would be difficult. But the dark faces were comforting. It was easier this way. He smiled pleasantly out at the stars pretending to be occupied or aloof, wondering what his boys were doing. Video games? Watching a hockey match? They were amazing little entities. Tiny, growing galaxies.

"You shore support?"

The writer turned to a beautiful face in the night.

"Yes," he admitted. "How do you know?"

"You're not drunk," she said in a British accent.

"Neither are you."

They toasted.

"Nefarious," he said.

"Last Tango," she said.

They paused and allowed the emptiness to fill the space between them.

"Are you a father?"

"You are perceptive," he told the woman. "How'd you know that?"

"You have the look of a martyr about you," she said. "Being away from your children and trying to have a little fun—I know, it's hard."

"How many do you have?" he asked.

The writer spied the little number eleven between her eyebrows and two lovely dimples when she smiled. She was distinctly in her forties, tall and lean, a classic brunette featuring a pair of steady legs that looked as taught as a cowboy's rolled cigarettes.

"Two daughters," she said.

"Two boys," he said.

"Cute," they said together.

The writer looked back at the stars.

"I'm Lindsay," the woman said.

"I'm Max."

"You here alone?"

"No," he said in a lonely voice. "I'm fucking the pit-girl." He realized that every time he said it, he did so with a different emotion.

The woman seemed to understand, the way that every sailor in the fleet seemed to understand.

"I heard your crew washed out today," she said.

"An epic fail," he admitted.

"Dan's a good, sailor," she said. "He'll bounce back."

"I wouldn't know."

The writer spotted Mac two boats over, her arm around Davey's waist as she led the crew in the Nefarious song.

The woman caught his eye.

"Mind if I ask what the hell you are doing here?" she asked.

"Research," he said. "I'm a fiction writer."

The two watched Davey pick the pit-girl up as high as a figure skater, twirl her and set her down and kissed her.

"If you were any good at fiction writing," the woman said in her pristine accent, "you wouldn't have to be here at all, now would you?"

The writer downed his cup of rum and climbed over two sets of safety wires to the deck of Nefarious.

"Darling," the pit-girl said when she found him glaring at her. She took her arms off Davey and threw them around him. "Where have you been?"

"On Bat of Hell," he said. "Watching you make out with your friend."

The pit-girl blushed and he could smell the rum that had already been processed in her body. She put all her weight on him and an unsteady finger to his lips.

"Take me home," she said before he could speak again. "Take me home and fuck me every which way."

CHAPTER 50

Kevin Jonson stabbed his harpoon in the sand at Sacred Cove, left it there standing tall, silhouetted against the stars and the falling Milky Way. From the shoreline, he watched the raft of sailboats break up, the sound of their motors poisoning the distant whale song. If the whale were healthy—he could tell by its song that it was not—like the sailors of Race Week, it would have arrived ostentatiously to display its sexual prowess, its advances measured in song. The canyon beneath would provide a perfect location for corralling its mating ballad, channeling it into a den of concupiscent cows. This is why his ancestors called this place sacred. This is where they came to hunt.

But this whale…

There was something wrong.

It was tired, frightened, lonely and lost.

Often, along the west coast, transient killer whales separated juveniles from their pod. They hunted the grey whale in packs, thinning the pod, encircling their prey, and then tearing it apart.

It came here to hide.

It came here to die.

Kevin Jonson recognized the loneliness he heard in the animal, sympathized, and one way or another, he would end its suffering.

In the distance, he saw a figure coming up over the hill, a square, shabby man staggering up the little parted trail of grass. When he was close enough to make eye contact, he stopped walking and spoke.

"My name is Christopher."

"I know who you are," Kevin Johnson said.

"I'm here to race the boats."

Kevin Jonson pointed to the boats.

"The boats are there," he said. "They are breaking up for the night. They race again tomorrow morning."

He watched the little man depart, knowing that he was not in Oak Harbor to watch boats. Bukwus was a Kwakiutl legend—sister tribe to the Makah, a long-haired dimensional drifter, a ghost associated with drowning victims who is sometimes known as the "King of Ghosts" or "Man of the Sea". On earth, he tries to tempt humans into eating ghost food, or steals their sacred maps and then lures them far away from home, turning them into Bukwus.

Kevin Jonson watched the little man saunter away until he was out of sight, then he lit some cedar to keep him away. In the gentle perfume of the smoke, he laid down in a bed made of maidenhair grass and watched the stars until the boats disappeared. When they were all gone and it was quiet again and he could hear the lonesome song of the bull and soon he began to drift into a deep sleep.

The sailors were hard on his psyche too, their aloof intensity, a drain and a bore. In short erratic burst, his eyelids fluttered, and the starlight warped into elegant, sublime features. The whale sang into the great void, calling out across the darkness to find his pod. He shut his eyes tight and felt the song in his bones, knew that it had come from a distance, the same distance that was but only a hair's breadth—yet also a chasm, so large that it was only from a great distance that one could see the true spectacle.

His body stiffened and he tried not to see the void behind his eyelids. It was madness to consider. It was madness to think about it all.

The whale called for him. He knew it was for him because in the inky darkness, only a consciousness can fathom the darkness. He opened his eyes, but instead of stars, he saw himself, sleeping in the grass, naked and alone.

The whale cried out again: a new song.

Are you prepared to harpoon me?

I am prepared to receive your harpoon.

Will I look straight into the eye of my hunter?

Which is none other than my own eye.

And see the naked face of my soul.

When you take a life,

whether it be physical or emotional,

you take with it a soul,

something that cannot be returned.

Will you keep what you have taken?

Forever?

The song lulled Kevin Jonson into a deep trance, and with smell of cedar in his nose, and with the whale in his thoughts, he soon fell into the darkness that he had been awaiting.

Together, he and the whale were not alone.

CHAPTER 51

The game was not to see how much she could take. She could take an enormous amount of bodily pain. The flesh, or more precisely, its complaining, could be compartmentalized, stowed in a locker, kept there until she needed what was inside.

No.

The game was to see how much he could dish out.

"You must be upset with me," the pit-girl said. "I've been naughty, haven't I?"

"I don't understand why you would kiss him," the writer said. "In front of your crew. It makes me look like a pussy."

He was going through it all again, wasn't he? She felt shame. Put it in the locker. She felt anger. Put it in the locker.

"You've seen me kiss others before," she said in a very, quiet and calm voice.

"Never so sweetly," the writer said. "You have feeling for him, I can tell."

The pit-girl unraveled his belt from around his waist; laid it on the bed.

"I'm drunk, darling," she said. "Davey means nothing to me."

The writer looked at her with more skepticism.

No.

It was loss.

No.

It was fire.

The pit-girl believed that lovers came in two forms, those who were cool as ice, or those who were on fire.

She needed the fire. She believed in lovers with the power to wound the heart, to break it, not heal it.

To stop it.

Shock it.

Make it live again and again.

Lovers who made you think suicidal thoughts, lovers who broke the frozen sea within her, lovers who play with mortality.

Theirs.

Hers.

Lovers who caught fire, or who were sized by fire.

Lovers who set themselves on fire.

But this was a first.

The pit-girl had never seen ice catch fire.

Max was different, wasn't he? And until she figured out why, he'd stay. She'd make him stay.

The pit-girl slipped out of her clothes; first her salt-sprayed coveralls, then her polyurethane, water resistant shirt. She unzipped her boots, still soggy, one at a time and watched the writer patiently, watched for the spark she knew was there.

"He's a friend," she said. "We sailed a little. Messed around like sailors do on cold nights." She fixed her pink panties, made them tight—the one's he despised and thought looked cheap. Sometimes, he'd tear them off of her. "Van Ise," she continued. "A long race—the course that circumnavigates Vancouver Island. Be sure to put that in your book, will you? Only two women crew members in the entire fleet."

She crawled onto the bed, moved her hair out of her eyes and poised her ass as high as she could lift it.

"I'll count them off, one by one darling," she said, and settled her head in a dignified pose. "Pick up the belt. Go on. You know what to do, don't you?"

The writer picked up the belt and she moaned when she heard the buckle ring.

"Yes, that's it," she closed her eyes.

The first strike was a loud and beautiful snap, like a fallen branch in a storm.

The force surprised her.

"One," she counted.

The second was harder; she winced, but stored it safely in the locker.

"Two," she said. "Harder."

The writer stopped and laid the belt on her back, then, with the back of his cool hand, he caressed the bruises she'd earned on the course today.

"Stop it," she said. "I don't deserve your tenderness, Max. Now don't be a pussy."

He picked up the belt and she counted to ten before she moaned again, each snap louder than the last.

"Again," she said. "I want you to lose control. I want to see it, you beautiful bastard."

The writer dropped the belt.

The pit-girl opened the locker and exhaled because she could hear the defeated in his footsteps as he moved to the other side of the room to pour himself a drink.

She didn't move.

She wouldn't.

"Finish what you started, you coward."

"No," he said, and sat down next to her and kissed her on the shoulder. "It's hard enough watching you hurt yourself."

"I love you," she said. "Now pour me a drink."

CHAPTER 52

Dan lay in bed—his pretty wife sleeping in his arms. She even snored pretty: tiny, civilized chirps, clipped by low, benignant octaves. It sounded like the beginning to his favorite Pink Floyd song, a set of notes designed to lull the listener into a drowsy trance. He sighed and watched her breast rise and fall. Perfect breast, the kind displayed on romance novels.

Sharing them would not be a problem, he thought. He'd shared them before, and more.

It was a messy night, on all accounts; he only remembered it in flashes and perhaps it was better left that way. Even when they were alone, they never talked about Round the County. The cook was a gentleman and did not threaten him in the least, but seeing your lover in such an intimate way never left your mind. It was like standing before a stained-glass window that is suddenly struck by lightning. You either see the event as a disaster, or the fireworks thrill you.

Through the wall, he listened to Mac and the cook. It sounded like an intense session: spanking, torn clothing, arguing. He slipped a hand under the blanket and held one of Martina's perfect mounds, brushed his thumb over a pert nipple and listened to her breathing change—then, he began to wonder what it would be like to witness his daughter feeding from his lover—sublime, he decided.

Dan rolled over onto his erection, waited for it to fatigue. Better get some sleep, he thought. It sounded like his pit-position was going to need his help keeping things tied down tomorrow. He'd spent the night avoiding her. But on a boat, that was hard to do.

CHAPTER 53

Ortun put away his guitar, closed the hatch to his girlfriend's Macgregor and leaned against the cabin for a smoke. It was docked on the outskirts of town, near a grassy hill, spotted with crab grass that was just high enough to hide a set of train tracks leading straight out of town.

Ortun heard footsteps on the dock.

"Where the hell are you going?" he said, and put out his cigarette.

The dark figure looked back at him, hunched his shoulders and turned back to the train tracks.

"Hey!" he called. "You didn't like the boats?"

Christopher kept walking.

"You ain't seen nothing good?"

Ortun closed hopped onto the dock and caught up to the bum. He hurriedly lit another cigarette and handed it over, but Christopher kept walking and made for the train tracks.

"But it's only day one! The first race! And shit! There was a wreck. And now Dan is sailing like a pussy so he can bow-out gracefully to raise a child. But he's a sailor, you see? Always has been. No way he's gonna let us down by going out with a whimper!"

Christopher never broke his gait. He just sucked on his cigarette—the orange cherry lighting his haggard face.

"Are you not entertained?" Ortun pleaded. "The protest ended in a brawl! A fucking brawl man! Sailors fighting over shit that when it's all said and done, won't amount to a hill of beans!" Ortun took out his flask and opened it. "And Dan's lucky charm, the pit-girl, she's pissed because he withdrew a protest. They'll fight! Oh it'll be one hell of a fight! Do you know why? Because they haven't spoken since the protest and their passive aggressive bullshit is gonna blow up in their faces. Oh man! Tomorrow's gonna be hell on water—you walking piece of crap! I give you a front row seat to a transcendent opera—a testament of will and strength and you make for the tracks? I play music for you. I give you cigarettes! Where the hell are you off to, anyways? You have better things to do?"

Christopher stopped, opened a bag of salmon jerky and offered it Ortun.

"Ah!" Ortun said taking the offering and chewing on the meat. "You like emotion, do you? That's your nepenthe! It's the only thing you really understand? The drama." He handed over his flask, and Christopher took a long pull from it. "Well, what about the cook? He thinks he's found true love, but he's too hurt to ever believe that he'll be loved the way he tries to love! How's that for fucked up? And Mac, nearly half his age. She can't be tamed, can she? And so she'll never believe that someone can love her for exactly what she is—a sailor without an anchor who isn't interested in settling down. She's too young! She's too proud to ever say that to Max, because she knows that real love doesn't come but once in a blue moon. Don't you see? They are captured by pride and affliction, forces of nature, but . . ." he laughed, and drank. "But by their very nature, they pull apart! How's that not entertaining?"

Christopher turned back to the waiting horizon, walked.

"Show me the magic trick again!"

He kept walking—walked until Ortun couldn't see him anymore.

"You bastard!" he said, and wiped his stinging lips. "You're missing the best part. Tomorrow, if Nefarious loses, it all unravels. All of it! The entire thing will be but a dream within a dream."

CHAPTER 54

Ortun opened his eyes and knew what would happen next.

It was cloudy, and he couldn't see much, but he could see enough.

Was he still in bed?

It didn't really matter, did it?

Even the surprises would be predictable.

You knew what the protagonist was going to do before he even knew why he was doing it.

Ortun looked out the porthole window, toward the grassy knoll that Christopher had disappeared over. The bum wasn't there—so he hit the snooze.

Hit it like he'd done a thousand times before.

Wished he wasn't hitting it.

Wished again.

Hit it again until finally he wasn't sure if he was on the deck of Nefarious or looking out the window from his bunk.

In the mirror, he watched as he cut himself shaving—the blood mixing with shaving cream, and morphing to pink. He could see every molecule diffuse into the lather, a slow kaleidoscope of change. His lips were parted, eyes darkened, and his diabetic skin was already pallid.

I could quit, he thought.

Not race. Just quit.

Go to the world of ghost.

Become a memory.

All the aches and pains and needfulness of the flesh and mind will leave in a wake memories—dissolved into the either—in front of my birth, behind my death. It will all end up in the same darkness. What if yesterday was destiny? What if the world of ghost is where I already live?

"You're late—you fucking Rockstar!" the pit-girl said. Her words slammed into his head like a ball of clay. "Boat time was seven a.m., asshole!"

He wished like hell that he could roll under the covers again, but there were no blankets on deck, just a cold morning drizzle to hide under. Again he looked for the bum. Again he reached for the snooze.

The crew was busy setting gear. They did not mind the drizzle, or the after effects of the rum and sex and drugs and...

Dan appeared.

"Mac," he said. "I'll do the chastising on this boat, got it?"

"Aye, skipper," she said, saluted and sassed away.

Dan frowned and turned to him.

"Late night?" he asked.

Ortun nodded.

"Was she pretty?"

"Not very," he groaned. "No."

"They can't all be, can they?" Dan said, and stepped up to Ortun to inspect his lousy shave. "Looks like a bum shaved you this morning."

"I only look in the mirror once a day," Ortun muttered, "and that's in the morning when I shave."

"That bad?" Dan said. "Well, can you rig this bitch to fly for me today?"

"Aye, skipper."

Ortun would have appreciated the fire in Dan's belly, but he already knew that they'd win.

It had to happen.

It was already written.

They'd get out on the water, and like angry make-up sex between lovers who were no good for each other—the crew would figure their shit out.

Nefarious did just that . . . and suddenly he was on stage, singing to the crowd.

He looked for Christopher in their faces.

"Nefarious kicked some ass today!" he heard himself tell the crowd. "Looks like a tighter race than we thought?"

The crowd cheered.

"But we know how this drama pans out, don't we?" he said, or was thinking. "Tomorrow Kai will win. And then it'll be our day. You see? Good and bad are infinitely tangled. It's a circle. It's what's in store for us all—and what's going to happen yesterday will happen tomorrow. Every race boat, every ant crawling on a fence post without a clue, every man and woman and every child."

He let the crowd steep in some guitar notes and then launched into his favorite song, A Poet is a Fool.

Left on the mountain

Moses on the mound

A poet is a fool

A fool with a foil crown

A poet is a saved child

A liar

And a clown

Afraid to let the good days go

And die

Without a sound . . .

But before he could close it—he was in his bed again, waking to the sound of his alarm.

Then in a shower.

Then he was at a breakfast table.

"You gonna finish that bacon?" Ewan said.

"No," Ortun said.

Ewan stabbed it with his knife, the rigging tool he kept strapped to his side.

"Nice show last night, Ortun," he said. "You were a little flat at the end, though."

"Was I?"

Ortun cracked open a Coors light.

"Sure, but you're a pro. You can sleep walk through that shit and still make us swoon."

He slapped Ortun on the back.

Duff leaned closer.

"You up late again last night, huh? Did you make her moan? Huh? What was she like?"

Ortun folded his napkin into a little ball, made it disappear in his sleeve and suddenly—a slap of ice water hit him across the face. He looked for the son of bitch who did it, but after he focused, he was staring out at the Salish Sea.

"You ok?"

The pit-girl was strapped in next to him, leaning over the side to keep Nefarious dead reckoned.

Ortun grimaced, looked out to sea, then to the little knoll where Christopher had disappeared.

"I'm not inspired," he said.

"Not inspired?" she laughed. "A bad day out here beats the worst day out there."

Ortun leaned over and kissed her the way he remembered when they had fooled around during Van Ise, hard and sloppy.

"Boy, you're not kidding, are you?" she said.

He gazed into her amber eyes, but only saw the writer looking back.

They'd never make it of course, but they danced the dance and did it right into the flames that would turn them into ashes.

"You don't actually love him, do you?"

"He has kids," she said. "Esther says that kids are little anchors, don't you know? And what business is it of yours, mister? You fuck a different girl every night."

Another splash hit him in the face, and now he was below deck, injecting insulin into his arm. He was shaking and his skin was gooseflesh; white on milk. He bit his lip, captured a purple vein and wiggled in the needle into it, watched the chemicals move slowly through the syringe: a liquid transfer of energy—life giving, molecular stamina. He relaxed the hold on his lip and the little capillaries opened and flooded with color.

Now he was holding a silver bullet.

A silver fifty-caliber slug awarded to the day's winner.

"What the fuck?" Bonesteel said. "We're still in this shit, like my hand's in a sheep!"

"What the hell are you saying?" Ortun asked.

"We're gonna pull this thing off, O-bro!" Bonesteel was shouting. "The skipper gave you that bullet for rigging his bitch to fly, don't you know."

Ortun tossed Bonesteel the prize.

"I have more of those than I can count," he said.

"Thanks mate."

Ortun walked away. Left the party behind him and found a pleasant dock where even the seagulls avoided. It was covered in tar and smelled like a cleaner his mother would soak the floors in. He closed his eyes and visited the cabinet where she kept it under the sink: twisted pipes and hoses vanishing someplace beneath the world and an old grey mop-head. There was a bag of potatoes, sprouting and rotting in the dank womb, their albino runners crawling along the floorboard, desperate for light.

On the horizon, a few boats were still coming in. He looked through the line of stragglers, past the roiling sea, to the edge of the horizon. He let it blur. Let it disappear behind the sinking, turquoise night and wished to see a staggering vision—an ax blow. A hammer. Something that struck at the nature of his existence.

He hit the snooze.

Shaved.

"Looks like Rhett is having a bad day," Dan said.

Ortun breathed in deep.

"Worst day on the water," he said, taking a sip of his Coors Light. "Beats the best day on land."

"How are you feeling?"

"Fine."

"You looked uneasy today."

"I rigged her to fly, didn't I skipper?"

"Yes you did."

Dan took out his little flask, took a pull and offered it to Ortun.

"No thanks."

"We're one up on Kai, thanks to you."

"Yeah?"

"Put twenty minutes on his clock."

Twenty minutes was an eternity to a race boat, but nothing to Ortun. Not today. Only a minute ago, he hit the snooze button on his clock. The sun's light was eight minutes old, the stars that hid behind the horizon . . . thousands of years. There was nothing new here to see. Today's embers longed for tomorrow and the ashes would never stop raining from the sky.

"How do you think Kai will rig for tomorrow?"

Ortun looked at Dan.

"He'll rig her for fair weather."

"What about the ebbing tide?"

"Marées vont et viennent," Ortun said in French, tides come and go.

Dan put the flask away. The only French he knew, Ortun thought, was Madam, please dance on the table.

"Ortun," he said. "Just remember this one thing." Dan patted him on the shoulder like a child. "There is no problem on earth that you can't make worse."

Ortun faked a smile.

"Thanks, skipper."

Dan turned and walked away.

"But I'm sure it sounds better in French," he said and turned a corner.

Ortun tuned his guitar. He let the amplifier scrape and scratch at the air. It made the crowd restless. He counted the band off while eyeing them all. The bum wasn't there. He could feel it. No stupid little baseball cap with an American flag, no tweed blazer with elbow patches, no smell of Mad Dog. In the distance, he watched a lone streetlight flicker on the hill where the little man had deserted. The funny thing was, the little shit had needed him first. Wandering the streets of Oak Harbor like a lost, sacred cow.

Adrift.

A mote of dust, touching nothing but space.

The little shit!

The little ingrate.

"This song is about karma," he told the crowd.

Ortun hit the first note and lost his guitar pick.

"Hey Ortun," Ewan said in the hot tub. "You were not your best tonight, where you?"

"No man, I wasn't."

"You need to relax," Ewan said. "Here, smoke this. Max rolled it. Said his grandmother taught him how to roll blunts back when he was ten."

"Bullshit," Duff said.

"She died of pancreatic cancer, man. He rolled them for her when she was too sick to do it herself." Ewan took a toke. "Who says shit like that if it ain't true?"

"A writer, you sorry sap," Ortun told him.

Ortun took a toke and tried to relax into the tub. He spread his arms and let the heat and steam escape from his skin; he felt like Christ on a burning cross.

"How does Dan wanna fly tomorrow?" Duff asked.

"He wants me to rig her for the tides," Ortun said.

"Oh," Ewan said. "And how does one do that?"

"You say 'fuck you' to the wind, and you set her short." Ortun grabbed a toy sailboat from Duff.

"Hey fucker!" Duff said. "That's mine."

"You keep your rigs tight," Ortun said, and turned the toy boom to stern. "And you wait for the devil's piss." He pushed the boat into one of the jets and it instantly caught the current. "Then you buckle your seatbelt." The boat slingshot to other side where the jet pinned it against the edge.

The writer settled into the tub and caught the boat by the sail.

Ortun waited for him to get comfortable and then eyed him skeptically. Maybe there was a surprise in him he'd missed.

"What's your game, sugar-man?"

The writer clouded over.

"Is that some sort of vague reference to my ethnicity?"

"Yes," Ortun said. "If you'd like it to be." Ortun moved closer to him. "Why don't you get on a boat and race?"

"I need to maintain an objective eye."

"Can you swim?"

"I'm a SCUBA diver."

"You didn't answer my question," Ortun said. "Can the guys on Tupac swim?" he asked. "I mean, aren't their bones denser or something?"

The writer passed the joint to Ortun and refused to answer.

"What's your book about?" Ortun asked.

"You," the writer said.

Ortun laughed, but it didn't feel funny.

"Have you written anything more interesting?"

"Yes," the writer took a toke. "The Makah."

"They let you on their reservation?"

"Yes," the writer said.

Ortun sat up, slicked his hair back.

"Neah Bay," he said. "A few houses. A grocery store. No bars."

"The end of the world," the writer said.

"What were you doing out there?"

"I'm a writer."

"No, I mean cosmically, man."

The writer thought for a moment.

"Same as what you are doing here," he said. "To fill the void."

"Nature abhors a vacuum." Ortun said leaning back. "Yes, she does."

Ortun hit the snooze button.

He let the alarm go off two more times before he rolled out of bed.

Coffee.

No sugar.

No cream.

Black. Black. Black.

Race four.

After today, one more to go.

Then he could find a dark hole.

Finish the job.

Burry himself.

Maybe try heroin again.

Black. Black. Black.

Then—warmth.

It would flood over him. Spread out. Close in on his heart. The hole would flood with light.

"Good morning," the devil said. He caught up to him as he walked to Nefarious.

"Sure," Ortun said.

"How are you rigging my girl, today?"

It wasn't his boat. Not entirely. The devil was co-owner, he knew, but never sailed with the crew. Dan felt that two skippers caused fuck-ups.

"Loose," Ortun said.

"Flooding tide," the devil said. "You tell Dan to be careful around Deception Pass."

"It's an ebbing tide," Ortun said. "The water is going out."

"Coming or going," the devil said. "The force that drives the water through a mountain, drives my blood as well. It carves an island, and it picks the flesh from bones and then turns them to stone."

Ortun stopped walking.

"What the hell are you talking about?"

"Oh nothing, I suppose," the devil said. "How's your skipper? Is he ok today?"

"He's fine, what's going on?"

"You've been too distracted to notice, I think," the devil said. "So I'll spare you the details."

"I know that he's having a baby," Ortun said. "It's not due for months."

"Ah yes," the devil said. "But Deception Pass is a dangerous inlet, is it not? I don't want my boat hurt."

"It's not your boat."

"Half mine."

Ortun stopped.

"Do you know why bananas are never brought on board a boat?"

"I never thought about it, why?" the devil allowed.

"Because they are asking for problems," Ortun feigned a slipping motion. "And so is telling a sailor to be careful."

The devil laughed.

"Don't let Kai intimidate you out there, today," he called out as Ortun hurried off. "Not the way he intimidates Dan. We're all counting on you! It's not racing if you are afraid to bump hips."

Ortun turned a corner and ditched the creepy man. He walked hard, scaring off the seagulls bathing in fog. He drank his black coffee. He zipped his overalls. Tightened is belt. When he came to the end of the dock, he peered at deception point. The tide had already gone slack, barnacles closed and the ripe stench of festering alga drifted in the breeze.

"It's going to be weird out there," Rhett said.

He was with Ivonne, his pretty wife, watching an otter eat a rock crab for breakfast. It floated on its back with its meal on its belly. All the crab's leg were missing, except one waving frantically in the air. Finally, the fuzzy little murderer snapped the last leg off, chewed on it and dumped living carapace into the sea.

"Yep," Ortun said. "Weird."

"You ok, sailor?"

Ortun wanted to say no. He really did. But how could he explain the fact that a little hobo man had disappeared and would never return? How could he explain that the little guy was sitting under some lonely bridge begging for change as hipsters passed by without a care? Who would show him humanity? Who would look him in the eye while he cooked a can of chili over a little hobo stove while he sipped from a bottle of Mad Dog? Who would pretend that his stupid little magic trick was real and amazing?

"I'm fine," he said, and ran out of breath.

"Remember," Ivonne said. "The worst day on the water beats the best day on land..."

Ortun wished it were true, but every sailor knew, there wasn't a lonelier place in the world to be lonely than at sea.

"Ahoy," the pit-girl said, and she peeked at her watch.

Ortun was transported to the deck of Nefarious. He went right to work. He carefully tuned the boat while the crew drank coffee and peered out through the fog. He loosened the forward halyard—let them hang of the mainstay like a pretty necklace. Checked every halyard. Tested the helm.

Dan appeared.

"I'm not sailing, today," he said.

The crew froze.

"Why the hell not?" Ortun Demanded.

"Something's wrong," he said. "Martina."

Ortun saw the worry in Dan's eyes. It killed him.

"Who's gonna skipper?"

"You are," Dan said.

Ortun moved to Dan, met him face to face. He let in the pain he saw in his eyes into his heart, but it didn't change things.

"I can't," he said.

"Then, we'll have to forfeit," Dan said.

"What about Mac?" Ortun asked.

"She needs more seasoning." Dan said. "Tag. You're it sailor. I'm headed to the hospital."

Dan turned on a heel and disappeared in the fog.

The pit-girl appeared.

"Where the hell is he going?"

"Martina."

"I knew it!" she said. "I knew she would keep him off the water!"

"She's in the hospital."

In that instant, they both knew she'd lost the baby.

"Shit," the pit-girl said.

"Dan made me skipper."

The words stunned her, and her face angered, and saddened, but even in her cloud of rage—she was clear headed enough to know that placing the tactician at the helm was not personal.

She nodded.

She was sober.

Clear.

"We need some dead weight," she said.

"The writer," Ortun said.

"He can't swim," the pit-girl said.

"He's a SCUBA diver."

"Doesn't mean he can swim."

Ortun pulled on the mainstay, released the pressure on the jib.

"He can hike it," he said. "I'll take the helm. You call tactics."

"Who's in the pit?"

"Bonesteel."

She took the mainstay halyard from Ortun, pulled until the jib lofted.

"We need him to grind."

"Not today," Ortun looked out at the fog. The tide would do all the grinding. "Get the rest of the crew. Tell them we have shit to deal with."

The pit-girl hurried off to the boathouse. Ortun waited for her footsteps to disappear and then he looked back out at the water. The bridge over Deception Pass loomed like a giant metal spider. A bank of fog was captured in its metal legs, and it rolled and rolled under its spans, trapped by the cold water and torn by the marine layer. Under the surface were glacial erratics; hummock of stone and carved mountain tops sunk into the icy fjord. He knew that two percent of all the tidal water entering and leaving Puget Sound constricted its way through this narrow, thirteen hundred feet of stone—a funnel, moving water under the bridge at nine knots. That wasn't fast, but it was powerful enough for thrill seeking kayakers to use the current to surf the standing wave called, Boxcar.

Deception pass was a fickle entity, a hushed and still vista from the bridge deck, but down at the business end, it was fierce. Under normal circumstance, Edmund would have altered the course. The tides were predictable during Race Week, and the sever currents could be avoided. But this year, the race needed to remain "technical" to qualify for the Farr 30 International Sailing Federation. The club had even sent a rep to Whidbey Island to scout the location and considered the idea of hosting a world-class race around the island.

The crew gathered.

"You heard?" Ortun said.

They all nodded.

"Let's win this for Dan," he told them. "Now get your scurvy asses on board. It's going to be a snail race today. Count on it."

The pit-girl, now a tactician, barked orders.

"You heard the skipper! Get your shit done. Racing ain't for fun! It's to keep from dying! Let's make like a worm in the rain. You looking for a nice soul to pick you up and put you in the grass where the robins won't eat you alive? You're on the wrong boat! Ewan, make like you know some shit and zip up that halyard like you were finished taking a piss!" Ortun knew what she was doing. It was like when he played football in high school. The butterflies in your stomach didn't leave until the first hit. She punched at the crew hard with her voice, a sparring match before the real thing. "Get those bitch bumpers off our girl! Douse that jib! Let's go, me bucko's. Get the bilge out of ye' stomachs!" she screamed and dialed her phone. "Darling, we need you. Get down here now! We need you to hike it for Neffy today. Dan's out. I'll explain later. Forget about the brisket! What? You can't swim? Are you crazy? But you're a diver!"

In parting fog, with a new skipper, a cook and a screaming tactician, Nefarious set sail for heat three. As they departed, Ortun looked toward strawberry hill, but his lucky charm was still AWOL. He knew that the universe was nothing without him, a temporal snag, knotted like a tangled mess of ropes, now useless. Somehow, he needed to untangle the mess, but that required effort. No one liked untangling shit, especially when shit was happening. He thought about Dan on his way to the hospital, eyeing the start in his rearview mirror. The truth was, this was going to be the last Race Week, wasn't it? Not the last event. The competition was fifty-three years running, but it was the last for this crew. Sure, there would be another. But not like this. Not with a crew that was madly in love.

Ewan, aging and taking too much time off to sail, left Duffy holding up the business. They fought endlessly about bills and clients and Ewan's long lunches with mimosas, which he drank so that he didn't feel like an alcoholic. Their hot tub cleaning service ensured that the crew bathed in the best water possible, clean and ph. balanced, just enough chlorine to not sting the eyes. They especially came in handy when the boys from Gardyloo dropped by and fouled up the tub. The word "gardyloo" was an old saying in Edinburgh, yelled just before someone threw slop into the streets from a high window. Ewan always added more chlorine after they entered and yelled it as he did it sprinkled in the water. But like his aging bones, Ewan's charm was wearing thin. He was the largest mainsail position in the fleet, and he was no longer able to scramble over the deck like he used to. They all knew he'd have to be put down soon. And Duff. He had wife troubles, teenager troubles, money troubles, which made him unreliable.

Ortun eyed them both; watched them settle into the serious moment ahead of them. Perhaps they saw the knot in the timeline like he had seen. Perhaps this was their last Race Week. Perhaps it really was going to end like this.

Jupiter neared their starboard side. Kai was tight on their bow.

"I hope Martina gets better before tomorrow," he said. "I want to take the trophy from Dan, not you."

Kai called out a tack, but it was a feign. Ortun bit and started a turn to keep out of his wind shadow.

"No! No! No!" called the pit-girl.

Ortun steadied the boat, steered alongside Kai and his hideous laugh.

"Now!" the pit-girl called.

She had already grown too big for her britches. She'd come on strong at World's, wild eyed and nimble. Her hair was long and red and there wasn't a single bruise on her body. She managed financial accounts for the William T. Hass Foundation, and she began to long for the images in the promotional posters they produced—the white-hot, knife edged bows of sailing yachts cutting through turquoise water. Excited sailors. Full spinnakers. Teamwork. Adventure. Ortun stepped in front of Dan. What's the weight of a keel and its co efficient of drag on a race hull? He asked, and her answer was perfect. Who gives a fuck? she said. If you don't know where you are going, any road will get you there.

"Don't fall for that shit again, Ortun!" she called out.

Kai turned his boat into Nefarious a second time, but steered clear at the last minute. The bow was snorting like a bull—it's hull stomping through the water.

Huff! Huff! Huff!

"Throw a flag!" the pit-girl said.

"No," Ortun said.

"Give us ten feet, you bastard!" she yelled at Kai. "Back off!"

Ortun turned Nefarious on a hard tack. He let her bow swing around and then turned at the starting line, killing just enough inertia to keep from damaging Jupiter's hull, but scratching her pristine gel coat.

"It's not racing if you are afraid to bump hips," Ortun snatched the flag and threw it in a locker. "We won't need this today."

Kai stopped laughing and reached for his flag, threw it over the stern for the committee boat to see.

"You pussy!" the pit-girl said.

Ortun turned his attention to Tupac. They laughed at the writer when they saw him providing ballast.

"Hey, you on the wrong boatman!" the skipper said.

"Can you even swim, motha-fucka?" the helmsman said.

Nefarious sailed by Bat out of Hell, who flew a flag with a red lobster today.

"Looking good, Ortun," Ivonne said standing at the barbecue. "Tell Dan we love him!"

The wind picked up and Ortun saw that the crows and seagulls had taken flight. It was breakfast time, and the Salish Sea was in reprise.

"There!" Ortun pointed to a patch of sky.

The pit-girl saw it too, a mat of dark, rippled water.

"I see it."

She called for a tight mainsail. Bonesteel answered with two powerful cranks on the wrench.

"Gimme your ass, dear!" he told the sail. "Both cheeks, love!"

Ortun steered the boat away from the fleet and the hull cut hard into the water. A heavy load landed on the deck with a smack—smothering the writer.

"Don't worry, Darling!" she said. "It's going to get much worse and you won't remember that!"

The crew scampered to the lee side.

"Hike it!" Ortun called. "Hike it for your skipper!"

Nefarious caught the current just in time, and for an instant the sail went luff. The hull righted and sat in the wash, slowly gaining momentum while crew untangled themselves from the rail.

The starting line was near.

"Wait for it—" Ortun eased.

"It's not coming," the pit-girl said. "We missed it."

"Wait."

Ortun could hear Kai's laughter closing in.

"Two minutes to start!" Ewan said.

Deep Pickle texted, NIFFY'S GONNA BLOW ANOTHER START-HA-HA! NOOBS 4SURE.

"Wait."

Ortun held the tiller with one hand, and like he was giving a blessing, he put his other in the air. His eyes burned into the Mylar, up the batten pocket to the main head.   The crew waited for him to close his fist.

"It's a hook!" Kai called. "He's gonna hook us!"

Jupiter stayed on course. Instead of yielding way, Kai went for the penalty flag. If the boats touched this close to the committee boat, Nefarious would have to round a buoy.

"Make him drink it!" Bonesteel said.

Ortun remained silent. Waited for the sail to go loft.

The power they needed was coming, hidden beneath the surface.

Nefarious would not need wind.

OH SHIT, texted Bat Out of Hell. ORTUN'S GONNA HOOK JUPE.

Ortun closed his fist.

"Now!"

He pulled the tiller hard to starboard, jibing Nefarious into the hiding current.

The mast began to moan and creak.

The boat accelerated.

Kai scrambled, turned his tiller to port. He looked off to the committee boat where he watched Edmund throw a green starting flag.

"Bastard!" he said. "Where's the penalty?"

Nefarious began to pull ahead.

"We're in their wash!" Kai's tactician yelled. "Hike it! Hike it for your skipper!"

The boats separated, leaving a silent triangular wake in the water. Ortun watched it disappear and turned the tiller to port. The main sail filled, leaving a shadow on Jupiter.

"Have me tea!" Bonesteel said. "It ain't goat's milk!"

Nefarious crossed the starting line the instant Edmund fired the gun.

Ortun jibed again, opening the lead and defending his high position. It left a long wind shadow, causing Bat out of Hell to tack.

"Nice move," Rhett called.

The race wasn't over. They all knew that with an ebbing tide, The Salish Sea had more in store for them. This was an emotional lead, and nothing more.

"Don't let it go to your head," the pit-girl said. "When we get to deception pass, you have to play the tidal cone less aggressive."

"Less aggressive?" Ortun asked.

The pit-girl stepped up to him, the way she did with Dan.

"Don't worry," she said in her little girl voice. "You did great on the start." And then in her big girl voice. "But that shit was lucky. You could have fucked us with a buoy."

Ortun locked the tiller.

"You have no humility," he said. "Or respect."

"You have too much of both," she unlocked the tiller, put his hand on it. "Keep 'em there, skipper," she said, and nodded at Hope Island behind her. "Point it away from trouble—not at it."

Ortun watched her step under the boom and disappear in the pit, where he thought she should stay.

"Don't worry," Bonesteel said. "It was a great move under the sheets, mate."

Ortun looked to port, where Hope Island was emerging and he tightened his grip on the tiller.

The pit-girl was right.

There were many island jewels embedded in Skagit Bay, all of them inviting and capped with evergreens, but this one seemed ominous. As Nefarious closed in, he wondered if the fleet saw it the same way he was seeing it. Maybe they were not interested in the fact that they were a mere mote of dust, cast onto the either, riding a jet of water that had already decided their fate. Maybe everyone knew this, and he was the only one who cared. He stared at his hand on the tiller then back at the island. Soon, the water in the straight would narrow, and the sea would squeeze through like an octopus through a wee-sized hole.

Aggressive or not, what power did they have? All the material and nonmaterial things Ortun had ever known were busy doing the same thing: approaching oblivion, squeezed through a channel, around an island named Hope.

And if they made it through unscathed, there were many more islands waiting.

What was the point of it all?

Ortun sat down on the stern and contemplated the course. Jupiter was falling further behind and Bat of Hell was tugging at Kai's ass. Tupac had just finished rounding the buoy and fought Artemis for position. There was a steady wind for all to take advantage of, but no one moved in closer where the currents were fastest.

Not yet.

The channel would narrow, and only a few safe spots to jibe would remain. The fleet would bottleneck and cutting in too close meant risking a grounding, or hitting the bridge.

Ortun cracked open a Coors light, one handed, and drank. The fluid hit his empty stomach in a hurry. He waited while the organ dispersed its contents throughout his body, thinking it all through. Someplace a train was blasting its horn urgently and the seagulls complained, squawking and molesting each other. He wondered about the commotion as the beer cooled his gut.

"Tighten that jib, sailor," he said to Ewan. "Aim high!" he said to Duff. "And stow that rope," he said to the pit-girl.

"You stow it yourself."

Ortun smiled a little.

This was real.

It would all never happen again.

And it was perfect, right?

Nefarious was set to finish strong. It didn't matter that they weren't in love today, not the way that Dan skippered. His job was to make Dan's boat fly. Bring it back in one piece. Come what may. But don't hurt the pretty boat. There would be another race—and then—nothing.

Zero.

Just as it was meant to be.

It would all disappear.

All of it.

Ortun turned the boat east, pointing it directly at Hope Island.

"What the hell are you doing, Ortun?"

The instant the boat changed course, the pit-girl was back at the helm.

"I'm going around Boxcar."

He pointed toward the ripple of water, caught up on the middle spar of the bridge. In a flood or an ebb, it could grow the height of a Boxcar, and moved just as sure of itself.

"Like hell," the pit-girl said. "I'm calling tactics."

"Today, I'm skipper," he said finishing the turn.

"You'll hang us up, you bastard."

Ortun secured the turn, watched Kai break his attack.

"See," she said. "Even Kai's tactician knows better."

"Because we're pushing through this soup," Ortun said defending his position. "He's drafting."

Bat out of Hell surged forward, straight toward boxcar.

"Suckers," Rhett called out.

"See you later, beijos!" Ivonne said.

The pit-girl lunged at the tiller and he pushed her away.

"Give me that thing," she said.

"No," Ortun said, "we'll fly around Boxcar."

"You're risking the boat," she said.

"I'm making time," he said.

The pit-girl lunged for the tiller again, but this time, Ortun did something that Dan would never do. He slapped the pit-girl. He slapped her with the back of his hand hard enough to send her stammering backwards into the pit.

"This tiller is my responsibility," he barked. "Mine alone.

"You fucker!" she screamed.

Ortun took no pleasure in the action.

None.

In fact, as she stumbled backwards, he caught the awkward, stunned look on her face.

Sad.

It was as if he'd walked in on a famed opera singer while she sat on the toilet. It was none of his business and there were some things that were never meant to be seen.

"Don't!" the pit-girl said to the writer, who had untangled his harness. "Let him have it!"

The crew, frozen, watched the two like a standoff in the Old West.

"I'm the skipper," he said to the writer. "I'd have done the same to anyone."

The pit-girl took her post—right next to him at the helm. Her cheek was red, but her sea legs were steady.

"Sail," she said. "It only hurt my face."

Ortun watched the writer take his position. Then the crew. And they all sailed under the bridge in fierce, unloving silence. He turned to check on Kai. Jupiter was tacking in and out of their wake, stalling until they could use the broken water to slip out of their shadow. In the distance, Tupac and Artemis stayed close to Hope Island, inside of the current. They wisely held back—gambling that the other boats would get pinned down in the currents that jetting into the straits. To port, Bat out of Hell was locked into Boxcar.

"He's going middle spar!" Ewan said.

The pit-girl took out her binoculars.

"He's caught," she said.

"Don't do it, Rhett," Ortun said. "Don't do it."

Nefarious closed the distance, a hundred yards off their starboard. Ortun aimed the tiller to get out of the current, but it was too strong. The only boat that could help them was the one stupid enough to risk hitting the bridge.

It was dangerous. Bat out of Hell was in trouble. If they pitch-poled, the nose of the ship would hit the wave, stop, and lift the stern out of the water. Any sailor thrown overboard was going for a long, deep swim into Davy Jones' locker. There would only be a slight chance of catching them, but not until they'd swung around, fought their way through the current, tacking into the wind—a slow-motion rescue at best. Maybe they'd get a front row seat just as the current pulled him under.

"He's going down!" the pit-girl pointed. "A pitch-pole!"

"They've got their dick out, fer sure," Bonesteel said.

Bat out of Hell went nose down into the ripple, ass up. The crew held fast, but when the stern came down, Rhett popped out like a cork.

"Man overboard!" the pit-girl shouted. She leapt at the radio, called into the mike.

"We see him, Nefarious," Edmund said from the committee boat. "Moving to intercept."

"The current's too strong," she said. "We've lost visual."

"We've got him in our sight."

"Like hell," she said. "We're closer than you and we have negative visual."

"We've got him sighted, Mac. We'll pick him up," Edmund said. "Continue your course away from the spar. We're advising all vessels to do the same."

"You piece of shit," she said. "This race is disqualified until he's out of the water."

"Negative," Edmund said. "We're on our way. Continue the course."

"This is all about those fancy guests you have aboard, looking us over for nationals, isn't it? How's it gonna look if a man dies out here?"

"Pretty damn good, if you ask me," Edmund said. "Now get your ass out of the way so that we can move in for a rescue."

Ortun turned the tiller, aimed the boat out of the hellish inlet.

The pit-girl eyed him.

"Dan wouldn't let his friend suffer like that," she said.

Ortun cracked open another beer, one handed and drank half the can.

"Dan would listen to his tactician," he said, steering Nefarious out of danger. "And I'd tell him to get the hell out of the way."

The rest of the crew agreed in silence.

Ortun sat down. He fished the second half of his beer and by the time he'd done so, the committee boat was circling Bat out of Hell. She'd broken free of Boxcar and righted herself, the way Farrs were designed to do. Ortun reflected on the sobering scene. The crew was climbing aboard, scrambling to steady their boat. He could hear Ivonne calling out, Beijos! Beijos!

"The bastard's gone for a swim," Bonesteel said. "He'll meet his maker if they don't fish him out."

The committee boat killed its engine.

Jupiter sailed by.

"I see him to your starboard," Kai said over the radio. "He's having trouble with the current."

Ortun took the binoculars from the pit-girl, spotted Rhett's orange vest. Just a glimpse, then nothing. The current was too strong for the committee boat, but their skipper circled Bat Out of Hell. If they missed again, to avoid a collision, Nefarious would have to start the engine.

"Turn on the blowers," Ortun said. "Get the engine ready."

"That's a DNF," Bonesteel said.

"To hell with this race."

Ortun locked the tiller, moved to the engine panel.

"It's about time," the pit-girl said, flicking switches.

Tupac and Artemis passed by, all hands on deck. They were pointing to starboard.

"There!" The skipper of Tupac said.

"Beijos!" Ivonne cried.

Ortun heard a distant splash, a single slap into the green, muted water. He turned.

"Crazy, bird," Bonesteel said. He pointed to Ivonne in the water. "There'll be two hearts in the locker."

Ivonne swam madly against the current. She was a strong swimmer and there was no stopping her. She would leave it all in the ocean. Here, in front of a crowd. Into the abyss. Every breath, her precious heat, her energy. She risked oblivion. Swimming away and never to return, every stroke for love.

"Beijos! Beijos!" she cried.

Save your breath, Ortun thought. He knew that the water was too cold for her, a shock, even in survival gear. Soon her muscles would seize, and the current would swallow her whole.

Beijos!

She disappeared from the surface, and Ortun held his breath with her. He scrambled to start the engine.

"No!" Bonesteel said. "Look!"

Ivonne surfaced.

"She's got him!" Edmund said. "We're moving in. Continue the course."

Ortun froze.

The crew cheered, but he couldn't hear it over the pounding in his chest.

"He'll get his wicket polished like a striker tonight," Bonesteel said.

It was the first time he understood Bonesteel.

"Yes, sir," Ortun told him. "That he will."

Ortun looked at the pit-girl.

"First, she'll kill him," she said. "She'll kill him for being out of his gear at the pass."

They watched the committee boat fish the two out. They wouldn't let go of each other, even as they were dragged on deck where they landed in a heap.

The writer appeared.

"I have seen the priestesses of Rati make love at moon-fall," he said. "And with a golden lamp, lie down carelessly anywhere to sleep."

Ortun and the pit-girl turned to him without words.

"Sanskrit," he said. "An ancient poem."

"Obviously," the pit-girl said. "Now get your ass back on the rail, we got a race to win."

Ortun looked off towards Sacred Cove, where Jupiter was rounding the mark. Kai had effectively used the diversion to run at West Point. They had good wind, but at the point he'd catch them. The currents were still flooding, and while the Committee boat took care of Rhett, he could fight dirty. Real dirty. It would be a knife fight—two Farrs in a dark alley—caught between a flooding ocean and a sunken sea wall.

"Tighten that jib, sailor," he said, feeling as if he'd awakened without hitting the snooze. "Aim high!" he said to Duff. "And stow that rope!"

It didn't take long for Nefarious to catch Jupiter.

"Your blowers were on," Kai shouted as Nefarious broke free of their shadow. "The committee boat will be hearing about that."

"You're a rotten bastard, Kai."

"The better to eat you with, my dear!"

The pit-girl called a tack and the crew instantly responded. It was her best move of the day, bringing the hulls together, they drafted on Jupiter's ass and pivoted into another set. The boats bashed and smacked hulls. There was shouting and cussing, but no parent to break up the fight.

"Lily-livered, action-taking knave," the writer cussed using his best Shakespeare. "Whoresons! Beggars! The sons and heirs of a mongrel bitch!"

The boats thrashed their way into Sacred Cove, edging and braying. The water was fast and the wind was waiting. Near an islet, the pit-girl saw textured on the water and called for the kite. Bonesteel went into action. He sang a song that know one knew, and by the end of it, the sail popped!

Nefarious advanced, stealing Jupiter's air.

"Three-suited, hundred-pound, filthy, worsted-stocking knave," the writer scowled.

The rest of the race was spent watching Kai fall further and further behind.

"Rhett and Ivonne are on their way to the hospital," Edmund said over the radio. "We dropped them into a zodiac and took them to Strawberry Hill. Last we heard she was bitching him out for not wearing his harness."

"Roger that," Ortun smiled. "We saw the ambulance on Canino Road a while back."

"Negative," laughed Edmund. "Sherriff said some hobo was run down by a train. They had to transport the happy couple in a squad car."

Ortun set the microphone down.

"Having the policeman between them is his safest bet," the pit-girl said. "You make sure we're not penalized for starting our blowers. We were attempting a rescue."

"Affirmative."

Ortun knew it was the little guy. He could feel it. He knew that he'd died on a train track, the same way that he would die from heroin. It was a poem. Not in the arms of a pretty wife, or under the sad eyes of sorrowful children—runes of love and grace, to care for in sickness and in health—but a vessel, a sestina of time and space, whose purposes was ever and ever to touch the face of god.

It was the same way for Christopher, and suddenly Ortun was ashamed that he'd tried to lure him away from the tracks. He realized this as Nefarious crossed the finish line to a starter's gun, watched the smoke rise through the sky and disappear into the ether.

It was he who was trying to lure himself away from the tracks, wasn't it? He who was running. He who was dying. And what hope did he ever have of loving such a thing again that he must leave it, to love it? To stay is to die. To leave is to watch it die slowly, and disappear like the silver cloud shot from the pistol, killing you in the process.

There were no exceptions. He could see it when he looked in the mirror while shaving—particles of god sloughed off by entropy in disguise, active or passive. It was still a pink-fucking elephant, the one that heroin told him not to think about. He had resisted as long as he could. Tried to disguise it as cynicism. He was too cool for this shit—he was not cool enough.

Fuck sailing.

Fuck it all.

And then, he'd purge.

Purge in the arms of a woman.

Purge in the stanzas of her kisses, or in song, or both.

Then he'd disappear long enough to ache for it again.

Be lost in her sultry, loving eyes and return again and again.

And there would be love.

Ortun was the last sailor on the dock. He waited for everyone to finish securing the boat and head to the hospital to see Rhett and Ivonne, Martina and Dan. There was no time to celebrate. Even Kai hurried off.

"See you at the hospital, big guy," he said. "Hopefully Dan will be skipper tomorrow!"

The marine layer remained; it rested upon the land and Ortun as he walked with his cold hands in his pockets. His pants were loose, on account that he was a diabetic, but his beard kept his face nice and warm. Some of the overcast was beginning to break up, the onshore flow that shifted in the evenings to bring a Chinook wind that soon part the holy, blue sky.

Ortun walked.

He walked right by his boat and past the naval air station into town where the late blooming, wild pink roses crawled out of the seawall.

He walked right by the laughter inside Toby's Tavern and right by the rum-tent where he could hear the band playing his songs just fine without him.

At the intersection of Main Street and Canard, he removed the heroin he'd wrapped in foil and unfolded the little package.

There was enough.

Plenty to do the job.

He closed the package carefully and walked to a thrift store where he made pleasant conversation with an old woman as he purchased a single, silver spoon.

"Will that be all?" she asked, confused.

"As a matter of fact," he said, "yes."

Ortun wondered what the crew was doing—not doing, but rather, how they were feeling. He'd made a living projecting his feelings onto others, but now, under the lash of this grey sky, he was open to emotions that were not his own. A poet is a fool, he sang as he crested Strawberry Hill.

A fool with a foil crown.
Too afraid to face the truth.
And leave this hallowed ground.

When he finished, he sat and thought of the little man's voice. My name is Christopher—I'm here to race the boats!

The hill, barely a hill, just large enough to rise above the grassy field that ended at the sea—was where the little bum had been king of all he surveyed.

King of the of the old rusty train tracks, slicing the world in two. King of weeds. King of the sad grey sky. King of sorrow. King of glory. King of the loneliness in his heart and the ghost that haunted it. King of memory. King of darkness. King of chains. King of the road behind him. King of his fear. King of rage. King of the horizon in front of him, where the Salish Sea beckoned him nearer. King of the silver spoon, clutched in his hand. King of the needle in the other. King of the little figure walking towards him— sauntering in the direction of this throne made of dandelions.

The figure drew near.

At first Ortun thought it was a police officer, set to arrest him for his contraband. But soon, he saw the black raven hat, and the handkerchief tucked into the breast pocket of a crummy brown jacket with elbow patches.

"It's you," Ortun said standing. "You're back."

"Yeah, I'm back."

"I thought you were dead," Ortun said. He hugged the little guy, stood back and gazed into his frisky eyes. "A man was killed on the tracks today."

"Must've been some other bum," Christopher said. "I came to see the race boats."

CHAPTER 55

As a child, Ivonne's father tired-out his two beautiful daughters by throwing coins into the family's pool. The girls had been blessed with their mother's vitality, but this was also a curse.

"Dears," he'd say in the spruce, Portuguese of a businessman, "yet again, I've lost money in the water. It's these old-man shorts I wear. They have silly pockets, see? And when I buy cigars at Jose' Arcadio Buendia before I swim, I forget I have money in them. As you know, my dears, I do not like being under deep water. It gets stuck in my ears and drives me mad. So, if it pleases you—you have my permission to retrieve the coins." This was a joke for as long as she remembered. Even after he passed away, he had mischievously arranged for uncle João to leave gold coins for them to find.

The pool was deep and large enough that Ivonne could barely detect the pieces shining at the bottom, and there was an alga that bloomed in the spring, which despite the pool boy's efforts, and her father's complaints, bloomed in the pool and tinted the water emerald-green like new leaves of a Hibiscus. When the sun crested Pico do Monte Negro in the afternoon, enough light would penetrate the surface for her to spot the coins, always left by father in the deep end: fifty Centavos and one-hundred Reals with silver imbedded in the center.

Ivonne was a tentative child, younger than her sister and less aggressive.

"Papi," she'd ask, trying to convince him to give her the coins from his pockets before her sister Raissa would arrive. "It's not fair. She always gets more coins than me. Why don't you give them to me now?"

Her sister was a much better swimmer, leaner and could sink faster. Raissa was born with father's glorious shoulders, broad and taught like Flavia's muscles, the family mare. The animal's muscles were so taught that its skin would glisten like an exquisite Antonio Meijueiro painting caught in evening's magic light. "Dear," he'd said. "She gets more coins because she doesn't hesitate, like you when you stand at the water's edge. You think too much, my sweet beijinho, you were born with the gift of imagination, which is better than muscles. But, because of your gift, you can think up more problems than are ever possible to exist."

Ivonne did not understand, and for as long as she could remember, Raissa was ever the victor.

One morning, while watching the sun crest over the mountains, she caught sight of a rooster just before it was set to sing its tribute to the new day. At first, weary, the scrawny thing scampered nervously about, looking for a suitable place to croon. It finally settled on a spot near a woodpile where the landscapers had been installing another one of the fountains her father had purchased. Upon reaching it, the creature seemed to gather itself, waiting for its moment. Then suddenly, the sun pushed through the long, flat-layered clouds steaming from the jungle, and burst forth in a golden ray that lighted the woodpile. The scrawny rooster perched itself upon the pile and took in one stupendous breath—filling its lungs as if there wasn't enough air in the world to hear the glory of its song. In the golden ray, its chest filled with sweet air, splendidly, it released its canticle into the hazy warmth of a new day.

Ivonne was mesmerized by the power and magic she saw, which streamed from the little bird in the form of mystic enchanted. It was as if the scrawny rooster had awakened all of creation from the dream of darkness—stood there without a doubt that it had fulfilled its cosmic role in the conception of a new day.

A new day filled with chocolate treats.

Love.

Father's cool hand on her cheek.

Warmth.

Light.

Her lovely sister.

Mother.

Family.

Kisses on the door step, hello and goodbye.

Polenta.

Silver coins.

From that day forth, she would let the light take her. Not the anticipation of the light. The light itself, and nothing else. No matter what harrowing, turbulent thoughts raced through her mind. The light would forever decide when it was time to act.

"How did you do it?" Raissa asked one day. "How did you learn to stay under the water so long, little sister?"

On that day, after beating her sister to the coins every day for a week, Ivonne was particularly motivated. She had planned to use the money to purchase a salacious swimsuit she'd been saving for to wear to Florianópolis Praia, which her mother refused to have any part of purchasing. Her sister had similar plans, but as the cautious, older daughter of a patriarch, she spooked easily. Ivonne was too young to know the power of her answer then, but the instant she jumped into the Salish Sea to save her husband, she realized what it was that her father was trying to teach her.

"I will tell you," she'd told her sister while counting the coins she'd collected. "The moment I enter the water, I don't plan on ever returning."

It is what saved her Rhett, she knew. The foreboding presage of her father's words come true, acted out in dreamy-green water, the same color she remembered as a child. Before diving into the sea, she found the limits of her imagination, for she could not imagine living without her true love. Not in a million years. Even with her imagination. Of course, her father could never have known that his act of dropping coins into the pool would prepare her for this reckoning, but no parent truly can; their deeds are merely wishes, desires and hopes that live forever in the shadows, for fear that their child will participate in the miracle of life without knowledge of the enemy within: fear.

The next thing Ivonne saw was Rhett, slipping away . . . his eyes, like coins, settling into the deep end of the emerald pool. She followed his silver eyes down into the abyss, never losing sight of them once. She could have followed the silver coins forever down, into darkness, into hell, into nothingness. It was beyond her imagination to do anything else.

CHAPTER 56

Dan awakened in the examination room. He had nodded off while holding Martina's hand, and while he was asleep, he dreamt of a voracious waterfall crashing over a cliff. It was a primordial scene, ancient as the wind and left alone in a shrouded corner of his mind. Translated into form, the water fell in mystical, silken waves. There was a Zen feeling to the whole thing, like watching molasses pour out of a jar and into stellar darkness.

He would like to have stayed there, he thought. Stayed there in a sultry landscape, where the temperature was the same as Martina's hand. The warmth had something to do with her capillaries. They ran close to her skin, a trait passed down by her grandfather, a German sniper who, in World War II was awarded the steel cross for marksmanship during the winter siege of Stalingrad. Martina's fingers were lissome, supple things, the kind you loved to clasp, stitch your fingers into while holding it. A simple pleasure, one he never took for granted.

In the dream, he found that he could move from any vantage point to another, as if he were tied to the landscape's physics by a single, conscious tether. The mist in the air carried with it the smell of her perfume and the sky was the color of her eyes. Where the waterfall began, an indigo pool flowed over a polished, massive boulder—a black obsidian that seemed to hold the world on its back. Mesmerized, he watched the translucent fluid spill over the stone in phasing, spate waves.

Dan froze at the sound of thunder.

The hair on his neck rose and he turned to watch the sky roil and shimmer in the darkness. There was a sudden heavy silence, and the sky gathered into dark barbs. Dan squinted his eyes, and then, from the silence, he watched the sky produced a single raindrop.

It was amazing that he caught sight of it, and in awe he watched in as it fell slowly: a perfect, tear.

When it struck the pool, it recoiled to form a lavender circle, then crowned on the surface.

Now, distinct, it floated.

A gentle orb, radiating life.

Dan instinctively moved to the water's edge. He wanted to capture the orb before the crashing waterfall destroyed it, but suddenly, his body appeared in the chasm below, where he could only watch the perfect sphere spill over the waterfall, to join him in the darkness.

"No!" he mumbled.

"No?" Martina said, looking through a magazine. "Honey, you're dreaming."

Dan frowned and sat up.

Outside the window, there was no waterfall, but he could spot the rum tent, and from the ruckus he knew that the race was over and there was no way to receive the results, sans his smart phone, which he dared not touch.

"Oh, Dan," she said. "Just pick up your phone and check the results."

"There are more important things to attend to," he said.

Martina smiled at him the way a mechanic does when the brakes stop squeaking.

Dan was frightened.

He didn't know it, but he was. Becoming a father was a terrifying prospect. Not the work and the time and the hours of sleepless nights, but the vulnerability. A boat was a labor of love, but a child, well, that was another thing entirely. Raising a child was like purchasing a boat without setting eyes on it once. Who would his child become? He thought of his old man, how disappointed he was that he'd never wanted to be a fisherman. It was a judgment. Sure as shit. But the old man had wasted his life. Dan hated being judgmental, and his life as a sailor afforded him the luxury of benevolence, so long as the jibe was straight.

"I need a little fresh air," he said.

Outside, he smelled the Salish. The ebb had finished washing the stink of low tide off the land, and now the flats smelled like fresh, cold oysters on the half shell. It was a relief to no longer smell the hygienic, chemical burns of disinfectant, though it did remind him of the smell of whiskey.

"I love this place," the devil said from behind him. "I truly do."

"You bastard."

Dan turned, moved at him.

"Don't you even," the devil said.

He lit a cigar and offered it to Dan.

"You did this, didn't you?"

"Ha!" the devil laughed. "Too cruel for my taste."

Dan wanted to punch the fucker, the way he'd done to his old man the night he caught him slapping his mother around after a drunken night at the bar. But he knew the devil would only enjoy it.

"I mean, come on . . . a miscarriage?" the devil continued. "Do you really think I have the power of death at my hands? Think about it? If I killed babies, what would be the fun in that? No, you should be talking to the other guy. That's his domain, not mine."

Dan pulled a drag off the cigar.

"You're a crazy bastard," he said watching the smoke leave his mouth.

The devil waved the smoke away.

"Danny, what you say is true," he said. "And please, if you don't mind. Know that what you call crazy, I call company."

"I believe you."

"You see—you're complicating things, Danny. We have a deal. Remember? You win, you throw a party in my honor. You lose. Nefarious belongs to me." The devil looked Dan in the eye and smiled. "It's nothing personal. But if I don't follow through, people will think I'm a bitch."

"I know the terms," Dan said.

"But I don't think you do," the devil said. "I don't think anyone ever does."

The devil stopped. Put his arm around Dan.

"Did you have the dream?"

Dan didn't answer.

"Don't be coy with me," the devil said. "Every father has it. It looks different, man to man. But it's always about vulnerability. The helplessness they feel. They see the void in front of them, and they fear it. They question, why would I invite another soul into this troubled dimension? It is a brave thing to be a father, Dan. Not to sow a seed like an animal, but to care for it, to cultivate it, and finally to reflect upon your creation. Have you asked yourself why?"

"Why?"

"Yes," the devil said. "Why are you so vain to think that all of humanity needs your genes? Trust me, the gene pool will be fine without the likes of you."

Dan was not insulted.

"Right now," Dan said, seeing the perfect sphere in his dream. "The only thing I care about is whether my child is going to live or die."

"Don't worry."

Dan shrugged the devil's arm off him.

"Don't worry?" he said.

"You heard me," the devil looked around as if someone was listening. "The baby's going to be just fine."

"But you just said—"

"I said I don't have the power over life or death—but I know shit."

"What do you know?" Dan grabbed him by the lapel. "Tell me."

"I know that Martina will have a lovely, healthy daughter. She'll be precious to you. You'll accept her for who she is—no matter what."

"What the hell does that mean? You said you know shit."

"I do, indeed."

"Tell me."

The devil smiled again.

"She'll have green eyes," he said. "Green eyes, like the sea you love to sail."

"Green eyes?"

"Yes," the devil said and strolled away.

CHAPTER 57

Edmund sat down at the bar and ordered a scotch and soda. It'd been a hell of a day.

"I'll make it a double," the bartender said. "On the house."

This thing was spiraling out of control. A hot mess of deep fried ape shit. And now free drinks. It must be worse than he thought.

"Hey," the bartender said. "That guy over there, the one in the tie? He's been asking a lot of questions."

Edmund grimaced and looked over at the stiff in a suit. The only other people who wore a suit to a bar where the town's morticians.

"What kind of questions?"

"Not your everyday questions," the bartender said. "Questions about tactics and safety."

"Oh yeah?"

"Yeah."

Edmund sucked in some of the stale air. The last time he felt like this, he lit a fire in the garage while his parents weren't home.

"Floyd!" he bellowed at the suit. "What'cha drinkin'?"

"Tonic water."

"With what? Like with gin?"

"No, just tonic water."

"Oh," Edmund said. "What's that even like? Didn't even know you could do that."

"Yes, it happens all the time, Edmund."

"No shit?"

"Really, it's quite refreshing."

"Well two tonic waters, then," he said to the bartender, who on account there was nothing to do but put two stupid looking lemon wedges in the glasses, instantly served them.

Edmund sipped at the drink, scowled.

"Jesus-fucking Christ," he said. "Put some gin in this! It tastes like ass! No. It tastes worse than that! It tastes like a sailor's ass who's been dragging' his ass through tide flats!" He'd lost his composure and the time for small talk was over. "So Bill, I heard you had some concerns about the course. What the hell's going on?"

"Sure I do," the stiff said. "A man and a woman nearly died here today."

"Hey, come on now," Edmund said. "The course isn't for wankers. Just two years ago, same kind of problem happened in Frisco."

"Yes," the stiff said. "But the hazards there are well known, aren't they? No surprises, see? When a boat gets busted, everyone should have known better. But that damn ripple. Such a surprise. Crazy the way it came out of the water today and pitched that boat like a toy."

The stiff leaned back in his chair and reflected.

"That rip was a freak incident," Edmund said. "Only comes once every blue moon."

"What about the whale?"

Edmund stammered. He hated whales. Every goddamned one of them.

"Yes, they do use the channel this time of the year to feed, but—"

"What if an accident happened with one of them?" the stiff whistled. "We run an international race, you know? If we hurt one, we'd have every environmentalist in the world protesting us. Now that's bad press."

Ivonne entered the bar, fiercely. She was looking for someone and she gazed right at Edmund like she was a pissed-off steer.

"You son of bitch!" she said.

Edmund stood.

"Now hold on, sweetheart!"

"How dare you!" she said, and she took Edmund's drink and splashed it in his face. "You should have closed that line, closed it down tight so that no one would even think to run it down!"

Edmund dried his face with his napkin, the tonic water burning his eyes.

"The other skippers avoided that rip," he said. "Why not Rhett?"

She moved to slap him, but Edmund caught her arm.

"It's not worth it," he said. "Rhett should have run inside of that rip, run inside just like the rest of the boats did today. He took a dumb-ass risk to make some time for his boat. We all respect that. That's racing."

"It's not racing!" she said, and snatched her arm away. "Those assholes pushed us into Boxcar. They waited to see what would happen to us. Well, now they know. Muertos!"

CHAPTER 58

The pit-girl found Dan in the examination room. He was holding Martina in his arms.

"I've been calling you," she said.

"I know," he said.

Catching them in an embrace was off-putting, like seeing an off-duty sign on a taxi, or a man in a muscle shirt with no muscles. A good sailor compartmentalized their affections, stowed it next to the lemons until the threat of scurvy arrived.

"Is the baby alright?" she asked.

Dan kissed Martina on the forehead and turned to her with a tear in his eye.

"We don't know yet," he said, in a sober voice. "Doctor is due for an update."

It was almost too much for her to absorb. This was the skipper who'd jumped ship and attacked a tactician while on a jibe because the ass-clown had caused the boats to trade a gel coat? This was the skipper who swooned strippers, sat them on his lap, guessed their weight and used them the next day for ballast on his ship? The skipper who smuggled gin into bars, on account that he was a cheap, nickel-squeezing bastard? Dan was crafty. A rogue. Smart, unlike Ortun, who was willing to risk Boxcar to make some time for his crew. Even though they won the day, everyone knew that it should have been Rhett's day had he not ended up in the drink. The poor bastard. Nefarious was lucky today, not good. It should have been Bat out of Hell's crew on the podium, making an honest run at tomorrow's prize. Ortun went belly up; soured at the risks it took to captain a crew to victory, too worried to risk breaking his skipper's boat to be as tenacious as Dan. Courage was not the absence of fear, but the triumph over it. She'd once read about a dog, lost at sea during a storm, swam five nautical miles through shark infested waters, landed on an island, ate baby goats to survive. This dog was her skipper, incarnate. Soul brothers. She even framed the article and gave it to Dan as a birthday present.

"We need you on the water, skipper," the pit-girl said, worried about her run at worlds. This year, something needed to give. Another year at Race Week was one less year to sail on the big boats. "Ortun's got no balls out there. He nearly fucked us."

Martina set down her magazine.

"It's not your place to be here right now, Mac."

The pit-girl smiled. Moved to hug her, but Martina sat up and put a hand in her face.

"This is all going to blow over," the pit-girl said. "You've got at least a baker's dozen in that pretty little uterus."

"Get out," Martina said, with tough German love. "Get out now."

The pit-girl turned to Dan.

"Go, sailor," he said.

The pit-girl threw the flower's she'd bought at Dan and stormed out the door. Her pants were wet and her shoes squeaked as she moved over the speckled linoleum floor. She couldn't slam the door on account that it had soft-close hinges installed, so she squeaked down the hall until she found a quiet place to sulk.

In the nursery ward, she stopped.

Drank.

Behind the glass she eyed a fresh batch of the little darlings busy ogling for attention. Their bodies were a fussy, stretchy mess—a loud noise at one end, and no sense of responsibility at the other. Everybody always talks about it, about how you don't know love until you meet your baby. But Esther was fine without one, wasn't she? She had many lovers, each a special jewel, and collectively, they added up to something more worth while than one of these.

The pit-girl carefully observed the litter while the whiskey stung her lips.

"You will outlive the bastards," she whispered to the babies, or to herself, not entirely sure.

The truth was—she liked the little anchors. Their baggy skin, and squishy faces tugged at her heartstrings the same way that old people and dogs pulled on them, a place where she let their likely foibles roll off her back without needing to call them on their shit. By nature, babies were selfish creatures, lacking the empathy to understand how they fucked shit up for their caretakers, but that was the point, wasn't it?

It was as if they required ransom, not sacrifice.

And there was nothing worse than a person—baby thing, or not—who did not understand the deal.

When Ortun turned down-wind on their final set and fell into Kai's shadow, he should have seen it coming. Own it! When Rigby didn't understand that Davey had sailed the straights with her during a magnificent winter storm, and they needed to sleep in the same sleeping bag for warmth. Own it! When Esther pissed herself in her car and ruined her seats? Own it! When that stupid bartender over served her and she ended up punching one of his customers? Own it! When she ordered a gin and tonic from a 7-11 clerk?

Accountability was always relative, was it not? And as far as she knew, there was only one person in the world who judged the actions of others—god, who didn't exist.

The pit-girl pulled another drink from her flask, drank until it was empty.

She heard footsteps.

"Here you go," Dan said, handing his over.

She had seen him slink out the room to find her, but ignored him until he offered her a snort.

"Just in time, sailor," she said.

"When a man drinks gin from a flask," Dan said. "He is either a scoundrel, practical or a cheap son of a bitch."

"You're all three," she drank.

Dan took a snort.

"The baby is going to live," he said.

The pit-girl let the news pull on her heartstrings for an appropriate amount of time.

"Congratulations," she said. "And so is Rhett."

"Rhett?"

She waited a beat.

"Yes, didn't you hear?" she said. "He nearly died today. Or were you too busy tending to your darling?"

Dan screwed the lid back onto his flask.

"You're a mess," he said.

"Seriously, Dan," she said with her hand on her hip. "If Martina can't handle a little morning sickness, what do you think she's going to be like—alone, with a baby while you're burning up Round the County? Or Blake Island? Or, shit! Worlds?"

"Who said she'd be alone?"

The pit-girl shifted her hip.

"So you're packing it in then?"

"I didn't say that."

"Oh, but you did," she said. "You did when you played the sportsman with Edmund at the captain's meeting, made excuses for sailing like a pussy. And when you pushed the start like a bitch, and that call to avoid the whale." She threw her hands up in the air. "Own it!"

Dan put his flask away.

"The conditions are different, sailor."

"What?" she said. "You think you're a father already? Oh why'd you have to ruin it all by having a baby? You're letting the crew down Dan. Everything's already changed, and the little anchor isn't even a tadpole." Dan looked at her with sad eyes. She hated it. "Without you, Ortun goes back to heroin. I can see it in his eyes. Duff becomes just a husband. Ewan, a burnout. And you will be a dad, Dan. Just a dad. Jesus! Look at what your father did to you. He was a dick from the time you were a baby. She slapped the window of the nursery. "And me Dan?" she almost shed a tear. "What about me? You know what I become? I become somebody else's Martina! Now come on, snap out of it sailor. We have a race to win."

"I heard from Ortun," Dan said.

She turned slowly.

"What did that fucker tell you?"

"You're off the boat, Mac," he said without much emotion. "Suspended."

"You bastard," she said. "I'll find another skipper. One that doesn't blow his starts."

CHAPTER 59

The devil smiled.

Here it was in action.

Veiled, but recognizable.

Plain, but when you looked at the thing straight on, it disappeared.

$$C_d = 2F_d / pv^2A$$

It was his grandest achievement: force meeting matter relative to its speed. That was the most accurate way to describe his little puzzle. Vortex drag, parasite drag, form drag: not even he could control it. In nature, it metamorphosed into chaos.

On a starry night, Einstein witnessed these mystic threads stitched into the heavens like carefully arranged, harmonious notes, and when he thought he understood, he whimsically deduced there were no accidents in the universe.

God did not play dice.

Then, after puzzling his life away at a chalkboard, hoping to catch another glimpse of the creator's handwriting—on his deathbed, he mysteriously laughed at his transcripts.

Maybe god did play dice, he thought. What the hell do I know?

Van Gogh saw it, and cut off his ear.

Martin Luther King saw it—and on his last night on earth, he told the faithful that he would not be on the mountaintop with them.

Lincoln saw the puzzle during a glorious ride through Maryland, and he told a dandy congressman without blinking, "My concern is not whether God is on our side—my greatest concern is to be on God's side—for God is always right and we will join him in his house." And then his carriage crossed the upper bridge at Keedysville, which marked the entrance to the battlefield at Antietam. Twenty-three thousand men died along the creek that day, their lives wrenched from the corporeal with lead and blade, the heels of boots, steel and stone. It was the single largest death toll of the war, and vermin had begun settle down to feast on his army. Here, the congressman at his side told him, "Sir, do not despair, for these flies are saints, and they are carrying the souls of your soldiers to the house of god—one tiny bite at a time."

Of course, to a sailor like Dan, chaos disguised itself as an impediment, and his feeble attempts to understand the coefficient was an effort to predict the consequence of an unstoppable force meeting an immovable object. Time and nature. Yin and yang. No matter the shape of the hull, no matter how smooth the water—against this force, there were small enough variations that no mind could fully understand it—tiny variations that, added together, broke bits and bones, schemes and dreams.

In the America's Cup final, the biggest, fastest boats of all, the AC72 rode on titanium fins. At their top speed, the hulls came completely out of the water, but even it was slapped back into the cosmic puzzle. Caught in a gust, Team Artemis's fin jammed a swell and flipped, killing a crewmember, a direct consequence of inertia meeting matter.

Look at that!

Something new!

Something different.

An errant bomb dropped on an Afghan village, where hysterical mothers and their children scurried away into the desert. A hurricane! Begat by the gentle strokes of a butterfly's wings, was sleeping in the wake of a saltwater trail.

In mathematics it was understood as statistical mechanics, in war it was known as fog, and sailing it was simply called drag.

These days, it's what delighted the devil most—watching sentient beings attempt to understand the true nature of a measureless void. The impossibly, possible. The stunning reality of time's eternal congregation with matter.

It was a trick, of course.

All in the mind's eye.

But, wasn't that the point of Race Week?

This was the first year he'd seen it affect the crew's morale. Not the logistics and planning, but the way the race had slowly over time, one tiny error after another, manifested as personal.

Emotional.

Their bonds were tested.

Their love for one another, eroded.

The child was the key.

He should have thought of it sooner.

While the sailors settled into the evening, he listened to their scheming, and brooding and troubles and their thin-skinned thoughts.

The pit-girl had already planned her treachery. After the writer declined to receive a spanking with his own belt, she left the bedroom in a tizzy and called Kai. She told the skipper that she intended to sail as pit for him during the final race, and he should inform Jupiter's crew. She knew that he couldn't resist. Dan heard the news that night, and countered by hiring the Indian tactician, whom he promised total control of their tactics. The Indian agreed. Ortun packed his guitar and wandered off with his new friend. The crew had not heard from him, not since the accident, and knew that it was possible that they'd never see him again. Duff and Ewan argued un-jovially, and when they tired of each other, Ewan joined the writer in the hot tub and challenged him to a game of chess. "You protect the queen too much," he prodded. "What you don't realize is that she is the most powerful piece. She is vicious. She is righteous. She is not to be captured by your fear." The writer resisted his advice, and soon lost his queen in a trap set by a pawn. Ewan laughed and knocked it into the water sending the writer into a tantrum and then to bed without finishing the game.

"Fuck you, Ewan."

"Fuck you, Rigby."

In the workout room, Bonesteel was amped. He finished a set of curls and hydrated with a beer. While toweling off in front of the mirror, he was surprised to find the pit-girl standing behind him with a leather belt.

Night fell. . .

The devil listened to the dreams of the crew.

He listened to their erratic, exposed thoughts until they were erased by the eternal, lonesome hum that has always haunted him, every moment of every day, for all of time. The hum that meant nothing, was nothing, could only be nothing and never was anything else.

CHAPTER 60

Kai found Dan outside of the morning briefing, stepped right up to him and pointed into his face.

"You Bastard!" he said. "You stole my tactician!"

"That's the consequence of stealing my pit," Dan said.

"You fired her!"

"I suspended her."

Kai walked to a wall, and then back. To the wall, then back.

"This is low!" he said. "Even for you, Swardstrom."

"It's not racing if you're not trading paint."

"That's paint, not people!" he shouted so that the other skippers could hear. "It's not racing if you can't maintain your own crew!"

Dan's pleasant smile disappeared.

Oh, Kai thought. That was it. The crew!

Kai spent thousands of dollars outfitting his boat, five years of upgrading sails, buying expensive paint and hiring pros to make some time, but he never once thought to fuck with the crew. Not the crew of Nefarious. Not the sailors who sang together in the bar after every race, win or lose. Not the sailors who threw each other birthday parties and watched the super bowl together.

"Where's your Ortun?" Kai taunted. "He didn't look so good after Rhett took a swim."

Dan put away his race notes.

"He handed you your ass, yesterday."

"Is he on another bender?" Kai said following him down the hall. "It looks like you're getting an early start on being a parent. With all this drama, you're more like a mother than a skipper."

Kai laughed. He knew that Dan wanted to sock him, but never would. Skippers don't sock each other. It was not sporting, but the thought of Dan losing his cool delighted him.

"Good hunting," Dan said, with nothing else to say.

"This is not going to be any fun at all at all," Kai called after him. "Watching Nefarious go down like this. The darlings of the fleet—going down like cheap wine." Kai followed him to the dock barking like a seal. "Look!" he said. "There's your pit. She's prepping Jupiter. Must be strange.

Tell me. Did she fuck her way onto Nefarious the way she got onto Jupiter?"

The next thing Kai saw was Dan's fist coming at him, fast as an untethered boom. A gold ring flashed before him, some white hairy knuckles, and then a red light.

But Kai's never stopped smiling.

Not for an instant. He smiled through the punch and the pain, even as the blow sent him backwards, where his heel caught the dock and sent him into the water. He was wrapped in bubbles—tiny crystal balls, dancing in the green rheum of the sea. Each bubble was a little mirror, and reflected in each was a wonton image of Nefarious. To his delight, she was wayward, struggling, a sick seal in a choppy sea; her hull dragging heavy in the chime and her keel askew. Behind her, he spied the golden scales painted onto Jupiter's hull, out in front, and he could hear Dan cursing and spitting. He'd blown another start, the fool! Typical. He was a shell-shocked warhorse, ready to be put down.

Now the bubbles were above him—their southern hemispheres foretelling the last minutes of the race, where Jupiter was crossing the finish, showered in champagne and confetti from the committee boat. He saw the cake and trophy waiting in the yacht club, and the people who did not bring a tuxedo to Race Week, who were now forced to scramble into second-hand stores to buy any cheap tux they could fit their fat-asses into.

"I'll see you at the party!" Kai said when he surfaced. "I hope you brought a cummerbund!"

CHAPTER 61

It was hard talking to pretty girls.

Telling them the truth.

They were so absorbed in their own idea of themselves, they rarely had the insight to see who they really were: a composite of lies, images and projections wished onto them by those who wanted their attention.

They desperately wanted to believe it, too.

That they were worthy of the attention they received, and often, they were not.

"Dan's gone mad!" the pit girl said. "Stark raving mad."

She was loading her gear onto Jupiter, throwing it at a crewman.

"He kicked you off the boat?" the writer said.

"Yes," she said, and threw another bag. "He's caught up in his own shit and forgotten about his family."

"I think he's doing just that."

"What do you mean?"

"He's thinking about his baby." .

"Not that family," she said and passed him her flask. "His real family."

"A child has an effect on a man that is completely unexpected."

"Oh, of course you'd say that," she said. "You're a father, and a sap."

The writer didn't drink.

"Darling," she apologized. "I didn't mean it like that. You're a romantic fool, and you know it."

"There are no good fools," he said.

"You know how I get before a race," she demurred, "and you know as well as I do that crew is thicker than blood. Write that down. Skippers have been leaving their families teary-eyed on the dock for centuries. Sometimes for years," she dank again. "And it's sad that Dan can't sail one goddamned race without hurrying off to Martina's side."

The vitriol surprised him. She'd always been sassy, but this was crass.

"Dan is going to be an excellent father," the writer said. "I hope he'll never be as good a sailor. Any man blessed by a child shouldn't be better at anything else."

The pit-girl put away her flask.

There was a puzzle in her eyes, the same puzzle he'd seen when they first met at the grocery store.

The fruit had fallen, and for a moment, he thought it better to leave it there on the floor, to leave Pandora's box closed. And from that moment, he began to wonder in reverse, what his life would look like without the pit-girl and her friends.

"I don't understand you sometimes, Max," she kissed him on the cheek and slapped him a little hard on the face. "You're the worst martyr I ever met."

"No," the writer said. "I'm the best."

CHAPTER 62

Dan removed the last of Nefarious' bumpers and before he pushed her off, he looked up, just one last time to see if his gut was right.

That's when he spotted Ortun; a hip gait, easy as cake, carrying a six-pack of Coors light, headed down the dock.

"This is my last race, skipper," Ortun said.

"Oh yeah?"

"Yeah."

"You going to take up bowling?" Dan said.

"Hell no," Ortun smiled. "I'm going to take up a more honest living. I'm going to stick a needle in myself and die in box car."

Dan looked at him as if he were serious, then realized that he wasn't, then realized again that maybe he was.

"You'll be pit, today," he said.

Whichever way, there was no keeping Ortun at bay from himself. He was his own best friend, and Dan knew he would never come between the two.

"A demotion," Ortun said.

"You know it."

"Who's playing the role of tactician?"

Dan nodded at the only crewman who wasn't wearing a shirt.

"Kai's guy?"

"Yep."

"Mac?"

"Suspended," Dan said. "She's sailing Jupiter."

Ortun smiled.

"Chaos," he said, and he clicked his heels like a leprechaun. "Permission to come aboard."

Dan tossed him a bumper.

"Permission granted."

Ortun pushed them off and he looked at the crew.

Bonesteel appeared.

"You're back like a shark, are ya?"

"Aye," Ortun said.

"Where you been?" Ewan asked.

"The future," Ortun said.

The crew laughed.

"Are we going to win this bitch?" Duff said.

"No," he said. "But, we'll win the day, won't we?"

Ortun led them through a chorus of the Nefarious song and everyone sang, except for the new tactician. He waited for them to settle down, eyeing everyone until they focused on him, and then he raised his hand and closed it to make a fist.

"Start the clock," he said, and an instant later the starter pistol was fired from the committee boat.

Dan started the motor and aimed Nefarious into the channel. The Indian had certainly changed the mood onboard. As he looked on, scanning the course, you couldn't tell if he was looking at you, or the horizon.

"Make your heading two degrees starboard," he said.

Dan didn't question.

The course the Indian laid was austere, and he seemed to catch minute detractions that called for the most precise corrections.

"Cut your motor," he said.

Dan cut the motor.

As they entered the channel and headed toward the starting line, it was clear he was spoiling for a fight. Dan watched him scan the proving grounds: every wave and wake, ripple and gust. He used his shirtless body to detect the wind on the water, absorbing every mistral.

"There," the Indian said.

Dan eyed the harpoon and turned the tiller.

Jupiter caught on.

"Hey Nefarious-ass!" called the pit-girl, and slipped into their draft, edging close enough to banter. "You're listing, starboard. Did your pit check the keel head-foil?"

"We're in good order," Dan called. "Have you checked your ego?"

"Looks like Eight Ball wants some action," she pointed to the Farr that was gaining fast on their position. "See you at the finish line."

Jupiter cut in tight and then pulled in behind them to draft.

The pit-girl blew them a kiss.

"Love you, darlings!"

Dan turned to the skipper of Eight Ball, who was dressed in a tuxedo.

"What's your business?" he called.

"Your wind, skipper."

"I'll throw a flag if you come any closer," Dan said.

"Nobody cares, Dan," the skipper said. "We all know your head's not in the race."

Dan cursed when Nefarious suddenly slowed and like a hot knife, Eight Ball cut into them.

"Looks like Kai has some goons on the course, today." Ewan said.

"Hold your course," called the tactician.

Dan hesitated.

Eight Ball was clearly attempting to jibe and cross the line early.

"Time!" Dan yelled.

"Two minutes," Ortun said.

Dan gripped the tiller tighter and looked to starboard.

The Indian pointed his harpoon, but Dan looked to port.

Ortun smiled; he knew what Dan was thinking. Today was shaping up like the last bad start, only this time, there was a pro onboard. Dan knew that Ortun knew that winning his way was the only option. Doing differently was like allowing someone else borrow your underwear.

Dan turned the tiller and Nefarious leaned to port.

"Eight ball," Dan said. "Corner pocket."

Ortun and Ewan raced to port.

"Hike it, you bitches," Dan told them. "Hike it for your skipper."

Eight Ball saw the daring maneuver, a jibe that pointed Nefarious' bow right at their belly.

"Oh shit!" Ortun said. "Chaos. It's coming."

But Eight Ball folded, left their cards on the table and tacked to port.

Nefarious took their wind, and Dan straightened the tiller.

"If you pull that shit again," the skipper of Eight Ball cursed. "I'll be the one throwing a flag today, Danny Boy!"

"You afraid to lose a gel-coat, Theodore?" Dan said.

"Get a life, you pirate!"

"Yar!" Dan growled. "And a gentleman. Mind if I pass?"

"Piss off."

Nefarious cut in front of Eight Ball.

"Don't mind if I do."

Dan turned his eye on Jupiter.

"Time?"

"One minute," Duff said.

Dan took his hand off the tiller.

"Bonesteel," he said. "Kill it."

"What was that, skipper?"

"Kill it. Now."

Bonesteel let the slack off the mainsail; let it luff until the halyard clips jingled like Christmas bells.

Ewan leapt from the rail.

"What are you doing, Dan?" he said. "Jupiter's on our six."

Dan turned to the Indian, watched him point his harpoon into the wind.

"Let's be friends," Dan said. "We're all one—big—happy fleet."

"You want them on our ass?" Ewan said.

"I want them in front of us, where I can see them," Dan said like a wolf. "It's time to find out if our pro is worth his salt."

The crew looked to the bow where the Indian stood, erect like a bowsprit, harpoon in hand. He was looking off into the distance, out into the channel with a mysterious intensity in his eyes.

Jupiter passed by—steady as she goes.

The course was set, steeped in green emerald, goose bump seas, ruffling in the breeze. It was a time for tactics, but not until Dan made his mark.

"You run out of gas, big guy?" Kai said?

"What the fuck?" the pit-girl said.

The starter gun fired.

Dan watched it spew bone-while smoke in the air and the report of the gun reached him again, a ricochet from the lumpy hills on the inlet.

It was time to overcome the monster.

Time to own it.

Take it on as his own creation,

Fight it here today.

He was no good at starts.

Never had been.

Now the monster was on deck with him.

Hassling him.

Now, now, now.

"What are you doing?" Ewan said.

"Softening them up," Dan said, watching Jupiter pass.

He waited.

"They'll take the first buoy," Ewan said. "We'll have to fight them for the straits."

Dan saw the monster pouting.

Stomping its horrible feet.

Spinning and spitting.

But it was his.

His perfect monster.

"The skipper is well aware of that," the Indian said.

Jupiter cut through the starting line. They were the first over, and the passengers aboard the committee boat applauded. Eight Ball crossed, and then Tupac and Blue Lullaby. The monster stomped harder as each boat drifted by. In the distance, it saw the pit-girl flipping Nefarious the bird.

Dan turned to Bonesteel.

"Crank it," he said. "Crank it you magnificent bastard."

Bonesteel cranked the mainsail taut as his six-pack—tighter than his prom date—tighter than a clam's ass at low tide.

Nefarious responded instantly, catching the headwind in her bosom with a snap.

The monster was at a loss.

Stunned.

There was nothing else to do.

Now that a blown start was out of the way, there would be no barging leeward of the mark, no penalty buoy to round—only a straight shot at the inlet where his master could rip into the course.

The monster tiptoed away from Dan, and with sad eyes, and without making a sound, it jumped overboard.

Dan hoped to never see the bastard again.

CHAPTER 63

The Devil slammed his fist on the counter.

"What a joke!" he told the bartender.

"What do you mean, sir?"

"You didn't see that?" the devil said. "He didn't blow his start!"

"A tactical decision."

"Pride!" the devil said, disgusted. "He's racing like a pussy!"

"Looks like he's in the middle of the pack."

"He shouldn't be doing anything differently," the devil said in contempt. "Dan's a wolf. He needs the adrenalin of a bad start."

It was true.

The wolf hunted its prey from behind, nipping at its heels, causing panic. Dan was a predator. He didn't know it, but his blown start kept him at the heels of his prey.

"I heard he's got a pro onboard."

The devil slammed his hand again.

"Kevin Johnson?" he said, and drank. "That guy's not interested in winning! He's got other plans for that boat. Don't you see? Dan will have us all in tuxedos before the end of the day."

The devil snapped his fingers and his suit transformed into a red-silk tuxedo. It was fabulous, he thought as he caught himself in the mirror. Classic style. Formal. A dinner jacket, single-breasted, seersucker lapel—just like the one his good buddy Kanye West wore at the Espy awards.

The possibility of not hosting a party started to sink in. What fun would it be without it being thrown in his honor? How many times has a party with tuxedos and seafood ended in threesomes? Roasted animals on a spit? Drugs that made you realize your life was a hyper-technicolor, re-awaken state ambulated by endorphins and testosterone that can easily be reset by a morning after pill? Well, there was that one party in the Jefferson Estate, but he was a Mason, and that shit was weird. The fact of the matter was, even the Russians were not up for hedonism these days, not even Putin.

Only the sailors.

Only the drunken, lost, wayward relativistic, put my cock in a beer can, amoral, live for today, son-of-a-bitches and bastards who sailed a boat. Only they were uninhibited enough to sacrifice an actual goat.

"This race is turning into shit, I tell you!" he said.

The devil opened his phone and texted the group, DAN IS AN ASS. STBY NEFARIOUS.

"The skipper's got a plan, right?" the bartender said. "Who sails a quarter-million-dollar boat without a plan?"

"Dan is a simple man!" The devil spit. "And isn't that the challenge—to steal the heart of the average man? You see? I can't let him have the last word. No! What fun is it to watch you people kill in the name of your holy Lord? You foolish, lizard brained, sacks of water can't escape your own amygdala!"

Ah. But Dan! He thought. His pet—the average man—so content to let the world burn—so long as the ashes did not fowl the deck of his own boat.

"You see," he said, buttoning his tux, "I've learned a thing or two about being the black sheep, cast from Heaven as it were. I've learned what it is to truly be broken, and for lack of anything better to do, I lost myself in the terrible loneliness of this universe. I saw nothing, was nothing, and committed myself to using whatever spark of consciousness I'd willed from the fires of creation to put a stop to these the commandments and scriptures set in stone—but I overestimated people like Dan. The chaos only makes him stronger. No matter how dim or fleeting, in the darkness, he continues to seek the light."

"Yeah, I guess that's right," the bartender said, pouring a shot. "He's always had a positive outlook on life."

"But I couldn't let it go," the devil said. "I tried. Once I had broken away from God's grace, I covered myself in ash, and I became my own God. Then, because I was bored, I lent you fools my powers and found it glorious to watch you suffer. But Dan's run amuck. At every corner, he turns lust into love, and greed into avarice, gluttony into joy! The deadly sins turned into virtue. Why, I am no more destroyer of worlds than I am the creator of new worlds! And he spites, thee! The average man. Isn't this what I wanted? Forever a figure to blame. But Dan has only taught me not to trust. And how to go insane."

"Look," the bartender said. "Nefarious is heading up the pack!"

"What?" the devil said.

"Yeah," the bartender said. "Maybe he does care about winning today."

"Well, I'll be damned," the devil said.

CHAPTER 64

The pit-girl watched Nefarious close in on Jupiter. Her heart was heavy and for an instant she regretted crossing swords with Dan. But then her dignity cut in. During a race, or whist being chased by a panther, the last thing on one's mind should be regret. In the end, we only regret the chances we didn't take.

She was a lightning rod.

Lightning rods were made to channel energy, not repentance.

She pulled hard on the main sail halyard, made sure it was taut.

No slack.

None.

Zero.

It was the best way to sail a ship.

No excuses.

And when there was doubt, it meant you hadn't checked your lines the way a good sailor was supposed to before you left port.

That was the point.

You sailed the seas you were given, and if you weren't ready for the shit storm, too bad if you're little boat sank in a sea of your own sorrow.

Dan had thrown her off the boat, which she respected. For once he didn't give into his instinct to be passive. But when she really thought about it, the reason her heart was heavy had more to with the fact that she'd begun to think of Nefarious as her home, and just who the hell was he to kick her out of it? Yes, she over salted people they way she did her fries, but out here, with these manly-men, a chip on her shoulder was not only required, but it was enjoyable.

Dan had been her mentor.

He saw through her aggressive nature, and even nurtured her.

She began to feel like a puppy cutting her teeth.

Who was he to nurture her?

Who was he to put her in the doghouse?

Nefarious flanked two more boats, catching their draft and slipstreaming around them. Dan's pro used the wind like a mousetrap. He'd catch each boat by the tail and one by one, kill their wind. Tupac, Occam's Razor, Ballyhoo, Blue Lullaby and Ballistic were now in their wake.

"Jesus-shit!" she said. "They just took Absolutely."

"The captain is well aware of their position," the new tactician said. "Now get in the pit, where you belong."

The pit girl stomped her foot.

"I get in the goddamned pit when I feel like it."

"Jesus, skipper," he said. "Where did you find this one?"

Davey called back.

"She's won at worlds," he said. "She knows when to be in the pit."

The boat, slowed suddenly.

"Really?" the tactician said. "Then who the fuck is feeding the kite right now?"

"Get in the pit!" Kai said to the pit-girl. "Now!"

The pit-girl dashed inside and grabbed the kite halyard like stolen handfuls of money, shoved it up the hatch to Davey.

"Fly that bitch!" Kai said. "Fly it for your skipper!"

It was too late.

The pit-girl watched Nefarious jib. On the deck she could see Bonesteel unzip the main sail, hold it taut and jam the onshore westerly down its beam. In an instant, Dan's trap was on their tail.

"I don't like the smell of your ass!" Dan called. "Slowest set I've seen you pussies run all day!"

Kai did not respond. He turned the tiller to keep Nefarious behind them.

"Watch it Kai," Dan said. "Section C, rule twenty, room to tack at an obstruction."

"Section C, rule twenty-point-one," Kai said. "Passing boat shall hail, and give the hailed boat sufficient time to respond."

"Is that your response?"

"Fuck you," Kai said. "That's not a response."

Kai turned the tiller hard and so did Dan.

"What was that?" Dan said. "Are you responding to my adjustment, section C, paragraph one?"

The boats were side by side, pulled tight as slingshots. The water between them splashed and stung the hulls

...stiiizzz

...stiiizzz

...the sound of frying bacon.

"You call that an adjustment?" Kai said. "I can't feel anything. Is it inside me yet? Is it now?"

"Oh you'll know when I'm responding, baby," Dan said.

Dan feigned a tack, but the pit-girl called him on it.

"No," she said. "It's bullshit!"

Jupiter caught the run an instant before Nefarious, and by some miracle, the kites did not tangle.

"You're sailing with a mad man," Dan called to her as Nefarious fell behind. "We'll catch you on the next set."

"Like hell you will!" she said.

The pit-girl watched Jupiter straighten and the catch the wind. They were making time. Her eyes were entranced, and she could sense the undoing of her shipmates. A run into the inlet meant it was Jupiter's race to lose.

Sadness entered her, but it was swept away by the wind at her back.

"Sailor!" the tactician said marching to the pit. "The skipper does the chatter while racing. Are you new?"

Davey dropped his halyard, moved at the tactician.

"No!" Kai said. "Stay where you are."

But it was too late—Davey was already throwing his fist at the pro, landing it squarely on his cheekbone. The next thing the pit-girl saw was a splash in the Salish sea.

"Man overboard!" she said, and raced to the rescue line, threw it at the douchebag who was being swept behind the boat.

"Damn you Davey," she said. "You never punch a man on a race boat!"

Today marked the seconded day of fisticuffs in her honor—Race Week had become Fight Week.

She was a liability.

An albatross.

A banana peel.

"Never—period. Ever. Exclamation point! You could have killed him," she spat. "But worst of all, we lose time."

Kai took Davey's position and killed the spinnaker, slowing the boat instantly. The pit-girl took the tiller and sullenly turned the boat back into the mayhem that Davey had caused—yet for an instant, she contemplated it as her mess that she was backtracking into.

For a long moment, she looked out into the sea and listened to the hissing noise of dead sails tacking against time.

Nefarious clipped them and the hissing was replaced by the sound of her shipmate's laughter.

She listened to it fade and disappear, and with it, Nefarious turned on the buoy marking the entrance into Sacred Cove.

CHAPTER 65

The writer watched the fleet disappear around Whidbey peninsula, Nefarious leading the pack. Their masts synchronized, hauled away into the cove like a line of ducks strung together. He was relieved to see them disappear. The clatter and clashing, the brash talking, bell ringing, flat clapping sailors were a drain on his introverted, propound sensibilities.

The ability to fake his way through this spectacle was long past its middle.

In the hush, he thought of his children. How they'd miss him at this point, and in returning, the consequence of chasing a life of interests, of adventure . . . and of course, love, would catch him. Yes, they'd miss him. But, what was there to miss of a man who does not dream? What dreary, dutiful life could he pass on to them less his paternal obligations?

At the beginning, she refreshed him. Aged him in reverse. But here in this harbor, he felt father time's hands slowly speeding up.

Nefarious was the underdog, and part of him wished the albatross to stay on their deck for the final race. It would be easier, he thought. Less messy. Less complicated. He'd partied with the crew for less than a win at a premier event, and they were something to behold: busted windows, promises, bones, bottles and condoms. It went on and on like this, and always accompanied by the yammering ring of their egos.

At this point, he began to feel as though he could do nothing to stop the storm waiting for him, all of it culminating in reverse, as if the thing unspooled before him like a melancholic poem, its stanzas read in reverse. He watched the cloudy sky break up over the harbor, were in his mind, they were gathering into a world-changing cyclone.

Only his world, yes.

And therefore, the universe.

He breathed and tried to lift it all off his shoulders: his unstable ex-wife, prone to depressive abjection, masking her contempt for mediocrity behind a pleasant smile and opiates; her recalcitrant efforts to resist the sacrifice of children and the energy it took to launch them.

It took more than snuggles and bedtime stories.

It took a tolerance for vomit, fever, fear, humility and forfeit.

She had not adjusted well, and soon, he found himself with the kids five-days a week, and she the weekend parent.

There was never a fight.

That's just the way it had been and now it was the way it was.

Until the pit-girl came along.

Through her, he'd learned to live outside of his life as a father. He was seen. When the boys were away, they'd get in the car and drive in random directions until there were only trees, lay down on a blanket and play like otters. By three-o'clock, they'd be back in the city, drinking cold gin until dinner, then roam the streets and analyze the intentions of hipsters, shop at lingerie stores, make out in alleys, then stumble into her apartment where he'd rip off whatever underwear she'd bought.

When they walked, she took his hand and he followed. Her hold was firm, not rigid nor loose. It said, let me take you with me and show you these things I've seen. We are like-minded. Like souls. Like fools. Friends on a journey. Lovers. Let me take you. Let me show you.

Where had it all gone wrong? Did the pain of their inevitable breakup outweigh the pleasures she had shown him?

He sat on a cold rock and began writing the poem he knew was inevitable.

How shall you be my ghost today?
For I love you as I love the dead.
Never ashamed
Never with dread.
How shall you be my ghost today?
For I love you as I love to sleep
Forever eternal
Without a peep
And nay a weep.
How shall I live alone today?
In wanting hope, that fades away?
You shall be my wish today.
Defined by you, as now I lay,
Inside the tomb

That blows away.
The backwards flow of ghostly streams
That haunt and haunt the poet's dreams.

Of course, he would miss the crew. They were his friends, too. But he knew he had to kill them.

All of them.

All his darlings.

He knew that after this race, he would slowly cease to exist, and instead of facing their rejection, he'd be the one who'd make them disappear, one page at a time. The people he cooked for. The people he drove to the docks and argued with and hydrated after their drunken benders, got them ship shape before the race . . . he'd kill them. Break them. Draft after draft, he'd perfect the story of their demise, and sadly, it would comfort him.

But in doing so, they'd live in their ruin forever.

It was the odd way that writers coped with loss: the grindingly slow, annihilation of time and space—bringing with it, the haunting, heartbreaking souls of the people you loved, and loved to hate.

The story was vanity incarnate, his, theirs, held before a distorted mirror, and it was in his power to shine whatever light he saw fit upon his subjects.

It would heal him, he hoped.

He'd do the world a favor by showing them exactly why a sane person should steer clear of a sailor.

Stay away.

Stay away and keep your heart.

He looked out at the water, and began to see that it was all happen in reverse, all the things they'd seen and done together. It was all unwinding before his eyes faster and faster.

Clouds eating rain.

An eagle flying backwards.

The retreat of thunder.

Planets running away into oblivion.

CHAPTER 66

Tupac turned tight into the windward buoy, trading shots with Wild Horses until they backed the fuck up like the bitches they were. They jockeyed for position to make the final jibe mark on the course, chasing down El Zorro and Abel Brown. It was some fucked up shit, the committee boat whoring out the course as a modified port-triangle. They were showing off for the suits in town, and as they made the leeward mark, just as they wanted, the fleet was lining up in a parade of sharks. This meant a tight, back stabbing fuck fest as they all turned toward the finish line.

"Yo' skipper, what the fuck's that niggah Dan up to?" LaPrell said. "That shit he's doin's wack."

The skipper took the binoculars from his trimmer.

Indeed, he thought. That shit is wack! Why was the number two boat suddenly off course and risking a penalty? They were headed out of bounds toward Sacred Cove.

"He must be tryin' to stay out the clog these assholes want us to parade in."

The skipper smiled.

"If Jupiter's lookin' for a knife fight, they better look out. Dan's a killa."

"He's a killa'," the tactician said. "But he ain't dumb enough to get a penalty by fuckin' wit dat whale."

"He must be ballin' his ass to the jibe," the skipper said. "Try'n to jam 'em up. Know what I'm sayin?"

"Yeah, skipper."

They spied an eagle on the course, drafting off Nefarious' main sail. It was a sight to see, almost majestic, but there was something ominous about it, too.

"His pro must have him tryin' to make some time," Decron said.

"Hell yeah," said Tyrone.

"Dan's gonna get dat ass," LaPrell said.

Nefarious swung wide, out from behind Jupiter, jibed and turned back in hard on the line of boats the way a wolf attacks sheep. Ninety-Nine Problems and The Great Gatsby cleared out, and the wind smoothed for Dan.

Nefarious accelerated.

"Look!" said LaPrell. "He's takin' 'dem mother-fucker's air."

It looked like Dan was going to pull the day off. A respectable win, with a steady wind and no penalty flags. Kai was going to be pissed. The skipper smiled.

"Them bitches gonna win!" LaShonnu said.

Nefarious began opening the lead and the crew cheered.

"Dan's a pimp," Decron said.

Yes, thought the skipper. Dan was indeed, a pimp. But why then was his tactician standing on the bow with a motha' fucking harpoon?

"What the——?" he said, and dropped the binoculars because he wanted to see whatever happened next with his own eyes.

CHAPTER 67

Kevin Jonson knew this to be the place. The eagle had arrived, just like the old stories used to say—stories that helped him understand that everything was a circle.   Just as it was imbedded into the whale's consciousness, so too had it been imbedded into his.

No maps were needed.

In darkness, both hunter and prey could find the cove.

It was in their bones, living on their flesh, living in the songs they shared, the dances and stories, the stars and planets, passed down from father to son, mother to daughter, grandparents to grandchild, cow to calf. It was a solemn, enshrined, communal circle not broken by death.

Only apathy could take it down, only contempt—and if it should come first, the end of time itself.

Sacred Cove is where the warm currents of the Salish Sea meets the shallows; where unhindered and free to wallow, grey whales hide their ancient ritual from the enemy.

But not today.

It was not so long ago that this cove, now a bucolic sprawl, served as a hallowed hunting ground, where beast and beauty gathered in pairs to trade their seed. Here is where they would sow the playful, lulling, ritual that produced a calf. Normally, their mating and calving occurred in the lagoons off Baja California, but the shoal in Sacred Cove mimicked the lagoon's conditions. The whales were canny enough to forego the migration, meeting halfway to their winter-feeding grounds, risking only the occasional killer whale.

Never mind the bucolic scenery. Makah were witness to cultures that came and went with the tides. Their home was Neah Bay, enduring on the most northwest tip of the haggard, edge-on, Olympic Peninsula. The mountains had come and gone too—pushed up by tectonic forces and eroded into sand by the certainty of chaos. For thousands of years, they subdued the ever-changing, windy and wild, scattered landscape as it shaped them into its masters. That whites would have their turn was of no consequence. They brought the unnecessary: news and devices, trouble and disease. The Makah had been tested. They were the only people in the continental United States to still inhabit their indigenous land: this land.

These waters.

No one else could live here a thousand years.

The eagle was still here.

It wanted a piece of the action.

In silence, Kevin Jonson watched the beast move into Sacred Cove. He slowly coiled his rope and collected his stones, tied them one by to his feet. The moment was here.

He steadied his hold.

Stood.

Breathed.

CHAPTER 68

Dan saw the whale enter Sacred Cove and hoped it was an illusion; a glistening, black oval in the sparkling water. But when the animal spouted, he removed his sunglasses.

There, between the committee boat and the spectator boat, sure as hell.

Ortun looked off into his gaze.

"Shit!" he said, grabbing the binoculars.

Nefarious seemed to be on the same tack as the grey whale, leading them toward the finish line. Ortun dropped the binoculars and snatched the mike from the receiver to call Edmund.

"No," Dan said and turned to the bow where his tactician was standing.

The Indian was perched like a crane, his harpoon raised.

Ortun turned just in time to see him heave his body in front of the boat, and without a splash, disappear.

"Chaos!" he said to Dan. "It's happening!"

Dan held onto the tiller, braced himself, though he didn't know what for. The air was charged, but everything was still.

Silence.

Then, for an instant, the boat stopped and a large object drummed on the hull.

Thud!

"What's happening?" Dan said.

"Judgment day," Ortun said.

Dan turned his main sail slack, killing the power and Nefarious crawled through what was left of the wind, slowly tipping from side to side. He peered over the rail to see what Ortun was eyeing in the water.

"Holy hell," Dan murmured as he watched the hull slip through a pool of blood—so much, that he could feel the heat at the surface. Hushed, he watched with Ortun, dumbfounded and afraid.

Bonesteel shot to the helm.

"We just fucked a whale, skipper."

The animal suddenly cried out from below, and they jumped high side.

"No shit," Dan said turning Nefarious to port. "And we lost our tactician."

The cries from below continued, a piercing woe that slipped in and out of anguish. Dan was no marine biologist, but judging from the amount of blood in the water, that fucking thing was going to die. And soon. Whoever, or whatever injured it had surgically severed a major artery—a stream of blood, spilling from the leviathan in twirling ribbons, languid and supine like the eddies he'd seen in his dreams.

"Ewan, get the hell over here!" he said, feeling nauseous. "And bring the docking stick."

Dan didn't know what else to do. For the first time at sea, he felt like shitting himself. Maybe pushing the creature away from the hull would keep it from blowing a hole in Nefarious; it certainly had the strength to do so. But it wasn't fighting. Not one little bit. The blow to the artery had taken its strength. It was a graceful killing. A willful death. He was starting to understand it now—chaos! Close to the surface, just beneath the emerald green water, rolling onto its silky, bone white belly covered in barnacles.

Then, he saw it.

The harpoon.

The man.

The beast.

It all happened so fast that he thought he was dreaming.

When the whale rolled over with the harpoon stuck in its side, the shaft rose and fell like the ticking hand of clock—and attached to the shaft was the lissome figure he'd last seen standing on the bow, holding fast, pushing it further into his captive.

There was no doubt about it.

Like a bullfighter, the Indian was its master.

The beast was his prey.

Dan tore his eyes away from the spectacle, but it was like trying not to look into a total eclipse.

When he saw Jupiter cross the finish line, he could still see the glare of the whale spinning in the sea, rolling over onto its belly, in its own blood, spinning against the weight of the dagger in its heart.

He heard one last breath expelled from the beast: a murmuring burst of bubbles that reached the surface, and then disappearing like magic.

CHAPTER 69

The devil set down his drink.

He'd had enough.

A thousand years.

A thousand times.

They'd let him down.

Why was this time so different? There had been countless eternities, and he'd live a million more; an endless, turning staircase of disappointment.

A turret of souls, rising into space.

Long ago, his tears were extinguished in the fires of creation, and when you are born into fire, you called it home, and when your hearth is home, there is nothing more vile than the anguish of being alone without tears. Not in a thousand lives, a thousand wars, a thousand deaths. There was nothing. He was born in fire. He'd seen it all.

"Looks like Jupiter wins the day," the bartender said.

"First, accept sadness," the devil said. "And realize that without losing, winning isn't great."

"Will you be having another, then?" asked the bartender.

"I'm not thirsty," the devil said.

Now his only companion was disappointment.

The devil frowned and left a wad of cash on the counter and hurried to the deck where he vomited into the sea.

A million fears.

The sting of a million suns.

Ten million years of improbability.

A million lies.

The pain of a million wrongs, forever tangled in the fabric of time and space, clogging the cockles of the human condition.

If there were a single truth, a single thought, a single grace, in all his lives, all his manifestations, it was that he was innocent. He had always been, and it was in fact man who had sinned. Man who had tasted the fruit and spited his master.

He was innocent.

He had never tasted the fruit.

He never would and he never could.

So, who better to torture man than him?

Who better to reduce him to ash with a single thought and then single handedly convince him that he was more than the whole of mankind—a million, million, points of lights—star scattered, shewn and blown to dust, blown into the cosmos, to die, alone.   Erased.

But not him.

He was ageless.

He lived many lives.

He rode with kings and conquered many lands.

He'd won their world in games of chance, watched it turn to dust at his hands.

He'd made fodder for cannons, destroyed a thousand men in the breath of a word; sent their wives into mourning, turned their children into bastards and whores and then judged their crimes from a bench. He'd worn a writer's cloak, kept a thousand mysteries in his sleeve, watched them unfold like galaxies spinning apart in an ocean of time, eternities to suffer and his word the last, at the turn of every page.

But he had done so without sin.

The average man was the sinner.

Not him.

The average man was a reprobate, and unlike himself, the average man did not know that he was a sinner, not really, or a even a god, and to his delight, that there was an eternity to prove it to him, to show him the fires of creation, the fires that stole his tears, turned the salt from stars into blood, forged metal into sword, and water into wine.

The devil removed his handkerchief and cleaned his mouth; gathered himself, cleaned the vomit from his lapel.

Perhaps he was wasting his time.

He had an infinite amount of it to show them, to prove that he was innocent, but when he saw the fleet headed back into the marina, bobbing and rolling side to side, he felt sick. The horizon was a long, inverted eggshell, bending up into the sky and circling outward. He was upside down, and a dark, tiny moon, pulled his stomach toward the void. Under his feet was the earth, a wiggly, fuzzy blue orb just out of reach.

He looked hard back into the sea, watched the boats squirming on the water and suddenly, he was no longer sentimental about the ugly little specks.

CHAPTER 70

Dan was on the edge of a dream. Or, was he dreaming? He found himself observing his life from the throws of his imagination, or was he captured in it?

Watching Jupiter cross the finish line was surreal, but not as shocking as killing a whale. He had told the crew to keep quiet until he knew exactly what happened. Losing the race was bad enough, but killing Race Week was a hook in his heart.

Race Week was his darling, and he knew her buttons. Knew every curve and sultry detail. Today, she had turned her back on him, and as fate would have it, in the cruelest of manners.

It was his style to win with a flourish, and even as a child while playing the game of Risk in the garage with friends, he'd only try to win after he'd conquer Iceland. It was no fun to win any other way, and losing without it meant he'd been defeated. He'd always blown his starts, but today, he tried to play by their rules. Held back his aggressive starts.

Kai would fall for the troll every year, even if Nefarious had to take a buoy. The aggression so enraged him that the remainder of the course, he'd make stupid decisions: overrule his tactician, risk trading gel coats, run a kite up early.

Not today.

Not only was Kai going to enjoy putting the kibosh on the antics that normally followed the last heat, but now, of course, Dan would be fighting for the meaning of his life, it seemed: Race Week, Nefarious, his new life as a father, his new life as a skipper who DNF'ed the race for the first time.

After the whale, surely, the suits would move on. They'd see the bloated, bloodied corpse in Sacred Bay as the omen it was. They'd grasp the attention that the accident would bring and move on to Vancouver, or the Bay Area. Race Week would die. The Whale Killing race. The Moby Dicks of sailing who had little regard for cute whales.

Everything coming he deserved.

Judgment day.

And the funny thing was, he'd always known it was coming, and not once did he stop to think that perhaps, it would be just.

That was the thing about making a deal with the devil.

It always was.

He always got what he was due.

Dan knew he would lose the boat, of course. It was part of the deal. He'd lose it, but wasn't losing it this way better than losing it the way his pit girl had suggested?

After giving up sailing to love a child—the child would break his heart, just as a child was designed to do.

Dan dismissed the crew on the docks, he'd finish the chores alone, a cathartic reckoning of sorts, and with every halyard he touched, came a memory. The first time he'd seen Nefarious, she was out of the water, lonely as he. God made man to live by motives, a preacher once told him, and he will not live righty without them, any more than a boat without steam or a balloon without gas. And surely, he had not lived before seeing her that day perched on her trailer, white as an angel's gown, sharp as a knife.

Nefarious wanted the sea and he needed a lover.

His first race was a catastrophe. After training with a pro for weeks, he scrounged up a crew and sailed Nefarious through the Bahamas to race in Nassau. A Farr was a race boat, but also, if you didn't mind pissing and shitting in a bucket, it had enough space to live aboard. When they steamed out of Florida, a tropical depression caught them by surprise. If he'd properly planned, he could have avoided it by steaming out of Jacksonville, but instead, to avoid the brunt of the storm, they found themselves in Haitian waters where pirates, notorious for killing the crew of luxury boats and selling them to Argentine oilmen, were known to patrol. Dan was nervous, but his decision was calculated, the kind you made while playing poker with a weak hand on the flop.

Nefarious made good time, a straight shot through topical skies dotted with cumulus, and by night, the tip of the Southern Cross was holding up the Milky Way. They drank and talked and slept in the bosom on twilight.

On the third day, Nefarious sailed into the horse latitude. They hit it like a wall, and suddenly the boat stopped moving. This is the place where ships of old would be stuck for months and sometimes needed to slaughter their horses for food. The air was still, flat as a frying pan, and no relief. The crew lived on warm PBR and Coors Light for days while trying to wiggle out from under it, but the alcohol suppressed their discomfort and disquiet. On the third day, from a distance they heard the blasts from a gun, shots fired at Nefarious, one of them ripping a hole in her new Mylar sheets.

The pirate ship was a converted fishing boat, rusted and broken, but with its twin diesel engines, it was fast enough to catch them the in the doldrums. Nefarious sat fat as a duck in oil, and he began to say his prayers, then, the front of the depression caught them. A breeze that smelled of grass and rain, which rolled over their sails as the pirate ship, approached. He tacked into the wind hard, cutting into their shots and then jibbing away, again and again until he built the momentum to raise the kite. When the sail filled, the pirates stopped firing. They knew what a Farr could do in tropical winds. On that day, he learned how to run full speed with his spinnaker hanging out like tits.

He touched another halyard. Now he saw the pit-girl, not flipping him off from the deck of Jupiter', but smiling in braces. He liked them on her: a jumpy, smoky-eyed vixen. The braces took the edge off her, but not the attitude. He'd sailed Nefarious to the Bay Area for nationals without a pit. They had missed the weight restriction and ditched the greenhorn in Oakland for being too fat. The moment he met her he asked how much she weighed, and she answered with her hand on her hip, none of you fucking business. He explained that he was a Farr skipper, and she asked the name of the boat. My kind of boat, she said.

Robin had a way of getting under his skin, and maybe he liked her that way. Maybe he could not accept her any other way. Who in life has time for lukewarm? Who does not spit it from their mouth, wanting the taste of heat?

Dan saw the uncoiled main sail halyard tangled on the deck. He considered the puzzle, the roping lines tangled in on itself, a snake, devouring its own flesh. Instead of straightening it, he sat on the deck and allowed an old sea shanty to comfort him.

I must go down to the seas again, to the lonely sea and the sky,
And all I ask is a tall ship and a star to steer her by,
And the wheel's kick and the wind's song and the white sail's shaking,
And a gray mist on the sea's face, and a gray dawn breaking.

He looked out at the horizon. The sun had fallen and the evening was settling into hues of indigo and lavender, red and gold. July's heat held back the onshore breeze, for now.

Dan took a deep breath and uncoiled the halyard. As he finished, he heard Edmund's footsteps and made out his plump shadow heading towards Nefarious.

"You really screwed the pooch this time, skipper."

His face was red and he panting from having hurried through the marina.

"Yep," Dan said. He was past Edmund, where the devil was waiting at the end of the dock.

"You killed a whale, you bastard! You killed it dead! Right in my water! Right there on my goddamned course!"

"I didn't kill it."

"What the hell do you mean?"

"My tactician."

Edmund realized what he was saying before he finished.

"That crazy Indian bastard?"

"Yes."

Edmund looked around, distraught and out of breath.

"Where is that son of a bitch?"

Dan looked out to sea but didn't say anything.

"You don't say?"

Edmund sat down on the dock.

"He harpooned it," Dan said after a moment; his voice unsteady, as if he'd seen a ghost. "He stabbed it right in its heart, then he swam to shore like an otter. Last we saw him, he was standing on Dugualla Point, watching the whale bleed out."

Edmund's face was pale and his eyes were dark and tired.

"You mean to say," he said. "Not only do we have a dead whale on the course, but a crazed Indian?"

"He's not crazy," Dan said, and a chilling image of the tactician appeared. He was holding on to his whale, sprawled with his limbs out and his arms holding the harpoon. In his eyes were bedlam. A cosmic, hunger peering into the near and seeing everything in the universe. Dan saw the edge, too. He saw the edge of everything he ever wanted, slipping away into the void of stars. "He got what he wanted. Which means we have work to do, don't we?"

Dan took out his phone.

"Who are you calling?" Edmund said.

"The cook."

CHAPTER 71

The devil listened to Dan's footsteps approach the end of the pier.

"Have you ever you ever just watched it all?" he said when he heard the footsteps stop. "Energy is a vibration, a pulse. The energy in this sea comes in the form of light to you. But, in blackness, there is no sea."

"If I close my eyes I can hear it," Dan said. "I can smell it and feel it on my skin."

"Yes," he said. "And hear it too."

He turned to face Dan.

"But what if you take that all away? What if you have nothing to smell or tastes or see, or hear or feel? What if you have no connection to what is real? What are you then, Dan?"

Dan couldn't answer.

"You are me," the devil said. "In the case of fast light, you don't notice the discontinuity because your retina retains the impression of the pulse, but you can't notice the pulse except in slow light. It's the same thing with sound. In the low note, you hear a kind of graininess because the slower alternations turn on and off.

The devil spoke.

Dan listened.

They were both defeated today.

"You see," he said with a tear in his eye, "all waves are motions and all motions are energy. You perceive them as waves, and all waves have crest. The crests are the top of the wave and the crest stands out from the undeviating darkness of the sea. But you cannot have the concave, without the convex. The crest and the trough. For anything to exist, there must be something hiding below. There must be something to give contrast to your senses or they cannot be excited." The devil could see Dan eyeing the stain on his lapel as he spoke, could detect the revulsion on his face, surprise, and empathy.

This was the average man?

This is whom he envied?

"The same thing is true of all life together, a contrast of existence with nonexistence," he continued, and calmly removed an envelope from his jacket. "Dan, your life—average thou it may be, is merely the vacillation of now-you-see-it, now-you-don't, now-you-see-it, now-you-don't." He removed his stained jacket and flung it into the sea. "It's a trick, you see? It's only the contrast of light and darkness, and without both, there is nothing in the universe."

Dan nodded politely, but he decided not to think about the puzzle. Puzzles were for land lovers, unlucky people without a boat and the wind to master. If he had any power in this universe, it was in the ability to choose his own dilemmas.

They both watched the red jacket in the water—floating on the oscillating surface of the blackness. After it sank into the abyss, the devil turned away from the water.

"Do you recognize this?" he asked.

"Yes," Dan said. "Our contract."

The devil removed his zippo from his pants and thought to tell Dan its story—that every time he lit it, a universe began anew, a bubble inside of another. But there was no point. This one was crowding in on him, and in the next instant, it would burst like a bubble and he would be gone. "I remember how eager you were to sign it and to begin your life as a sailor."

Dan smiled nervously, and the scar under his eye frowned.

"I wanted Nefarious more than I wanted my own life," he said, looking him right in the eye. "I couldn't live without her."

"And now?" The devils said, igniting the contract in front of him. "In this instant, indulge me, what are you feeling?"

Dan watched the contract burning, then looked out to the water where the committee boat was hauling in the last of the buoys. They were blasting rock-n-roll music, loud enough to raise the dead. No one had a clue that the future of Race Week was unraveling inside the corpse of a whale, drifting to shore, set to rot into lore and legend.

"I want to save this race."

"Yes," the Devil said. "You are not so average, are you? Without Race Week, there is no Nefarious. There is no Martina. There is no daughter. There is no you."

Dan smiled again.

"I hate to admit it," he said. "But you are right."

The devil looked at the burning contract.

"It was a parlor trick," he confessed. "A slight of hand. If only I could really take a soul. But what is dead may never die. And what is alive, will always live." He announced as the envelope tuned to ash in his fingers. "The contract is no longer valid. Nefarious belongs to you, now."

"Why would you do this?" Dan said. "I lost."

"Because without Race Week," the devil said. "There is no me."

CHAPTER 72

The writer was working on another poem when his phone rang. He was half finished: Gas Can and Match.

There are some flowers born to give pause:
Their scent, a nepenthe, aimed at attraction.
There are some fires, once ignited, aim to consume
the world. They are started by lighting,
or a smell, a touch, or a kiss.
There is a wayward rock in the world,
hiding in the shallows, waiting to wreck a ship.
It is hiding there, barely touching the surface,
waiting for you to sail into it.
It has been waiting for ages because
it's waiting for meaning.
It can smell your approach and
the moment you drifted over the horizon,
the living skin of organisms
encrusting its basalt, began to tingle at
your approach.
There are some books waiting to be read by you.
They hold the secrets you desire to be answered.
The words are there for all of time.
Your time. And the moments you
spend thinking of matches, the one
you will someday ignite, will be used

to burn the books one by one.
There is something delightful in watching
a book turned to ash.
The words will be inside of you,
and you will give birth to stanzas
that will smell of gasoline, and flowers,
sex, musk, and whiskey, and fear, and hope, and love.

He let the phone go to voicemail, but he could not finish the poem. He did not want to finish poem. So he got dressed and prepared for the evening's affairs. To his great misfortune, he'd found a tuxedo and he half-assed assembled it into something dapper. Because anything resembling a tux had been purchased, or stolen from the rack of every thrift store on the island, the mess he'd be wearing, found packed away in an old cardboard box at the back of a store, still smelled of cologne from the nineteen-seventies. It came complete with lavender ruffles, a set cufflinks and cummerbund.

A text appeared on his phone.

URGENT, CHECK UR MESSAGES, texted Dan.

The fleet was in and no doubt Dan required some equipment moved from one dock to some other dock, or a meal that needed to be prepared, or Ortun's required insulin or Coors Light. The truth was, the writer's heart wasn't into it anymore and he especially didn't want to nurse Dan though his epic loss on the course today. Losing a boat race was never one person's fault, but there was so much depending on him that Race Week might as well have been called Dan Week.

The writer sighed and took the message. By the time he was done listening to it, he'd spilled his glass of champagne.

Next thing he knew, he was dialing the phone.

"Hi Polly," he said. "It's Rigby. Oh, sure you remember me. I danced the rabbit dance with you last year. Yes, the one with the cowboy hat and the olivine shells. You moved too fast for me to keep up that night. I hope I didn't embarrass you in front of the other elders. Listen, I need to get ahold of Bub. Something important has come up. He doesn't have a phone? Where is he? Oh, at the senior center? Well, it's important that I talk to him as soon as possible. No, don't hang up. I had to call you three times to get this connection. Would you mind bringing the phone to him? Yes, of course I'll wait."

The writer put on his hat and removed his stupid as bowtie.

There was no way he was going to make it to the party in time.

CHAPTER 73

Kai fixed his tie in the mirror. He didn't need it, but it was a sanctimony.

A gut check.

Reassurance.

Who was the man in charge here?

The man he saw, or the man watching him?

They looked the same to him, but there was a trick.

The real Kai was the one who didn't blink first.

He slapped on some cologne, smiled and practiced his speech.

I'd like to thank the race committee and Edmund, our area judge. Their love of Race Week, and his stewardship over the years, has made this boat race what it is today. Edmund is exactly the man to take this course to world-level competition, where the entire sailing community will have its eyes on the Salish Sea, where their attention belongs. Too my crew. Your hard work is inspiriting. But I'd like to especially thank our pit, Robin Mac Brádaigh for pointing us in the right direction. Without her steady hand, I would not be standing here with this big fat trophy. In fact, I'm hiring her as Jupiter's tactician for worlds in Vancouver. As they say, never mess with a woman who thinks like a man and looks like art. She is the one who will ruin you.

Thanking the crew was a new thing for him. But he loved twisting knives.

And Dan Swardstrom—to hell with you for denying what has been mine for over seven years. This race does not belong to you. It's not Dan Week! It's Race Week. It's bigger than you. You are not the victor today, and in my eyes, you never were, you rotten scoundrel. Eat it, Danny. Eat anything you want! Including your own heart!

Kai tightened his bowtie one last time and stared at the mirror until the poor bastard looking at him blinked.

CHAPTER 74

Martina massaged her belly and looked off into the Salish Sea. The horizon was draped in twilight and she decided that her dress, a strapless, silk evening gown, matched the color of the edge of the darkness.

She packed it just in case.

It wasn't that she believed Dan would lose; she just believed that Kai wanted it more this year. Her career as an executive officer for Amazon had taught her to weigh her options, and if possible, when there was no consequence, to plan for the best and worst-case scenarios.

She was also a German.

But she was unsure how Dan would take it, packing a fancy dress for Race Week, and now that the fates had spoken, her decision was correct.

"Who was that?" she asked.

Dan put his phone away.

"Rigby," he said.

He was removing the bowtie she'd bought for him.

"What does he want?"

"He wants to save our asses," he said, peeling off his jacket.

CHAPTER 75

Kevin Jonson stood atop Wabash rock watching the flooding tide whirl into the shape of a galaxy. From the rock, he could see it move as a single unit: bits of wood, foam, lost buoys. On the edge of the gyre was the whale, bathed in the warmth of the delta, it's mass too ample to spin into the circle. Instinctively, the great beast used its last bit of energy to move to the center, to keep from being slung ashore. This only caused it to roll onto its side where, just below its pectoral fin, he could see the wound he'd caused, still bleeding.

He was a hero, but he felt utterly alone.

The tide had taken hold of the beast, keeping it out of the straits to wash ashore on county land. The creature would not be delivered by the strong currents of the Salish sea, instead, it would land here, rotting until government scientist dissected it, who would determine that it had not died of natural causes. This he knew would spark debate, and the spectacle would become the foundation of criticism.

He longed for the time when such a feat was accomplished by the entire tribe. Once the whale was killed, a crewmember would enter the water and cut a hole through the bottom and top of the whale's jaw, to which a towline and float were attached. Theses floats were made from the hides of seals, clubbed by warriors who hunted them in dark caves with torches tied into their hair. After the whale's mouth had been sewed shut, water could not enter it and it was towed to shore by the paddlers who'd chased it down. It would be received by the elders, who would bless it with songs.

The phone rang.

"Yes?"

It was his father.

"How are the tides?" he asked.

"Not good," Kevin Jonson said.

"It's not in Sacred Cove, is it?"

Kevin Jonson didn't answer.

"Son, you did a great thing. The elders will be proud and mother has already begun making a new song and dance for the family."

Kevin Jonson didn't speak. He didn't want to hear another song in a gym.

"We will perform it at powwow, and we'll roast a pig and pretend it is the whale. No one will know the real story but us Makah."

Kevin looked out once again at the whale.

It had landed.

It was time to bless it himself.

Alone.

"Hey son, hang on. Polly is coming. Holy hell. She's running. Looks like she has something important to say."

Kevin Jonson froze.

Though there were no chiefs in Makah life, Polly was an elder with much authority. Her son was the warrior who pulled the trigger back in the nineties when the tribe last tasted whale. She also had many songs and dances to share at lodge and she managed the tribal museum.

"Son, she says the writer fellow just pulled up to Washburn's with two school busses. Imagine that. You know the guy they call Rigby?"

"Yes," Kevin Jonson said. "The cook with the hot girlfriend."

CHAPTER 76

Swarar's cove is at the bottom of a chasm, the writer thought: a dystonic passageway, fastened in the world of Alice and Wonderland, through a rabbit hole and straight into the heart of Cascadia. On the other side, there existed a breach, and through it, an unbroken thread of time stretching from deep inside. It was an unknowable chasm, threaded by events, lined up across the greenery, circling out until it reached an ancient, milky-white, mile-high glacier.

Today, the glacier has been eroded into rivers, emptied into the sea and can only be seen through the tiny, magical, keyhole of the moment.

The elders were here; surrounding the beast, dressed in traditional cedar-bark kilts and flowing capes and dresses adjourned with polished olivine shells that rattled when they swayed, or popped, or skipped. So soft was the sewed cedar, gentle katabatic winds of eve played with the frills on their edges. The elders stood shoulder-to-shoulder, singing in their ancient tongue. A woeful, wispy language: a song that welcomed the whale to its willful passing, a heaven-sent prayer and blessing.

The writer stepped quietly through the chasm, lined in cedar and exotic shrubs and unbroken webs. There is a mist in the trees. Mystery. He hears the singing. A song that he recognizes as Makah, but it is sung with an exhilaration and urgency he doesn't remember hearing at lodge. The drum is steady. It is precise, but it is also captured in the trees and branches, kept a bay: a secret.

He pauses; closes his eyes. Waits. The sound becomes light: images he does not understand. The night has caught them and for a moment, he feels on his skin what the purpose of the drums, the incense to his senses, the smell of salt and blood, the wayward prayers and chants welcoming the whale's spirit.

"Are you sure this is the place?" Dan said.

The writer knows this is the place. He knows the drums.

"Yes," he said.

"What if they're pissed? What if they don't want us here?"

"We brought them here, remember?"

"I know," Dan said, removing a spider web from his face. "But, this sounds like some serious shit."

It did sound serious.

The writer had only seen the Makah whale dance in theater, on the floor of a new gymnasium, a building the Office of Indian Affairs approved two years ago along with a new jetty out to Waadah Island. They only performed it when an elder died, on account it was their most precious song, and to perform it without harvesting a whale made it superfluous and non-genuine. So they saved it. They saved it for death and powwows and sometimes a special birth like the time Polly was blessed by her nineteenth grandchild, a tribal record. But it had not been sung in front of a whale for nearly a generation, not since the troubles that came with asserting their treaty rights back in the nineties, when the world lined up pro Makah or anti Makah. Their controversial harvesting of a grey whale back then was spectacle.

This was real.

This was how it was supposed to be.

Their voices sank into the song, falling downward, spiraling back in time to the days on Neah Bay hidden by fog and the Olympic mountains, dappled in holy light, blessings, food and subsistence.

Three thousand years ago, the Makah lived here in villages, dwelling in large longhouses made from red cedar. Cedar roots were used in basket making. Whole trees were carved out to make canoes to hunt seals, gray whales and humpback whales. Much of their food came from the ocean: whale, seal, fish, and a bounty of shellfish. Women gathered nuts, berries and edible plants. And all of it, every leaf, and every bone, and every tradition, handed down by elders through song and oral tradition. The power of love. The power of people.

The writer begins to walk again, but every footfall is a step into the past. The drums sing with the elders, in reverse. The language is untangling. The dance moves backwards.

Dan's warnings are mushed: reversed they are encouragement.

"Do you want this whale to disappear or not?" The writer whispers.

Dan doesn't answer. He points.

"There," he said.

It is a beast; a landed, crashed submarine. Its lines are fusiform by nature, sleek and regal, cut for the sea. There is one fin reaching out, erect, where a child is standing, measuring her height against the appendage. The Makah are busy with oars and ropes, working with the beat of the drum to pull it further ashore. There are open wounds; the color of steak; medium rare, the color of the edge of night, the instant the sun has fallen over the chasm at Strawberry Hill.

The writer inhales the pungent incense, allowing it deep into his senses. The incense changes his consciousness: he sees the sun setting in reverse: it is rising, and yesterday is waiting for him like a promised kissed on the breast of a new day. He turns to whale, its eye of is being removed. In the fog and the smoke, it is being cut from the beast in retrospect: a portion of flesh placed back into the socket. He sees flesh being heaved off brawny shoulders and gently placed back onto ribs, and vertebrae. The knife lacerations are replaced with smooth, black, flawless skin. Pink flesh is slowly disappearing. The Makah are singing. Chanting. The sky lights up, washing away stars in a bleached light. They all disappear, every star except Venus, waiting in the corner, waiting on the edge, just beyond the skyline.

The writer moves at the whale. He is carrying a carefully carved, squared-off wedge of flesh on his shoulder. He is walking backwards, with ease, even in the shadows cast by the cedar. Each step is sure; he lifts his foot, it rolls off the heel, ends at his toes. Another step, backwards: toe-heel, toe-heal. A branch pops under his foot, and he feels the fibers come together. Blood . . . light pink, and warm, moves from his body and out of his soaked clothes and into to the flesh he is carrying. The warmth leaves his skin. The smell of salt leaves his nose. He carefully sets the flesh onto the animal: a cavity near its heart, along the seventh and eighth rib. There, he can see the pericardium, threaded with bulging veins—the protective tissue covering the mighty heart of the beast. He places the flesh onto the seventh rib and it sinks into the cavity and comes alive before his eyes. Steam is leaving the cool air, absorbed back into the cuts that are closing; sewed together by time and the long blades of the elders and their warrior sons and daughters and cousins and friends.

The writer stands before the great whale. He can hear its heart beating. A father is helping his daughter with a large blade cut into the head; a wound opens, crimson and wet. The elders are dancing. They raise their arms in tribute, calling for grace and tenderness and bounty and love to fall over the land and the sea, to protect the canoes, to keep their harbor safe, to bless the tribe, to fall in love, to be in love, to wish and hope for love, to win for love, to fight for it, live for it, grasp it, sink into it, drown in it, give it. The noble smell of burning cedar lingers. A heavy smoke. Magic. Some of the meat is already being roasted on cedar planks. In reverse, the smokes from the flames are returning life into the flesh. The writer's hunger is leaving and his thirst is quenched. He walks toward the open wound, following the smell of salt. In the flesh there is a form. He draws nearer. A voice is whispering in his ear. Singing? Chanting? Is it in his own head? He studies the form.

A body.

It is him, sleeping in the flesh.

The girl helping her father carve meat from the head sets down her blade. She and the writer are the only people who can see the aberration. She moves toward the writer, motions for him to kneel and whispers into his ear.

"Repair the pieces of your broken heart," the child says. "Pick up those shards that remind you of success—her strength, her complexity—and leave on the ground what did not allow her to be whole with you—her depth, her edges, her dimensionless emotions." The girl matures into a woman, blossoming, mellowing, and then aging into a gnostic elder before his eyes. "Remember," she says in an ancient voice, "few have the strength to endure the act of love. For to love means to risk all, to give another not only the path to your heart and soul but also the chance to reject any part of your path. To travel together requires a sacrifice many can never make, so they wander lost, alone, safe. You were brave to suffer her. As will be many more. You will heal. This cedar is pure. Now awake! And step away from this corpse."

CHAPTER 77

Tupac arrived. It was dead-ass party, but they were lookin' sharp as a motha-fucka. They were late, of course. But who the fuck cared? No one was here. You know your party ain't shit when the first mutha fucka's to arrive is yo' token-ass-black friends.

"Skipper, where's everybody at?" Leroy said, tipping his glass into the stream of a champagne fountain.

"They must be playing it cool?"

"Cooler than us?"

"Hell no," they bumped chest and fixed each other's bowtie.

Kai appeared from behind a tower of seafood on the buffet table.

"I see you dressed for the occasion," he said eating some type of tentacle. "You look like a gentleman."

"You mean a white-man, you racist motha-fucka."

"Hey, cut me some slack, slick bra'. I'm Tai, I know your struggle, too."

"Yeah, I guess you do," the skipper said taking in the posh setting. "I'm not tryin' to hate." He allowed the little man to jump up and chest bump him. "Congratulations on your victory and shit, you mad bastard. You handed Danny boy his nuts, today."

"Yes I did."

The skipper filled his glass with champagne.

"You like octopus?"

"I don't eat that shit."

"Oysters?"

"Not unless them mutha' fucker are fried in cornmeal," the skipper said and changed the subject. "Say, Kai. What was the business at the end, today?"

"Yeah, what the fuck?" Leroy said. "Did Danny choke?"

Kai thought a moment, and there was doubt in his eyes as he tried to explain.

"We were beating him fair and square," he said. "Then he came on strong. I thought he'd catch me on the run, but he hit something in the water, maybe a log."

"Must have been one hell of a log," the skipper said. "It stopped Danny cold, like he had a reverse gear."

"His bad luck," Kai said.

"Yes indeed," the skipper said, taking in the sight of the pit-girl at the door. She was on the arm of Davey and tucked into just the right kind of dress: a vivid scarlet number with a lace upper body revealing her bare upper back, shoulders and sides. She winked at his crew and made her way over to the fountain. "One man's misfortune is another man's gains."

"Yes," Kai said. "A toast, to Swardstrom's misfortune."

The skipper didn't raise his glass and neither did his crew.

"What time is your award ceremony?" the skipper said.

"You're trying to skip out early," Kai accused.

"Well, shit. I did hear there's a little party going on over at Bat Out of Hell afterwards," the skipper said. "Rhett was let out of the hospital but he's on bed rest now."

"A party on a fucking boat?" Kai said adjusting his cufflinks. "That old bastard should stop living on that thing. It's a race boat, not a god damned bachelor pad."

The skipper adjusted his cufflinks, too.

"We gonna tie up next to them. They's cookin' some skrimp. We're gonna pop out and see how he's doin'. Check in on Ivonne, too. She if she needs any of our assistance."

"No," Kai said. "We can't have a party without black people. Are you crazy?"

"Yeah, I hear that," the skipper said. "But we gonna bounce after they give your captain-Ahab-ass what you been trying to harpoon since I first set my eyes on you, know what I'm sayin'?"

"Fine," Kai said. "And just a little help to my brotha', so you know, it's pronounced 'shrimp' without the 'k'."

"Fuck you, man," the skipper said. "That's how my auntie Evelyn it, and her auntie, all the way back to the to the Jefferson administration. So that's how I say it."

CHAPTER 78

Ortun tasted the oysters. They were sweet and musty. Perfect. But they only reproduced the effect of eternal pleasure, wrapped in light and warmth, for an instant. Not that an instant couldn't be forever. He could taste the salt rollicking on his tongue but he knew it would leave, absorbed into his consciousness, measured for preference, delight and then it would squirm into the past until the next delicious oyster was devoured. How long could this go on? How did normal people trick themselves into believing that every day was new?

Even the sting of losing, and the weak ache he felt in the pit of his stomach would squirm away, packed against his wish to live on the blade of tomorrow, the pain of yesterday day.

"You want an oyster?" he asked Christopher.

"No," he said adjusting his bowtie. "I want to see the race boats."

"The race is over," Ortun said. "Tomorrow they will sail away for another race to win, or lose, or DNF."

Christopher mad a sad face.

"I know," Ortun said, sliding another oyster into his mouth. "Tedious, isn't it?"

He fixed the little man's bowtie, adjusted his cummerbund and looked up at the spectacular chandelier. It was the centerpiece of a grandiose room without windows, curved archways and vaulted ceilings: rosy-warm crystals shinning like a handful of stars holding onto each other in a vast, consuming darkness. Ortun wished that he could be the chandelier, ever and ever casting light into darkness.

Kai greeted arriving sailors and dignitaries with a glass of champagne in hand, the sparkling spectacle presiding with a sovereign eye.

The pit-girl caught Ortun's starry eyes.

"Don't be sore," she said, slapping him on the back. "Dan's gonna win again."

Ortun frowned. He looked away from the chandelier.

"He didn't lose today."

"No?" she said. "That trophy disagrees with you."

"I don't mean the race," Ortun said. He wanted to tell her about the whale, but he knew it would be unbelievable. An accident. An illusion. The entire scene was surreal. No one onboard mentioned the situation, not even Bonesteel. "Today, I think he's had a taste of something better than racing a boat."

"Like what," she scoffed.

Ortun looked up at the chandelier again. The crystals were glimmering, winking at him.

"Happiness," he said with watery eyes.

"You don't mean being a father, do you?"

"No," he said.

"Then what are you saying? Nothing makes him happier than being on a boat, you know that. If he thinks he can leave all this without regret, he's headed into the worst kind of heartache."

Ortun decided not to engage. The pit-girl had already decided to be threatened by Dan's evolution, and changing her mind would be like pulling a shoe out of a shark.

"I heard one of the suits hired you to sail in worlds," he said.

The pit-girl curtsied. She'd raced for Kai during Race Week, and crossed the line the way that a preacher does when he decides to become a pedophile.

"Word gets around fast," she said. "Esther will be proud."

Ortun smiled.

"It suits you," he said, and thought to slapping her on the deck of Nefarious. How she had broken him, reduced his will to viciousness. It was her way: to pull her opponent into the mud so that both of you were dirty.

"Imagine me a pro!" she said. "I leave for Australia in two weeks!"

Ortun looked for the writer.

"What about Rigby?"

"I haven't told him yet," she said, pretending to be bashful.

Ortun raised his eyebrow.

"What?" she demanded.

Ortun though for a moment, and took a deep dramatic breath.

"Rigby is a romantic," he said. "And you don't know the two most important rules when it comes to romantics."

"I don't like rules, Ortun. You know that," she said. "But humor me."

Ortun looked up at the beautiful chandelier again. He couldn't see the stars, or the magic, or the moody spell it threw into the void.

"Rule one," he said. "Don't fall in love with a romantic."

"And rule number two?"

"Don't break their heart."

The pit-girl was bemused by the accusation, and then she was stupefied. She winched at the disapproval she saw in his eyes and he thought about how it wasn't so long ago that he had nearly fallen for her. But he could detect her ability to slip out of emotional constraints, and therefore her ability to empathize, and in doing so, removed from her conscience the soul of her lovers as easily as a mistress slips from her black leather boots. Sentiment was for suckers, her friend Esther had told her, and she repeated again and again, a means to manipulate and to be manipulated. The pit-girl normally avoided sentimental fools like Rigby, and aimed to be a woman lost in her own wayward love, relishing the new, unconquered corners of her lover's heart as she explored their cockles with a butterfly net and a machete. But, the instant she detected intimacy, it was time to explore a wild new place.

"When it comes to love," she said. "I tend to go with my imagination."

"You can't depend on your imagination," he told the chandelier instead of her. "Not when your eyes are out of focus."

She looked up at the chandelier.

"Ortun?" she asked. "Are you ok?"

"A man may imagine things that are false," he said, "but he can only understand things that are true."

"And where's the romance in that?"

"Vulnerability is the essence of romance."

"I think your blood sugar is low," she said, not understanding what was so interesting in the lights, and why no one was particularly happy to see her at the party. "And where is Dan? He better not be sulking."

Chapter 79

Edmund downed his heart pills and chased them with a shot of Jameson from his flask. He grimaced and waited for the tightness in his chest to wither; waited for it to be swallowed up in the sound of clinking glasses and polite chatter which soothed his stomach like milk and scotch. When the pain left, he took two deep breaths and proudly scanned the crowd of sailors dressed in their formals.

Race Week was almost over.

One near-death.

Two smashed hulls.

Three jailed sailors.

All par for the course, but tonight is when the real troubles began.

The party at the end of the race was the crown jewel of fuck-ups, where these assholes blew off steam the way a broken boiler blew up a church. There was just no denying it. Dan's party had to be stopped. The ol' boy would understand. There was just too much at stake. Sure he called it tight enough for Kai to stay close, maybe even win. But the race needed to evolve. Race Week was the only course not taken serious in the Northwest corridor, primarily due to Dan's sophomoric party that inspired every dumb-ass to register so that they could dress up in togas and pretend they were in college again, assuming they didn't drop out or even knew how to spell the word university. Dan would understand. He loved the course more than anyone. Almost as much as he loved to party.

And look! They were behaving like real human beings for once, and if he squinted his eyes, let the chandelier's light cast a spell, it all looked kind 'a normal. No goats. No hookers. No orgies. He'd lost the virginity of two daughters at Race Week. Lost the trust of a wife. Lost the use of sixty-percent of a liver. It was time to pump the brakes, even if it was required that he help Kai win. And so far, it was working. Mercy to god, the entire thing stayed together like a blueberry-ginger pie—a dessert that only tasted good if it was cooked by a baker who'd mastered every ingredient. Even Bonesteel was on his best behavior, laughing quietly with a glass of champagne in his hand like a real gent.

"These bubbles' make my nose feel like it's having a lady orgasm," he was telling Drunk Bob.

"You like getting banged in the nose, then?"

"Don't be a tizzy-devil, mate. Talk like that with your mum, eh?"

"I don't like drinks that tickle my nose," Drunk Bob said. "I need something harder."

"Champs only mate. In case you brought a flask."

Of course there was tension. These were the saltiest men and women that have ever been cooked out of bone; a stew of testosterone and hardboiled ovaries sautéed in cheap, Trader Joe's bourbon. When the stew cooked on the stove, it smelled like a boiling mop after it'd been used to clean up the floor of a dirty picture show.

Edmund handed his flask over to Drunk Bob.

"Easy does it," Edmund said. "Just hold on until after the award ceremony. Then we'll duck out and head over to Rhett's place."

They'd need to blow off a little steam. Yes, they did. After a week of racing, they deserved it. So long as it didn't get out of hand. A party on one boat, he calculated, could not provide the inertia one needed for an orgy. And good luck trying to get a goat onboard to roast. No. There would be no animals roasted this year, not unless you counted T-Bone steaks and pork-chops, oysters and shrimp, and you'd be a real asshole if you did.

"I don't think I can hold on," Drunk Bob said. "I think I might throw a chair."

"No. Don't do that."

"I think he might, Judge," Bonesteel said. "Look at him."

Edmund looked at Drunk Bob, who wasn't drunk.

"Shit," he said. "Where's Dan?"

"Don't ask about the skipper's whereabouts, eh?" Bonesteel said.

"What do you mean, sailor?"

"I mean what I said," Bonesteel said, a bit self-righteous. A new emotion for him.

"You tell your skipper to get his ass here pronto so that Kai can finish gloating. Tell him to do it before this fancy-bitch turns back into the whore her momma made her." Edmund snatched the flask away from Drunk Bob and took a long pull. He drank until his tongue was pulled into the little vacuum created when you sucked hard on it. Then he drank again. "This race won't survive another party like last year. It's time to grow the fuck up, sailors. Kai is the future. The suits are the future. Being a grow- ass man is the future. Race Week is bigger than one asshole and his asshole boat."

The pit-girl interrupted, glass in hand. "Don't be too hard on Dan," she said. "He's still trying to cope with his loss today."

Edmund assessed her. The dress made for attention. The makeup, wicked. The hand on her hip, sassy.

"I'll be as hard on him as I like," he said.

"If it wasn't for him, there wouldn't be a Race Week."

"That's hogwash," Edmund said.

"But it's not," she said.

Edmund stepped a little closer, so that only she could hear him. He'd heard about her jumping ship.

"Do you know the difference between a wolf and predator?"

"Why, no I don't Edmund. Tell me."

"A wolf hunts in a pack. It works with its crew to take down big game," he said. "It will even sacrifice its own needs to play in the game. It knows that, without the pack. There is no game."

"And a predator?"

"A predator works alone to accomplish its desire. It hunts alone. It feeds alone.

"I like the sound of this," she said.

"But when it can catch no game," he said, putting away his flask, "it finds a pack and tries to fit in. Stay's just behind the alpha until it gets what it wants."

The pit-girl was angered, but composed.

"You don't frighten me even a little," she said. "You wanted Dan to lose, to impress your suits."

"Yes," Edmund said. "I knew that tossing meat at Kai's boat would upset Dan. Get in his head. I only allowed you to sail on Jupiter to maybe take Race Week beyond Dan's juvenile imagination. But make no mistake. I used you the way that you use people to get what you want—only with a little less charm, and not so much tits."

"How does that make you any different from me, you bastard?"

"That's my point," he said. "It doesn't. So, don't stand there bad-mouthing your skipper when it was Dan who put you on a boat in the first place." He adjusted his belt, letting out some slack. "I don't know what he sees in you. Maybe you have a past. Maybe you're like a daughter or a kid sister. But if I were him, I'd be happy if you moved on to greener pastures."

The pit-girl slapped Edmund hard across the face, and then she smiled.

"I'm not a predator, you fool," she said. "I'm a lady."

Edmond excused himself, digging in his pocket for more pills. More people were arriving and the mood was changing. It was the mood of a feral bull lazing out to pasture, ready to fuck a cow, a fence post, and a farmer's wife. Its black eyes narrowing on sultry shapes, its nostrils flaring at the smell of sex and the need for cocaine or ecstasy or whatever the hell these fools were into these days. The more they drank, the more of their briny hormones cut into the dank, Whidbey night. He'd seen it before. And this was not the place to let their commotions out of the bag. Just ask the owners of the Alameda Yacht Club, aristocrats who enacted a lifetime ban on anyone known to have sailed on, or stepped foot on any boat previously registered with Whidbey Island Race Week. The proclamation was announced in a full-page ad in the Yachting Chronicles, where they listed every infraction, including "the leaving of human excrement" in a punch bowl.

"Ortun," Edmund said, rubbing the sting out of his cheek. "Where the hell is your skipper?"

The freak was staring at the celling like he was in the goddamned Sistine Chapel.   "He is cooking whale my favorite way, bone-in, on the grill," Ortun said. "Stuffed with sliced lemons and herb sprigs, brushed with its own oil, and cooked over hot cedar coals."

Edmund grimaced.

"You need an insulin shot, son," he said.

Edmond shook his head grimly and stepped onto the stage. He sucked in some air and barked into a dead microphone, but his voice could still be heard in the back of the room, where the crew of Roanoke and Cherish were drinking from a bottle of rum. The skipper of Cherish was trying to lead a sea shanty, but there wasn't enough liquor in the crew—not yet.

"Listen up you harlots, bastards and son's a' bitches, by which I mean every one of you." He wagged his finger at the crowd. "I've known most of you since you first stepped foot on one of my boats. And yes, Race Week is supposed to be fun—but also respectable, do you hear me? Now listen. This is our opportunity to show some class, which has been sorely lacking around here."

Someone booed and he eyed them until they withered.

"Now, I see that some of you brought your own bottles. That's just my point. Not classy."

"But Edmund, I seen you been drinkin' out of a flask tonight."

"A flask is classy, you imbecile."

"That ain't hardly classy."

The crowd began gathering around the stage, looking like a herd of steer. They accepted his chastising, but he knew it was only because they weren't drunk yet.

"What's this about you calling a tight race today so the suits could see Dan loose."

"Now come on Roger, you know that ain't the truth. Ol' Edmund here always calls it tight."

"This was the tightest I ever seen," the main sail of Artemis said. "Hell, I ain't been in nothing that tight since prom night."

The sailors cheered.

"Now listen," Edmund said. "You're being ridiculous. I don't have nothing against Dan and his crew—even if I know it was them that took that took a dump in a punch bowl a few years back. I don't judge a race like that. But you assholes gotta grow up sometime. This race is becoming known for its parties and not sailing."

"But you met all your wives here, Edmund."

"That I did," he said. "But that's another story, ain't it?"

Some of the suits entered the room. They eyed the herd of steer and then Edmund, who smiled at them like a carnival barker.

"Now why don't we hear from this year's winner, Kai Kraiputra, skipper of Jupiter." He led the steer in a chorus of pitiful applause and handed the microphone to Kai. "Keep it short," he said. "Real short."

Chapter 80

It was about time.

The sooner he put the trophy in his hands, the sooner he could close this party down. No way he was going to pay for another round of appetizers, for Christ-sake, these people didn't even know that the caviar was from Portland. It was like feeding a living trashcan.

One thing was missing.

Dan.

Where was he?

Of course he wouldn't show. Coward. He didn't even have the common decency to show up and lose like a man.

All the better.

"I'd like to thank you all for fighting your best today on the water. It is such an honor to have my name on this esteemed trophy. I am humbled that you would celebrate with my crew and me. I would like to thank my opponent for running such a fair and competitive campaign against me, even though he doesn't have the balls to be here."

The crowd began to grumble.

 "I would also like to thank the many volunteers who worked tirelessly to help us achieve this accomplishment. I would also like to thank my family and friends for their unending support, my fraternity brothers, and the baristas at the local coffee house who know exactly how to make Ceylon tea the way my mother made it back home."

The crowd of sailors watched him raise the trophy over his head. They were stunned that it wasn't Dan.

There was more grumbling. Footsteps across the stage. A black man took the microphone.

"Yo Kai, I'm really happy for you," the skipper of Tupac said. "I'll let you finish, but everybody up in here knows that Dan is one of the best sailors of all time."

The crowd cheered.

"And you ya'll know that Edmund didn't call that foul today so that this phony could win this shit here today, know what I'm sayin'? When was the last time an area judge let crew jump ship just before a race? Rule seven, paragraph thirteen clearly states 'a crewmember wishing to transfer must notify the committee twenty-four hours in advance". It ain't been that long. That's some shit right there. And yo, I don't know if you mutha' fuckas' know it, but this caviar is from Portland!"

The crowd exploded.

Someone threw a chair.

A bottle broke.

"Now give me that trophy—we ain't punks. And this race ain't about pomp and circumstance, Kai. It's about liquor and bitches! Always has been. Always will be."

Kai tried to hold on to the trophy, but Jabari was too strong. He took it and threw it out into the crowd where his crew caught the prize.

"D-Money, take that shit over to Dan."

"Aye, aye skipper."

Chapter 81

Dan drank a bit of whiskey and sat down in the seat of his car. He sighed and looked out of the window to see if he could spy any boats, but the water was dark. Surely, the fleet had returned to the marina by now. Across the bay, he could still make out the Makah, some of them working with flash lights, but many of them were wearing small torches, tied up into their jet-black hair, finishing the last steps of dismantling the beast.

The trees were closed in around the bay, keeping the ceremony an awe-inspiring secret, harbored in darkness. He felt detached from it all. Not in a morose way. More mellow than anything. Maybe even a little sentimental. Tonight, there was something in the stars. Something that crashed him into the whale, something that wanted to see the magic happen. Was it possible that his entire life had been aimed at this moment? All the sweat and salt-stinging waves that lashed him, the cut under his eye and the fight that caused it, was it all a small part of how the magic worked? Foolishly, he'd believed that he oversaw his fate, used his power to forge the very bones in his body, and used the bones to walk safely over the embers of time. But this was arrogance. It reminded him of the instant he'd seen the egg in his dream fall over the swollen waterfall, how far he was away from saving it, even though he didn't possess the power to stop its destiny.

The whale was small for a grey whale. A juvenile, who'd wandered too far from the protection of its herd, most likely chased into the Salish Sea by transient killer whales. Confused by the terrifying chase, it exhausted every muscle and found itself locked in Sacred Cove as a refuge. The tragedy of the whale, in his mind at least, was no different than a kill he'd watched on a nature show, where after separating the juvenile from its mother, the killer whales took turns beating it down. When they were finished with their sport, because the skin of the grey whale was too tough to penetrate, they removed the large tongue as a trophy to play with and a delicacy.

It was clear now that the whale wanted to die. It was relieved to give into the beauty of its death, a reprieve from terror as it was pushed through the hot gates of pain and suffering. When he had looked into its black eye from the deck, he wondered if in that moment, the thing knew its death was eminent. That its death was the reason it had been born. And Now, he wondered the same thing about himself. He wondered about sacrifice and loss. How there were infinite ways to sacrifice oneself and some of them required fearlessness. At times, it meant sacrificing everything you ever wished for, or every person you cherished. Sometimes it was only noshing your teeth through the disappointment of loss and wayward doubt. Keeping a stiff upper lip, win or lose. This did not lighten his mood. In fact, it was the cause of a new consciousness—one that crystallized the moment he saw the crimson blood mingling in the green, Salish Sea. Life is not a journey, he thought. It is a dance. And sometimes, it was a dangerous one at that.

The thought caused him to tear up a bit—what was one to make of a universe with such an expressed desire harm you, and all at once love life enough to allow you to exist? He looked out at the water, blurred his eyes and remembered a poem that Martina once read to him in bed. He mouthed aloud what he thought was the first verse.

I must go down to the seas again, to the lonely sea and the sky,
And all I ask is a tall ship and a star to steer her by,
And the wheel's kick and the wind's song and the white sail's shaking,
And a gray mist on the sea's face, and a gray dawn breaking.

Somewhere out there, in the cold green water were the remaining stanzas he couldn't remember.

Dan drank, then started the car and drove through the dark roads of Whidbey Island. The centerline guided him into town and the poem played in his head. A good poem was always there in the background, like hot blood coursing through your temples at night. He could see the grey mist on the sea's face, holding on to the horizon, running into the edge of time. He could hear the wind's song. Or wished to hear it.

He drove. He ignored the ache in his heart. He ignored the light on his phone, blinking since he started the car: a flood of taunts from skippers waiting their turn to berate him for losing to Kai. They'd accuse him of not having the guts to hand over the trophy. Man to man. Sailor to sailor. Of being a poor sport. Less than a gentleman. But in fact, now that it was done, losing was a relief: amnesty from karmic duty.

When he really thought about it, Race Week was always the same. June would roll around and he'd begin hydrating. He'd order two kegs of Elysian and send Ewan to pick them up in his van at the Tavern. He'd rent a home on the shores of Oak Harbor, a beige, sterile mansion cluttered with "Life's A Beach" towels, gnomes and dried starfish bookends. There would be enough rooms to house his crew and all their fuck-buddies. There would be a master bedroom far from the madness to house him and his fiancée.

He picked up the phone and called Martina.

"Is it done?" she asked.

"Yes," he said.

"Good boy."

Somehow, she'd been there through all the lunacy of it all, and done so without judging him. She was a patient woman who stayed his hand, mellowed him without smothering the flame he'd keep lighting, even while drunkenly, hopelessly crawling on his belly through beer bottles and condom wrappers scattered on the floor. She let him hear the pop of a sail, watch it instantly fill with air. She let him be innocence, every time he sailed. She let him believe the lie of sailing, that the energy to push a boat was free, and that on the water, a sailor was free.

"I can't wait to meet her."

"How do you know it's a girl, stupid?"

"Because I am a cursed man," he said.

He put away his phone.

In the marina, he gazed at Nefarious, aglow in the evening. It was his first love, but real love had come in the form of a freckled brunette with flawless skin.

There are countless beautiful women, but only a handful of them possessed the elegance required to stop it from looking ugly. Martina's beauty was understated, perhaps because she was disarmingly unaware of it. She did not require make-up; her skin was flawless. She did not require ornaments; her conscious was clean. She was all about simplicity, making things easy, helping those around her to relax and be happy. To be in her company was to feel that you were someone who deserved her attention, love and respect.

Dan spoke to her through the distance. I think I should have loved you presently, he told her across the darkness. And let you catch my eye in doubt and joy. I should have married you before the baby. Let you catch me with love, heavy on my heart. I should have let you take my heart sooner. Let you catch me before the water turned black in the night, where I could not see through the murky, silt and seed of those who would not have me love you. I would have caught your sighing, heaving breast. The taste of your lips. I'd have savored them. And laughed with you on my chest. I'd have fallen for your follies, willingly, my love.

In languid waves, images of Martina floated before him and his thoughts rode the emotions on a sea of nostalgia. It felt like doom. It felt like birth. It felt like the end of something sweet. It felt like the beginning of a new life.

He looked away from the boat for a time. He let the stars blur and warp—shifting, glittering diamonds caught in the night. He thought about his love of sand castles, standing tall for a time. The stars were caught in the same scenario: shinning for a time, then absorbed into darkness. Forever.

The writer came to mind. He sailed different seas, but they were both sailors by his estimations. He made sandcastles, too. Watched them erode. Dan was an empathetic man, but he had no time for romantic notions. The sea would take everything. At the end of the day, doe-eyed optimist who broke their own heart received the same dessert at the buffet. Like every good guest, if they were willing to eat the food at the great feast, then they needed to eat the cake, too. And like any good guest, when the feast was over, they needed be a good sport, put on their coat and leave.

Rigby met every half-witted, alpha-type Mac let herself be entertained by, but it was clear that he was a romantic. Dan saw it the moment they'd met. The poor bastard. There was no way of warning him. Mac was Hestia, daughter to Zeus, goddess of fire personified. And Rigby was Icarus, son of Daedalus who dared to fly too near the sun on wings of feathers and wax.

It was none of his business, but he liked the guy, and becoming friends was not convenient. But there were too many lonely nights on a ship, too many lonely bars for a sailor not to wander into. Too many cold nights in close quarters. Too many drinks. Too many halyards. It was only a matter of time. Every sailor new this. And every non-sailor who dated a sailor, did not.

Davey was a decent sailor, and a decent man. But watching him move in on Rigby's girl during rehearsal made him sick. They'd eye fuck between sets, and it threw him. It was like driving horny teenagers to prom, and never asked Davey to crew Nefarious again.

It was all to Rigby's great misfortune, but as fate would have it, the writer helped to save Race Week. Not only was it fortunate that he knew the Makah—who by now had carved the beast into small enough pieces to roast—but in working with him under the cover of cedar, fog and tribal drums, he came to realize that Rigby was truly possessed by the passion and adventure of love. Was willing martyr. Was fool for Mac. And yet, Dan knew that he had the same feelings for Martina. She would have his heart, forever.

He sauntered into the dark marina, slipped aboard Nefarious and pulled out a lawn chair.

"Where do you want to go, sweetie?" Martina said, appearing from the cabin.

"What do you mean?" Dan asked.

"You have a boat," she said. "The world is your oyster. You can go anywhere."

"Take me to the seas again," he said settling in, "to the lonely sea and the sky. And all I ask is a tall ship and a star to steer her by."

Martina smiled and started the motor. She drove Nefarious out of the marina and into the dark bay until the water smoothed. He gazed at stars. The gentle wind and splashing water lulling him into a pleasant dream.

And then, from across the bay, a bottle shattered.

Chapter 82

Bonesteel thought it was a little early to be smashing bottles, but what the hell? You can't stable a wildebeest, can you? The party had gone sour, and no one even cared enough to reserve the hookers at the Oak Harbor Parsonage. This was Race Week. Race. Party. Play. Get some ass and tits in your face.

What had gotten into them?

"Time to light a baker's dozen!" he shouted, and threw another bottle.

The crowd of sailors cheered. They were drunk, but not from whiskey or rum, but from champagne, which as everyone knew, was a mean kind of drunk. The night was young. Not even ten o'clock.

Bonesteel took hold of a fire extinguisher and emptied it on the crew of Avalanche, who danced in the cold carbon dioxide.

"You stinky boys need a shower!"

"We need rum."

"I need rum," he said. "Where are you headed?"

"Nefarious, to give Dan his trophy. "

"Right! He deserves it after that mongrel race."

"He has rum," they said.

"He has the clap, too," Bonesteel said. "Not fit for a goat."

"Is he roasting goat this year?"

"Na," Bonesteel said. "I brought one, but let I let 'em go after that pissy end."

"Why do I smell barbecue?" a sailor said.

"Must be shrimp Rhett's cookin'" another said.

"Na, mate." Bonesteel said taking a whiff. The entire bay was smothered in the sweet perfume of cedar and salty meat. "Smells like mammal, though. Sea mammal, if you ask me."

"You're crazy as fuck, Bonesteel."

Bonesteel hosed the men down again, emptying the extinguisher and then he threw the container through the window of a second-hand store. The glass exploded and the sailors ran away.

Bonesteel stayed. He stayed because, after the window shattered, a mannequin in a wedding dress fell into the street.
He picked her up.

"A right, lass," he said. "The love of my life!" He kissed the dummy on the lips and stroked her hair. "I will name her Agatha," he told the empty street. "After me favorite auntie from Bloemfontein." He rocked her gently and considered her eyes and sang a song that Ortun once sang under the rum tent. It had been playing in his head all evening.

I have a pact with the shadows.
So I can be seen in your dark corners and alleys.
I follow you because you are the plight.
And I will let you carry me, if I can catch you in the light.

He sang it to her quietly at first, but then, as he remembered the words, he slowed down and whispered in into her plastic ear.

Ney, the night.
To add salt to your soul.
And sugar to your spice.
Let you see my horns and many thorns.
So that I may watch you fall.
The sight of every fright.
Not in darkness.
Only light.

He looked deeply into her marbled eyes, the color of ocean green. He was bedazzled. They were the color of a day at sea, lost in the azure and darkness found only at the edge of the horizon. In the storefront window, her plastic skin had been sun-bleached and her hair was the color of rust, but her glassy eyes stayed true.

I love when you go maniac.
Because love is love in whatever form it knows.
No norms.
To join their soul unto death.

Through the eyes, love attains the heart. And these peepers made him wish that she were real. So real. So fixed. They told stories, a menagerie of animal lust and provocation. He could feel it in his bones. The men were gone now, and in a moment of weakness, he stood her, and took to his knee.

I wish for you to see me.
Creating new paintings, memories...
Love touching my face.
Lurking in the shadows.
A man without a place.

Though they were unflinching, he could see his own reflection in them, lit by a sulfur-fused streetlight. Agatha showed him her darken soul, bleached in time, and soaked in his own wishes for a fallen angel, left on earth to watch without judgment, the torment that the human heart can endure. Aloof. She'd seen the parades through Main Street. All the humans pretending to not be vulnerable. Lost and abandoned.

But she knew the truth was only a seed, set to live under the hot soil after a bushfire. Her eyes gave him the proof that he needed. The proof that a lover bleeds. It was a revelation. She'd been propped up in the store window, watching the parade. Watching those legionnaires march two by four as they marched off to war. She didn't care what they were made of. Didn't care that they were made of blood. Yes, she was made of plastic—but plastic was only a rearrangement of carbon, and carbon was exactly what he was made of.

Closer and closer.

Learning how many steps.

Pacing.

Coiled.

Aiming.

For the heart.

"Hey, buddy?" a cop said getting out of his car. "Where the hell did you get that mannequin?"

"If you're referring to me wife," Bonesteel said. "You better be ready to eat some shit."

"I'm not ready for that at all," the cop said removing his handcuffs. "How's about I cuff you to that bitch and put you in the county jail?"

The cop took out his baton.

"Maybe if you'd been in a real fight copper, you wouldn't be so keen for another."

Bonesteel tore his shirt from his body and howled into the moonlit night

The cocaine was starting to kick in. He felt great. A fight. Some more liquor. Some more cocaine. Kick this cop's ass, then figure out how to make love to a plastic doll. A Great night on all accounts.

"You're the drunkest sailor I've ever saw," the cop said.

"You know what mate?" Bonesteel told him, and flashed his guns. He Kissed them and then his plastic wife. "You're the softest copper I ever saw."

"What boat are you headed to tonight?"

"Nefarious!" Bonesteel said.

"Of course," the cop said.

Chapter 83

Ivonne tucked the blanket under her love. Though he would soon be fit as a bull, she needed him to be weak. Just for now. Just for her. This is what lovers did for one another. They were vulnerable. In times of strength and weakness, they had the courage to be authentic. It was what she loved about Rhett. Though he put up a fight, he knew the rules.

"Stop it darling," Rhett said. "I'm not going to die."

"You shut up husband, and let me take care of you." She poured him two fingers of whiskey for medicinal purposes and made him finish it.

"I can't drink this Trader Joe's crap."

"You know I would never buy you that."

"What is it?"

"Glenmorangie."

It was their bottle of Glenmorangie Pride 1981, reserved only for victory.

"Why are we drinking this?" he swallowed. "It's a hundred dollars a shot."

"Don't be dense," she drank. "It is a victory that you are alive today."

Lace looked at his beautiful wife. He almost became teary eyed, but knew she'd like it too much. Life was sweet. Life was good. She really loved him for who he was and not his boat, or the lifestyle he could afford. Ivonne was a rare gem in a slag of rough-edged women who would settle for nothing less than a soul mate.

"Pour me another," he said. "And start the motor."

"Where are we to sail in the night, my love?" she asked.

"We'll raft up to Nefarious," he said. "Console Danny boy."

"My love," she said and kissed him on the cheek. "Surely, Dan is at the award ceremony."

"I doubt it," Rhett said. "If I know Dan, he's found a way to avoid it."

Rhett finished his drink.

Ivonne launched Bat out of Hell and steered her to the center of Oak Harbor where she spotted the navigation lights of Nefarious. She called Dan on the radio.

"S.V. Nefarious," she said. "Prepare to be boarded."

She saw Danny sitting on the deck.

"I'm afraid that Dan is not much in the mood for a raft up, tonight." Martina said.

"Tell that sorry puppy that we have Glenmorangie."

"Aye aye," Martina said. "Permission granted."

Ivonne turned Bat out of Hell astern so that her port side drifted toward Nefarious in the black water and then cut the motor. The world went silent and the two boats eased together as gentle as sleepy lovers.

"Are you feeling sorry for yourself, skipper?" she called out to him on the deck.

"I'm no good at losing."

"Bull crap," she said, and threw him a line. "You're the best loser I ever saw."

She lowered the bitch bumpers one at a time and waited for them to catch.

"That Glenmorangie better be older than you, darlin'."

"You wouldn't know the difference if it was old enough for prom."

"Trust me," he said cinching her line. "I'm too old for prom." He looked up and saw her smiling at him. "And besides, every prom comes to an end."

"Not if you live in the moment, Danny," Ivonne said. "Permission to come aboard." She kissed him on the cheek, as was the tradition during a raft up.

"Permission granted."

They hugged.

"Where is that old bastard?"

"I tied him to the cockpit."

Martina appeared with two crystal glasses.

"I hear there's Glenmorangie?" she said. "What's the occasion?"

"Yes dear," Ivonne said, presenting their fancy dresses. "Just look at us! It's prom night!"

Martina laughed.

"Yes, it would appear so," she said. "I think I will have just one tiny-tiny sip. That should be enough to acclimate Bullet for a sailor's life."

"Bullet?"

"Our daughter," Dan said. "But, so you know. This is not the first time I knocked up a prom date."

Ivonne filled the glasses. One she poured with a finger and the others, four.

"Dan and I will drink for Bullet," she said. "You may have one tiny sip, but then I make you drink my famous natal nectar. It is made with panther piss. I have some onboard for Rhett's sciatica. It will give your daughter the ability to fight off predators like the men we are in love with." She drank her Glenmorangie and let the grubby softness catch fire in her mouth. It burned a path down her esophagus, splitting her neatly into two pieces. When it cooled, she whispered. "What is it about scotch? How it gets into me, stings me, and by the time it disappears, everything is better?"

Chapter 84

Dan looked out at the water. More boats were headed their way. He tried to clear his thoughts; stared into the torpid water. But the idea kept nagging him. Was this the end of something good, or the beginning of something better? He did not know for sure but the boats kept approaching and one by one. They lined up port to starboard and tied themselves together in a string of pearls.

A new party had begun. Quietly at first. A secluded soiree that moved from boat to boat. A good party is an act of intimacy, the best ones being held in a kitchen. During a raft up, each skipper maintained a different decorum and their boat became an intimate affair. If you were fit enough, and not drunk enough to step over the web of halyards and lines, you could choose the energy level you wished. Some of the sailors made their way to every boat. Some stayed put.

Dan made his way to Tupac, where the crew presented him the stolen trophy.

"This shit belongs to you," the skipper told him.

When he refused, the sailors chastised him. LaPrell found a bottle of Shiraz and poured it into the trophy. They made Dan drink, and when he did, they cheered.

The skipper threw his arm around him.

"You see Dan, this week ain't about you," he said. "You come off like it never was. That's why people like you."

Dan took the trophy and held it above his head. The Shiraz, the Glenmorangie and wine was starting to crowd down onto the bitter edge he felt and made room for sweet sentiments in growing in his heart.

I must down go to the seas again, for the call of the running tide
Is a wild call and a clear call that may not be denied;
And all I ask is a windy day with the white clouds flying,
And the flung spray and the blown spume, and the sea gulls crying.

More sailors packed the deck. The night was warm and a sultry zephyr blew kisses into the bay, scented with summer berries and musty animal sex. The men and women could smell the musk. It mixed with their sweaty skin, which left their bodies at the slightest breeze. They danced on the deck to funky music. They slapped Dan on the back. They messed up what was left of his silvery hair.

"Everybody shut the fuck up!" the skipper said. "And listen to my boy, D-Money's song."

It took a few moments for them to quiet down, and the quite passed from boat to boat until the night was silent. D-Money stood on the cockpit and swayed back and forth until he found the rhythm of the lazy, crawling sea. When a swell lifted the entire fleet, he sang:

Dan is tha' killer

The Playa that'll

Fill ya with a bullet tip

Hallow points

Rip throughout yo' ship

Best play invisible

If ya wanna be around

Dan's gotta block

He's that silver haired clown

With the scar like a frown

Wit da destiny

To make yo heart stop

'Cause playa hatin' niggahs are left on the dock

In Race Week it's do or die

Battle cries, cause

Playa

It's a war zone

Best dip quick

Take them panties off yo' ship

When ya spy

Danny hits deep

The lights are in a two tone

In da red zone

You can score

Or be denied

Better pack up

Soul and niggah ready

Fo' da ride

Decide if ya get stuck in the flood tide

Too brassy

Too crazy

Ready to ride

Slidin' I'm slippin'

To keep a playa in our navy

Blared in a Farr

Mashin' da pound

Keeps me in an untouchable frame of mind

And he'll a snatch yours before he takes mine

Like they say

Bitches only talk when they spoken to

So don't talk.

So what you got to say?

Cause now Dan's spoken to you,

And just like that, you'd a stowaway.

Dan could see it clearly. He could see that Race Week was a
magnificent hallucination, and that he was a key part of the myth. Sailing

was myth. A game of hide-and-seek. The most important rule was seemingly the simple: find wind for your sails. Now you see it, now you don't. They were no more content to live forever in bliss than they were content to live in hell fire. No more content to live in a steady wind, than they were content in none. They were playing a game. A game called Race Week. He was the captain of this game. The captain of a great hallucination. The captain of Race Week. The captain of a Farr 30. And although they were only playing for trophies, bullets and bragging rights, they were absorbed in the game, hook line and sinker. He had never believed that he could never fall for the mind trick, but he had.

Dan stepped over the lines to the port boat, The Shackleton, where he found Ortun sitting on the deck with a guitar in his lap and a Coors light.

"I knew you would have the trophy one way or another," Ortun said, and he took a drink of his beer and strummed a chord.

"It's been stolen," Dan said.

"You're not the first person to steal a prize."

Ortun pointed at the pit-girl, who was busy making out with Davey.

"All is fair," Dan said. "Right?"

"I like to think that there are some things we hold sacred," Ortun strummed. "Without love, we're animals."

"You might be right," Dan said. He drank and watched the two maul each other against the cockpit. "But it's none of our business."

"No," Ortun said. "I wish that were true, skipper."

Dan looked around, wishing his cook could see the sloppy make-out session with his own eyes. He felt guilty and complicit. The disappointment and the illusion of love shared between his cook and his pit pushed down the sentimental feeling he was experiencing like nausea. But the cook was a writer, and writers were masters of propagating their own illusions.

"We make our own villains," he said looking away and out at marina. There, he caught the cabin light of Jupiter, tied up on the dock. Behind the boat, the great chandelier of the yacht club had been turned off and Kai's cockpit was the only light on the water.

"Wise words, from a wise skipper," Ortun said.

Dan frowned. He looked at Ortun strumming his guitar and for the first time he did not despise the life of an artist, and began to see the performer in himself, a desperate actor in need of an audience. When he thought about it, there wasn't anything important to win at Race Week, and when you really thought about it, there was nothing important to lose. Somehow, in his mind, and therefore, in the actions he choose, it all became fantastical.

"You got a song to play, sailor?" he asked Ortun.

"I do," Ortun said. "Been playing it all night, skipper. Have you been listening?"

And so, it was, in the same way that his cook and pit were engaged, he was engaged with Kai. They were epic lovers absorbed in themselves and with ever so many different beings involved in their plot. He was no different than them. No different than all the other beings, artists or writers or sailors or break mechanics or mothers, or luggage handlers who become completely absorbed in their own narrative creation.

"I mean the words," Dan said, drinking some Shiraz from the trophy.

"Sure, I got words."

"Sing them for me."

Ortun hit a hard note and sang loud enough for the fleet to hear.

Free me of pain

Make me forget our sins your devil helped create

Then wash away my tracks, your devil's lasting freight.

For you can release me

Today

Forget the rubble forest

The boiling sea

These lies your devil said to me.

turned my soul sour by my deeds

Sins caravanned, my vein bleeds.

Take me to your galaxy, saint

Rocket me away from this deadly cave

How fast the sun can set

And we plunge into the dark

My vein's a rollin'.

The vessel's rollin'

Down the stream.

A point hungry for its mark.
As I soar, your devil lays in wait
Eyes me as his prey
We have danced between ecstasy and hate,
Wrap me in your arms and seal my fate.

Dan applauded when he was done, but it was a slow unhappy applause. The fleet joined in, for Ortun's song played across the water where it landed in their hearts and ran away aching like a wounded animal. When it disappeared, he slapped Ortun on the back, smiled, knowing that after tonight, he wouldn't see him for a very long time.

The music on Tupac kicked in and laughter rose. More boats joined the fleet, Kiva, Bravo Zulu, Time Bandit and Cherish. Dan made his way to all of them, sharing the Shiraz in the trophy. On Time Bandit, he bumped into Bonesteel.

"Aye, Skipper" Bonesteel said. "Me wants to introduce you to me new ol' lady."

Dan looked the doll in the eye.

"Madam," Dan said. He lifted her stiff arm and kissed her. "You could have done better."

"Na skipper," Bonesteel said. "We're to marry tonight! Cranwinkle, the main sail on Cherish is a minister. I want you to be me best man."

"If he's a holy man," Dan said. "He won't allow it."

"But skipper," Bonesteel said covering the ears of his fiancée. "She don't give me no back talk. Her skin's smooth like a fresh jar of Skippy's.

She never says 'no', if you know what I mean—and she can't have no babies so there ain't a need for rubbers!"

It was a match made in heaven, Dan thought.

"I give you my blessing."

The crew of Time Bandit cheered.

Dan smiled and drank a little Shiraz to celebrate. When he brought the great trophy from his lips he licked them and saw a flotilla of dark figures on the water, canoes with raised bows standing off the water erect like a wolf's' head in tall grass searching for prey. Mother of pearl eyes were embedded in the bow, set in the faces of carved figureheads. A pack eyeing the fleet.

"Makah," Bonesteel said.

The pack was led by a plumb rowboat, with a single occupant rowing furiously.

"What the hell?" the figure in the boat was saying. "A party? For me? I hope you don't mind that I brought my friends."

"I thought you were going home?" Bonesteel said.

"No," the devil said. "I brought food."

Bonesteel handed his fiancée to Dan and threw a line to the rowboat. It was a perfect throw and the crew of Time Bandit cheered.

"What'd you bring us?" Bonesteel said reeling him in.

"Dan knows," the devil said. "Don't you?"

Dan didn't expect to see the Makah ever again, let alone their flotilla moving at the fleet, heavy with baskets and people pounding on drums.

Edmund appeared and sniffed the air. He could smell the sweet aroma of meat roasted on cedar planks.

"What's he talking about, Dan?"

"You wanted it to disappear, right?"

"Yes you imbecile," Edmund said. "Not like this. I meant bury the damn thing, or haul it out to the straights and sink it."

Dan laughed. From what he'd seen on the beach, there would be nothing for men in business suits to worry about, or government officials. Race. Party. Play. Race Week would live another year, and that's all he ever wanted from the start.

"The Makah would never waste a blessing," Dan said. "Trust me, they won't leave a scrap."

"What about the tactician?" Edmund said. "The fool hasn't wash up on a beach someplace?"

Dan had seen him on the beach while the whale was being butchered. The writer told him that the "saddle piece" found midway between the center of the back and the tail is the property of the harpooner. It is taken to his family where a special ceremony is performed, and the meat and oil are distributed to community members.

"I'm sure we'd only find him if he wanted us to," Dan said. "And if it weren't for him, this party would be shit without a caterer."

The devil boarded, helped aboard by Drunk Bob. He hugged Bonesteel and stuck a Cuban in his mouth.

"My little bastard!" he said. "I miss you, like the devil." The devil laughed and then he caught Dan's eye and moved at him with a slinky smile. "Don't worry," he whispered nodding at the canoes. "They don't believe in me. Not the way sailors do. To them, I'm more of a boogeyman."

Dan turned to watch the Makah men and women, dressed in breech cloths and skirts made from animal skins and grass, tying up to the fleet. He spotted his cook, still in what was left of a tuxedo, hauling baskets onto the deck of Bat Out of Hell.

The devil seized the trophy and held it like a fat baby, hugging it lovingly at the tapered middle. The polished silver was cool to the touch and its surface played with the moonlight and the stars. He seemed legitimately surprised to be holding it.

"And now, a taste," the devil said.

He looked at Dan and with his eyes; asked permission to which Dan granted because he saw him always as a sympathetic creature. The devil grinned and took a long sip of the Shiraz, drank until it began to spill down his satin shirt.

"It tastes sweeter this time," he said.

The night was alive and the world abuzz. The stars hung on a string and the horizon silhouetted more canoes drifting closer; silent, swift shadows floating on the backbone of night.

"Yes, it does." Dan said mesmerized by the ovate paddles, each adorned with a spirit animal: eagles and whale and wolves, painted onto wooden blades that cut into the water without a splash.

"Why do you think that is?" the devil toasted. "Why is it so succulent?"

Dan didn't answer. Instead, he thought for a moment and by the time he'd figured it out, he'd again spotted the little light in the cockpit of Jupiter. It was the only boat in the fleet parked in its slip, a lone stallion left in dark stable.

"Because wine and vinegar come from the same grapes," he said drinking from the trophy once again. "Every story needs a villain."

The devil smiled and then he sized the trophy once more, drank, and licked his lips dry of the sweet Shiraz. He then turned to the men and women of the fleet and said, "Listen up you louts, you sinners, you bastards and son's a bitches!" He raised the trophy triumphantly in the air. "Best Race Week ever!" The men and women cheered, and their calls spread across the fleet, punctuated by air horns and bells.

The devil returned the trophy to Dan.

"You're right of course," he said toasting himself. "There's nothing worse than sugar without spice."

Chapter 85

The writer hoisted basket after basket over the railing of Bat Out of Hell. Eager hands took them aboard.

"Smells so good!" Ivonne said. "What is it?"

"Whale meat," he said. "Shhhhh."

"You've got to be kidding me?"

"Tell your guest it's salted roast cooked on a bed of rosemary," he said. "Courtesy of the Makah."

He tied the dinghy up and secured it with a tight round-turn and two-half hitch, taught to him by the Mac. It was the first knot she taught him because it defined her. It is a highly useful, and reliable knot. It is a constrictor. The tighter you pull on the line the tighter it gets. It is one of the few knots that can be tied or untied with tension in the line. It doesn't jam. It doesn't give. But what she didn't tell him was that it was also difficult to master.

"Nice knot," Ivonne said. "You been practicing?"

"Everyday."

"We'll make a sailor out of you, yet."

The writer doubted that very much.

"How's Rhett?"

"He's fine," Ivonne said helping him aboard. "I drugged him."

The writer kissed her on the cheek, as was the custom.

"Welcome aboard," she said.

 "Where's Mac?"

Ivonne sipped her wine and pointed with her eyes to the foredeck.

"There," she said. "She's been drinking."

The writer looked to the foredeck where he spotted Cybil and Davey, taking turns kissing her on the neck.

"I see."

"Honey," Ivonne said. "Don't be mad. It's Race Week. It is what they do. They are such good boys and girls all year long, and then they come here to—"

"Race. Party—"

"Play, darling."

They both looked on as Mac continued to play. She put her arms around Davey and laughed. Kissed him again, then kissed Cybil.

"Excuse me," the writer said.

Ivonne stopped him, looked deeply into his eyes, held him by both shoulders. For a moment, the writer thought she could see inside him, past the swirling stars outside of his galaxy, and deep into the black hole in the center.

"I'm so sorry," she said. "I can see that your heart is breaking. You are in love with a sailor, and so this means you are in love with drama." She touched his cheek, and brought his eyes back to her. "The saddest thing about loving a sailor is that you do not get to see your heart shatter—we keep our love ashore, and like cowards, we have our drama in bars, in hotels, during a long cold night at sea. While we are at sea, your heart is sinking. Bleeding to death with worry. It is why I sail with my love to every port." She drank a great sip from her glass. "I was wrong to take your eyes away. To make excuses for her. You need to go to Mac. Let her see what she's done. If you don't do it now, you will always remember this moment as the end of your life, and not a beginning."

The writer let her see the ache and pain he'd hidden in the center of his galaxy, the pain he'd smiled through as every handsome, chisel-chinned, manly, blockhead danced with her, bought her drinks, courted her without fearing his redress.

Ivonne had seen it in his eyes and it was the first time he let someone see it. "And then you should get in your dingy and leave," she said. "Go away, and find a beautiful drama that suits you."

The writer set down the basket of meat and moved to the trio. He wasn't sure if he was moving forward or backwards in time. The deck of the boat swayed, set against the velvet darkness and stars, pinpoints of light, scattered amongst sky, reflected by the sea. As he moved through time and space, it was almost as if what was about to happen, had happened, or would, or was. He wasn't sure. But he knew that a wound was opening. Or closing.

"Max?" the pit-girl said. Davey stopped kissing her neck, but she did not push him away. "Darling. Come make out with Cybil."

Cybil moved at him, put her arms were around his shoulders and she kissed his neck.

"Make out with me, Max," she said.

The writer removed her arms.

"You've become incredibly unattractive during these last few days," he told the pit-girl. "I think I might die of fright."

She moved to slap him, but he caught her hand.

"Take it easy, sailor," Davey said, stepping between the two. "It's Race Week."

"Fuck off, Dave," the writer said. "I'm not a sailor. I'm a writer— you cargo thieving-half drowned wastrel."

"What?"

"Has that earring caused an infection?" the writer said. "Then use your other ear."

Davey grimaced. Set his jaw.

"How dare you defy me!" the pit girl said. "How dare you." She tore away from him, squared her shoulders and stared him down until he saw it again: the demon who possessed her.

"Oh Max," she said through her teeth. "You don't understand the golden rule."

"Treat others the way you want to be treated?" he said, looking at her smeared, red lipstick. "I don't think you're interpreting it the right way."

"No," she fixed her hair, and set her bra straight. "There are two kinds of people in the world. Players. And Playthings. Guess which one you are."

The demon.

The incubus.

The sinner.

He saw a tendril from the creature leave her skin in a mist, hover above him and enter his own body. It was intoxicated, inebriated, a phantom haunting bone—terrified, and searching for a heart string, dignity, integrity, any thing to shatter in the night.

Davey saw it, too. He saw that she was a wreck. A mess in a pretty dress. He moved to her side and pushed the writer back.

"How's this gonna go?" he said rolling up his sleeve. "You want to hit me, bro? I dare you."

The writer eyed them both, knowing they wouldn't last. Love endured suffering, but it cannot endure contempt. The tendril would soon be inside Davey, and it would bring out the worst he could show her. She'd do the same to every lover. Then she'd hate them for showing her the wreckage.

The writer held on, pushed the tendril away.

"No," he told Davey. "I can do worse. I can let you have her."

The writer took a step backwards, and turned, kept walking through the stunned party, silenced by the sadness of it all.

The pit-girl followed him to the dingy, cursing.

"Come back here, you damned romantic fool!" she cried and took off her shoes and threw them at the dingy. "You martyr! You coward! You should be above the clouds, or below the clouds, not in them in them!"

The writer unhitched the round-turn and two-half hitch knot on the boat. It came easily undone, just as it was designed. He paddled away furiously. He paddled hard, paddled until the shouting and the party and the smell of booze and sex was behind him. Paddled until his heart beat against his chest so hard that he could feel it pushing into his neck. He paddled until the taste of her poison kisses were washed away by his own sweat, and her profanities were replaced by the sound of oars hitting the water.

When he was far enough away, his heart smoothed and he stopped rowing to let the boat drift for a time. In the starry darkness, he finished the last poem he would ever write for the pit-girl.

Your Last Goodbye

Fall into my arms
You fool, my heart is yours to take.
My lips are yours; my soul adores
O' my projected self, of late.

So fall into my arms, you pirate.
Steal my lips, this night.
Make them wet, as in your depths,
Delight my every fright.

A phantasm;
A wicked magic show.
From which my dreams,
and all that seems
a mortal must'n know.

So wet your lips and kiss me.
Tease me on this night.
Taste me.
Devour me.
It is our sacred rite.

Make me disappear

Until the dawn does break.

Fall into my arms, you swank

That thou love you mayst take.

Kill me. Use me. Savor you, I fear.

Excite me. Tell the bastard I was here.

As if thy soul, hath come too near.

And at this moment

you will be mine.

A rapture to forsake,

And nay a curse.

And nay a fear.

And nay a heart you take.

For I am released, but for now

To stay, to forget the salted earth

The rubble forest, the boiling sea

The lies you now forsake.

So take me in your arms, you waft.

You lithe and luring, rake

O' that my demons may know

And fear to show

The curse of your mistake.

And deeds best seen in darkness

Are waiting for your spine

The break of day.

The stars at night.

To craft your words as mine.

It's the reason the devil is bound by hell and hate.

And why I am here: redemption's sake.

And he hath known, ever and ever

The sorrow and the ache.

So kiss me, now.

Kiss me you, vamp.

I know you know the stakes.

For the sweetest things do sour

By the action of your deeds.

Deeds, perpetually caravanned

A vein I now do bleed.

In that dark, sexy corner,

No others will resuscitate.

Kiss the places on my body

I have shown to you,

For you shall be kissed there, too.

And I will have my turn to love, as any fool would do

To revel in this maple sap,

Bearing scars you drew.

Dripping with the sultry musk

The scent of skin

To crave the taste of you.

I will leave it there,

until I am crazed to remember you.

And I am stung by the loss of hurtful creeds

Sung and sad anew.

So take me to your galaxy,

You starry-eyed ghostly ache.

Do it for thy own true love

and languish for my sake.

So that these days are gone:

The sins of men.

A siren do you make.

A cockled heart, aglow to know

The fool I now do make.

When he was done, he rolled the poem up into a beer bottled and threw it into the starry darkness at Nefarious.

Chapter 86

Dan paddled to Jupiter. He tied up and climbed aboard, carrying the great trophy.

"Permission to come aboard!" he called, but no one answered.

From the marina, he could hear that the party had started up again, and from the distance, he could hear his sailors singing the Nefarious song. The string of boats were locked up into a circle, and before his escape, he'd managed to visit them all. None of the skippers were willing to be the first to leave, and the boats would be locked in a circuitous party until dawn. He saw that Bat Out of Hall had raised a flag with a black whale painted on the face and that a disco ball, hanging from the mast of Tupac was spinning, casting out little diamonds of lights on the water.

Dan saw a dark figure in the porthole window, slumped over a table with crumpled maps. He smelled cedar incense and heard rhythmic mumbling that sounded like a praying, or chanting.

Dan knocked on the door but the figure did not move.

"Kai," he said. "Time to join the party, sailor!"

Kai did not stir so Dan opened the door.

"Sailor," he said again. "Time to—"

Kai lifted his head, but it was not Kai. It was the little drunk man.

"My name is Christopher," the little drunk man said. "I came to see the boats."

"I know who you are," Dan said. "Where the hell is Kai?"

The little drunk man didn't say anything. He only gazed at Dan mysteriously.

Dan set the trophy down. There was something queer going on and he wasn't in on the joke. He looked around for the devil, waited for the trick to end, but after a long silence, nothing happened.

"Please give this to Kai when he returns," Dan said. "Tell him that he won it fair and square and that without him, there would be no me. No tonight. No Race Week."

The little man put his head back down on the map and fell asleep before Dan's weary eyes.

On the water, he paddled a leisure pace, thinking about the nature of things. The stars had moved sideways and the moon was just now slipping behind the black trees at the top of Strawberry hill. As it disappeared, he remembered the rest of the poem.

I must go down to the seas again, to the vagrant gypsy life,
To the gull's way and the whale's way, where the wind's like a whetted knife;
And all I ask is a merry yarn from a laughing fellow-rover,
And quiet sleep and a sweet dream when the long trick's over.

When he neared Nefarious, he paused and watched her sway gently in the calm water, nestled in the family of boats. Maybe the trick was that he blew starts on purpose because he already knew he could win. And what was racing a Farr without a whetted knife? Win or lose, he already knew in his heart that he had crossed the finish line better than his competition, better than his father could have dreamed, better than his mother had hoped, better than the devil thought, who'd told him a secret tonight: the child would be born with green eyes, the color of the Salish Sea.

Dan quietly tied up the dingy, hardly causing a wake on the lovely, black water. He slipped by the crew, still drunk, still singing the Nefarious song and slinked his way to Martina's side, curled up in a blanket, asleep on the floor.

He kissed her, and she awoke.

"When Ivonne swam for Rhett," he whispered. "Would you have done the same for me?"

"Yes, Danny," she said in a dreamy voice. "You are my sailor and I am your sea princess."

And he laid his head upon her breast to fall asleep, a drowsy, sloppy, mess.

Made in the USA
Columbia, SC
01 July 2018